# Geraldine

# Geraldine

John Mead

The Book Guild Ltd

First published in Great Britain in 2019 by
The Book Guild Ltd
9 Priory Business Park
Wistow Road, Kibworth
Leicestershire, LE8 0RX
Freephone: 0800 999 2982
www.bookguild.co.uk
Email: info@bookguild.co.uk
Twitter: @bookguild



Typeset in Adobe Garamond Pro

Printed and bound in Great Britain by CPI Group (UK) Ltd, Croydon, CR0 4YY

ISBN 978 1912881 772

British Library Cataloguing in Publication Data.
A catalogue record for this book is available from the British Library.

MIX
Paper from responsible sources
FSC® C013604

Dedicated to my wife
for her support and willingness to grow old with me.

*'From the deepest desires often come the deadliest hate.'*

*– Socrates*

# Chapter One

It was nearing dawn as the police river patrol boat slipped its moorings in Wapping. The sinuous river was a glistening gunmetal grey and sluggishly ebbed, causing the small boat to bob as it pulled away. Sergeant Hunter was pleased with how the young constable managed the boat, steering it with confidence and an ease that denoted a feel for the currents and eddies of the river. The dark sky was a uniform dull grey, hardly distinguishable from the river, and the mist-like rain made visibility an issue. However, the weather was little more than a reminder that it was early November and the cloud and rain would soon clear to make way for a watery sun.

The boat's engine increased its beat, they were heading upstream against the tide to St Katherine's Dock for an early morning sweep, then intended to turn back to check on the various basins, inlets and moorings downstream to see what criminality they could spot. As they got underway the sergeant settled himself, comfortable with the swaying of the craft, he looked out over the empty river and his gaze settled on the small mud and rubble beach of Wapping Old Stairs. A bright blue, at the very end of the emerging concrete jetty below the stairs, catching his eye.

'Bring her over to starboard a little,' he instructed the constable, anyone else might have ignored the small piece of jetsam as a discarded rubbish sack or plastic bag, but the river police tended to have an eye for things out of place on the river. The boat engine slowed and the slightest turn on the wheel allowed the tide to push it to shore, the constable knowledgeably judging the distance so as not to run aground. 'It's a body,' the sergeant confirmed. The head, face down and wrapped with wet, light brown, shoulder length hair, had been hidden by a boulder that had arrested the body's movement downstream with the tide. 'A woman from the look of it.' Her blue dress, still buoyed by the river, swayed with the tide which tugged at the upper body now stranded on the shore.

Detective Inspector Matthew Merry did not consider himself a sluggard and had been quick to respond to Superintendent Malcolm Swift's phone call just after seven in the morning. He had already been up, helping his wife get his daughters fed and ready for school, and had simply skipped his own breakfast and left his wife to hold the fort on her own, heading straight out with hardly a word other than a hurried goodbye. Even so, as he arrived in Wapping High Street he could see that things were in full swing and he was likely to be the last on scene, his only excuse was that he lived further out than either of his colleagues.

'Inspector Merry's here, sir,' Detective Sergeant Julie Lukula informed Superintendent Swift, spotting Matthew emerging from his car, that he had carefully parked a couple of hundred feet away, not far from Wapping nick.

'Bugger,' Matthew muttered under his breath, for once he would have liked to have arrived before the superintendent and sergeant. His governor, Swift, didn't even have to be there but old habits die hard. Neither Julie nor Swift appeared to take any downtime, they both still seemed to have retained the habit of being perpetually ready for action from their army days. Although Julie Lukula's army service had lasted longer than Swift's. She had done seven years as a regular and a redcap whereas Swift had gotten out early after a training accident – with the parachute regiment – left him unfit for duty and with the slightest of limps. Or perhaps, Matthew reflected, it was simply that they were both single and childless. Both were casually dressed but both had an air of authority and self-confidence that made any uniform redundant. Matthew was tall but increasingly portly with a naturally pessimistic scowl and – wearing a long black overcoat, suit, tie and sporting a dark grey cloth cap to cover a growing bald patch – looked like an off-duty undertaker.

'It doesn't open for a few hours yet, you know,' Matthew informed the waiting pair. The uniforms had taped off the Thames side of the street for about twenty yards either side of the Town of Ramsgate pub and the narrow alley that ran down to Wapping Old Stairs. He had given his details to the constable on the perimeter and now ambled over trying, though obviously failing, to sound as if he were in a good mood.

'Missed breakfast I take it,' Swift deduced, knowing Matthew to be a man of regular habits who was easily put out if he missed a meal. 'As you can see everything's in hand so you needn't have rushed. SOCOs and the photographer are working on the crime scene and the surgeon is with the body.'

'I was just explaining that I have already been up to Wapping nick,' Julie nodded back the way Matthew had come from, not bothering with any pleasantries in her desire to press on. 'Ray Rosen's already arrived and is setting up the incident room.'

'What do we have?' Matthew wanted to get up to speed so there would be little need for Swift to hang around.

'Body, female, washed up on the beach at the bottom of the stairs,' Swift informed him before Julie could speak, 'found by the River Patrol at six forty-two. They checked for life and radioed it in then had the street and alleyway shut off, kept the alleyway and shore as untrammelled as possible until the SOCOs turned up. Julie arrived as the SOCOs did, she suggested that the river police ferry half the team round to the shore and they did the same when the surgeon arrived. It has meant that the SOCOs can check the alleyway and stairs while the others work the shore.'

'We have been waiting for the all clear so we haven't seen the body or crime scene as yet,' Julie stated. Then remembered to add,

'While I was up at the nick I spoke to the inspector to organise the collection of CCTV and to start canvassing the area.'

As always the efficient Sergeant Lukula made Matthew feel at a loose end. She was experienced, qualified, well organised and long overdue a promotion to inspector, so their working a case together seemed like overmanning. He was equally pleased to get Ray Rosen as the office manager as Matthew rated the experienced detective sergeant the best man in the Met to run an operations team. Ray would have made inspector, or a higher rank, himself by now if he hadn't had a long period of light duties while he fought his alcoholism; he was approaching his eighth anniversary of being sober.

'Do we know if this is where she was killed or just dumped?' was all Matthew could think to ask.

'The sergeant, from the river police, who found her …' Swift started to explain. Then, sizing up a car that slowed down almost to a stop as it passed the scene, changed track to ask Julie. 'We are taking the numbers of cars that stop, names of pedestrians showing an undue interest and that sort of thing, aren't we?' the superintendent asked Julie.

'I did detail a couple of uniforms on to it but I'll check where they are actually doing it,' Julie said, annoyed she couldn't see where the two constables were and set off to give them a bollocking.

'As I was saying,' Swift continued with a wry smile, something he had done a lot less since his promotion a month ago, 'the sergeant who found the body spoke with me when I arrived. He thinks it unlikely from how they found her that she was killed there, more likely to have been dumped in the river upstream and brought down on the tide.'

'Any idea where?'

'Until we get an estimated time of death he couldn't say, though he didn't think she'd been in the water long. So, as a start, he has gone along the road to check out all the places accessible from the street. However, he also pointed out that if she came off a boat the body could have travelled a lot further.'

'We will need to start compiling a list of boats known to be in the area, the clippers and the pleasure boats are likely to be the main river users,' Matthew was starting to feel impatient, standing in the chill wind sweeping down the street, though he knew in reality little more could effectively be done until the police surgeon gave her initial findings. However, he decided to deal with the most obviously unnecessary deployment of manpower by addressing the superintendent's presence, 'You don't need to hang around, you know.'

'I'll wait to hear what the surgeon has to say,' Swift stated, knowing Matthew was right but as he was here he thought he might as well stay a bit longer; he had time before the first of his many meetings planned for the day was scheduled to start. 'The chief made it clear, that despite my replacing one and a half superintendents, my role needed to be more operational than of old as money needs to be saved,' Swift's voice took on the sing-song accent of his Welsh upbringing, a sure sign he was embarrassed by knowing that Matthew was unlikely, as part of the cuts, to get the chief inspector's post he had recently vacated. 'I asked again about your position but they are looking to cut the number of DCIs so replacing vacancies is a bit of a non-starter.'

Matthew was tall but Swift was an inch or so bigger, with a boxer's build, his black face resolute and stern; although his eyes showed the sympathy he felt for what he assumed must be Matthew's frustration. Matthew smiled back in recognition of his governor's attempts on his behalf, though was embarrassed himself that he had little ambition to become a chief inspector, not feeling ready to move on as yet. Had the job been offered it might have been one thing but, at present, he wasn't putting himself out to move on.

'It would help if you completed all the requisite training, I understand you've virtually done so but it'd strengthen my hand if you were already acting-up,' Swift pointed out with as much good humour as he could muster in the chill of the damp morning air. There had been a time, little more than a year ago, when he didn't rate Matthew and the inspector was facing a sideways move. However, free of the need to impress, Matthew had seemingly come into his own and was now building an impressive reputation.

Matthew was saved making any response to his governor's veiled criticism by a SOCO coming out of the alleyway to inform them the path down to the river was clear. Nothing of any obvious interest being found in the alley, though some items had been bagged and the photographer was working on the stairs.

The steps down to the beach were slippery, as much from the earlier rain than the retreating tide. At high tide the beach could completely disappear under water, while at low tide it ran – a ribbon of sand, mud, building rubble, discarded ship ballast and stumps of old pilings – at the back of the buildings on Wapping High Street. A river police patrol boat bobbed twenty yards downstream, its bow pushed up to the shore, a diver standing by in the stern watching two river service constables in waders searching the shoreline. Even close into the shore a fall could put someone in danger of the river's currents and tides so no chances were being taken. The victim's body was neatly laid out in a supine position on a large plastic sheet put down by SOCOs before the body was moved. The surgeon stood at one side, on the low stone jetty running from the steps into the Thames. The damp laden air coating everything with the wet, muddy smell of the river.

'Good morning,' the surgeon, a middle-aged, matronly woman, hailed them. She had obviously finished but was watching the activity around her, turning to say, 'Malcolm, surprised to see you here, checking up on the underlings?'

'I have to have eyes everywhere in my exalted position,' Swift quipped, they had known each other for some time and a friendship had grown up around their professional meetings which were often conducted over a corpse.

'Well I can't tell you very much,' she explained, nodding back at the body, as Matthew manoeuvred past to get a closer look, 'but

I have a couple of observations for you. Starting with the obvious that you won't get any DNA or trace off the body, as it's been in the water for a few hours, and the ethereal nature of the crime scene explains our haste in moving the body. Given that most of this area was underwater only a short time ago the scene is of very limited value and the SOCOs tell me they don't hold out much hope of discovering anything.'

'She was obviously attractive when alive,' Matthew noted out loud. Her shoulder length, light brown hair was still wet and clung to the woman's face, exaggerating the finely drawn cheeks and chin. Her thin lips were pulled back slightly, showing a glint of evenly spaced teeth in the residual of a smile. *Not a beautiful face,* he thought, *but a pleasant one denoting a strong character.* The body was slim, narrow hips, with long legs. Her breasts were fulsome and still filled her bodice making him wonder if they had been cosmetically enlarged, the silicon would preserve their shape even while she was supine. Only her feet were overly large for her size and, without shoes, looked out of place. Her whole, otherwise elegant, appearance in a smart blue, knee length dress was marred by bruising around her neck, the signs of strangulation in her face and the greyish blue colouring of her glistening, wet skin. 'Her jewellery seems all in place,' he stated, noting the gold chain round her neck, pearl earrings and expensive looking watch and bracelets on her wrists and rings on her fingers, including a rather masculine looking wedding band, 'so robbery is unlikely to be the motive.'

'Actually, it is a man,' the surgeon matter-of-factly informed them, 'though as a woman he is undoubtedly striking.'

'A man! Are you certain?' Julie, who had come down the steps as the surgeon spoke, couldn't help expressing her disbelief.

'I was aware of the anatomical differences between the sexes even before embarking on years of training as a doctor,' the surgeon informed them with deadpan expression, 'but now, with my extensive experience in the field, and a few other places, I think I can conclusively say the victim is a male.'

‘Wow, would have had me fooled,’ Julie admitted squatting at the edge of the low stone jetty to make a closer inspection of the body. With only the smell of the river noticeable and the shiny wetness of the body, giving it the look of a mannequin, the relatively fresh corpse did not make her stomach churn as would normally happen.

‘His breasts are prosthetics and I would hazard a guess they are tailor made, along with the bra, as they haven’t shifted despite his having been in the water. Although there is no sign of any knickers. What I can also tell you is that he was probably strangled, though the post-mortem will confirm the exact cause of death. SOCOs are still checking the far end of the beach and the waterline but they are pretty certain this isn’t where he was killed.’

‘Time of death?’ Swift wanted to know, he couldn’t help admire the surgeon’s calm, professional manner, just the thought of having to touch a cold, wet corpse made him shiver, while to her it was the meat of her daily existence.

‘Can’t be that precise at the moment, you’ll have to wait for the PM to give you something more accurate,’ the surgeon didn’t like to be drawn on things where the degree of uncertainty might mislead, ‘but at the moment I’d venture sometime between one thirty and two thirty this morning.’

‘So she … he hasn’t been in the water long then?’ Matthew asked, still confused by the blue dress and outward shape of the body.

‘No, it doesn’t appear so. The river police sergeant has seen more than his share of bodies taken from the water and he described it as a fresh corpse,’ the surgeon explained. ‘He said it’s most likely that the body came from a boat as there are relatively few places it could have washed up here if it had been dumped in from the bank.’

‘He’s already looking at a particular site up at Pier Head,’ Julie informed them, standing back up. ‘He and a couple of SOCOs are searching the gardens up there.’

'That's only a few yards up isn't it?' Matthew pointed out, looking along the fast emerging shore and trying to identify the old pier head. 'You should be able to see it from here.'

'SOCOs are already searching the beach along there,' the surgeon confirmed. 'One of his shoes turned up further down the shoreline, where they are searching now, being lighter it travelled further downstream.'

'Any handbag or ID on him?' Matthew wanted to know, he was beginning to wonder if the victim's realistic appearance as a female might be a possible motive for his killing. Perhaps a new acquaintance, who had been unwittingly fooled by the dress, becoming violent on discovery his date was a man.

'No, that's what they are searching the waterline for,' the surgeon explained, pausing to savour the moment of what she was about to tell them. 'None of you recognise him then? I realise the face is distorted somewhat by the strangulation, and death always changes appearance, even so I'm surprised you can't put a name to him.' The three detectives looked at each other, momentarily re-studying the victim's face, before admitting defeat.

'You didn't come down Wapping Lane then?' although the surgeon guessed that at least Julie and Matthew had done so, only Swift looking clueless as the other pair frantically searched their memory of their journey here. 'You'll need to confirm it but I'd stake my pension on his face being on the posters plastered all over the front of the club, not ten minutes from Wapping rail station.'

'The club near Watts Street?' Julie knew the club but hadn't given it a second glance on passing it.

'Yes,' the surgeon stated with a degree of smugness that wasn't lost on the three officers, 'and, if I'm not mistaken our man here is their star attraction: Geraldine Driver.'

'Given the timings it's possible he had been at the club earlier, possibly had been attacked there,' Matthew jumped to the conclusion, though no one disagreed with him, 'we should get over there to ascertain if it's part of the crime scene.'

'I need to be getting on,' Swift told them, nodding his thanks to the surgeon, realising he was now cutting it fine getting to his first meeting. 'Obviously keep me in the loop but is there anything more you need?'

'More feet on the ground,' Matthew said, hardly needing to consider the request as everyone knew that the more officers deployed at the start of the investigation, the greater likelihood of success.

Swift took a deep breath of the chill river air, to give himself a moment's thought, 'Everyone's up to their neck at the moment,' though the superintendent realised this applied as much to Matthew and Julie as anyone else as both had ongoing cases and court appearances to occupy their time, 'but you can have the new constable, Harry Bainbridge, he needs the experience. As well as Hayden, as the Myers case is going cold she can work with you for the moment.' With a goodbye and a further 'thank you' to the police surgeon Swift was off.

# Chapter Two

Julie, Matthew and the police surgeon, who still wore wellies and protective clothing, had to walk in single file down the short, narrow passageway leading from the river steps to the Town of Ramsgate pub. They did so in silence emerging into the noise of a busy street scene. The area cordoned off had been extended further up the Thames side of the High Street, causing chaos to the early rush hour traffic and commuters heading down to Wapping rail station. Onlookers were being directed to move on, along the opposite pavement, while traffic was being directed to turn back and find alternative routes as forensic vans and the black coroner's van – there to collect the body – were double parked and blocking the High Street.

'I'll give you a hand,' Julie said to the surgeon, hoping to make amends for her earlier unintended gaff of doubting the doctor's assessment of the victim's sex. 'You're parked up by the police station, aren't you?'

'Yes, thank you, Sergeant,' the surgeon smiled, then turned to Matthew as he pulled off the protective gloves and overshoes he and the other detectives had automatically donned before entering the crime scene. 'You are lucky Malcolm still takes an interest you know,' she pointed out, referring to the superintendent having been present, 'but it won't last, the job will eat up his good intentions. Having time to spend being a good leader is a luxury long past, I'm afraid.'

Matthew was too slow witted to think of a response and simply motioned a goodbye with his hand, along with a 'thanks' and instructions to Julie to wait for him. A constable, waiting for his attention, quickly informed him that Sergeant Hunter, of the river police, and the SOCOs thought they had found the place where the body had been put in the water, just a short distance away at Pier Head.

'Hi, Julie,' Matthew phoned Julie as he stood watching the SOCOs working in the gardens at Pier Head. Uniformed officers were questioning each of the residents occupying the few houses on either side of the small, well tended communal garden which ran – at right angles to the High Street – down to the river, 'I think I'm going to be tied up here for a while. They have found the victim's other shoe in the bushes and a piece of cloth matching the victim's dress snagged on the river wall. Is Ray actually in the incident room?'

'Yes,' Julie informed him, she'd been waiting patiently in her car, sipping what passed for coffee from the police station machine, 'and I checked that Hayden and Harry are on their way. I also got the impression that the inspector from the river police would like a word, he was asking where you were.'

'Good, as I want to see him, we'll need to hold a press conference later today,' Matthew was checking off the mental To Do list he'd worked out as he watched the progress being made at Pier Head. 'I also want to speak with Ray, so can you get over to the club where Geraldine Driver worked and see what you can find out? I'll get over as soon as I can.'

Inspector Graves had been manager of the River Police service for nine years, he'd been in the force for thirty-one years and served in the unit for twenty-seven of those. No matter what the time of day his uniform always looked as if it was fresh from the dry cleaners. He was known as a stickler for detail and procedure but was also good humoured, sociable and understanding of the stresses his officers faced on a daily basis – a good leader. Every inch a man who had found a niche in life which suited him completely and he'd stuck with it and thrived as a result.

'Inspector Merry,' Graves welcomed Matthew, 'I have been talking with Sergeant Rosen and seen that he has everything he needs for the incident room. He strikes me as very efficient and everything appears in order.'

'Thank you,' Matthew responded in kind, 'your people and other officers from the station are proving a great help presently, but I have one further request.'

'Of course,' Graves stated, he wasn't in a position to refuse in any case but he was glad the murder investigation team were putting their demands in the form of requests, it indicated a level of professionalism that seemed to be slipping from some units and special teams within the force.

Matthew explained he'd contacted the media office to organise a press conference, a brief statement and appeal for witnesses, to be held at the police station later that day. 'We believe we have an ID for the victim and hope for confirmation by the end of the day, so I'd be grateful if you could set things up here and also take part, to briefly explain the role the River Police have played.'

Inevitably Graves was more than willing to take part, to promote the service he so loved, and Matthew knew that including them in the story would result in wider coverage, the press relishing the traditional policing values of another era the river service seemed to embody.

Matthew then checked in with Ray, each updating the other on progress.

'I've already got an address and some background on Gerald, Gerry or Geraldine Driver,' Ray informed him. 'No police record but he's on Twitter, Facebook and a blog; all of them as Geraldine – no hint of Gerry. Pictures from the blog seem to match those taken by the crime scene photographer. Twitter is picking up that he's our victim: "River body that of well known female impersonator", that sort of thing. He lives out at Epping, married, no children.'

'No report of him missing I take it?' Matthew's assumption was confirmed by a shake of Ray's balding head, reminding Matthew of his own increasingly noticeable bald patch. 'Can you get on to the local station for me and have someone go to the house? Make it clear the identification hasn't been confirmed yet so it is only a general inquiry and not to unnecessarily alarm the wife. I'm on my way to meet with Julie at the club we think he worked at, and we'll go to his house from there.' Ray nodded, again giving Matthew pause to think how he might look in ten years' time, though in practice Ray's years on the booze had done nothing to help him keep his youthful looks.

'OK, thanks, when Hayden and the boy,' Matthew continued, alluding to Harry Bainbridge's youthful good looks which, coupled with a keenness to participate, managed to make him look and sound like an over-zealous sixth former, 'arrive, send them down to Pier Head and Old Stairs to keep an eye on progress. And if you haven't done so already, make certain we have the CCTV from down there as well.'

On his way out Matthew didn't get further than the front desk, as the duty officer stopped him, 'Your victim's car has been found, reported by parking enforcement, outside the Turks Head in Tench Street, within walking distance of the crime scene,' the trim, young female officer crisply informed him. 'Must have parked in a hurry as they left it on a yellow line and there are plenty of bays round there.'

*Or why not drive it somewhere quiet and set fire to it, destroying any evidence*, Matthew thought to himself. Then seeing Hayden and the boy – he'd have to stop thinking of Harry Bainbridge in those terms before he committed the faux pas of addressing him by the sobriquet – enter the station. 'How timely,' Matthew greeted the pair. 'Hayden,' he'd never found out why Hayden detested her first name but no one ever addressed her as anything other than Hayden, 'can you go down the road to the Town of Ramsgate and take charge of the crime scene. Sergeant Hunter from the River Police will be there or at Pier Head and he has a good take on things. Harry, go with her and get a couple of SOCOs to secure the victim's car in Tench Street, the constable here has the details. I'm off to meet with Julie, keep me informed of any developments.'

All three constables had barely said 'yes, sir' in confirmation of their tasks before he was out of the building, his terse words and task focused manner injecting them with a sense urgency.

'The game's afoot,' Harry enthusiastically stated, to the inspector's retreating back, causing the two women to raise their eyebrows, if smiling indulgently at the young officer's beaming face.

Julie had pounded the club's front entrance doors for some time before searching out the small rear exit, leading out to the carpark, with a shabby sign denoting it was the stage entrance. Here her impersonation of an energetic battering ram finally produced a result and the door was opened by a tired looking woman of similar age to Julie, wearing an overall and speaking with a thick East European accent. After some careful pronunciation on both sides Julie managed to impress on the cleaner that she needed to speak with someone in charge, while the cleaning woman explained that would be the assistant deputy manager who was in the office, the way to which she pointed out to Julie.

During the day the club, the Blue Snake, looked like a large, black box dumped on the corner of a side street in Wapping Lane. Its uniformly navy-blue exterior, with painted over and grill covered windows, gave no insight to its neon lit night time luminescence. The interior was a surprisingly pleasant pastiche of the modern romantic style, making it look more up-market than it really was. It was laid out cabaret style: with a low stage and small dance floor at the front, tables and chairs on the main floor; with booths, notionally giving more privacy, around the outer edge and in the gallery above. However, Julie only caught a glimpse of the interior as most of her short journey to the office was down a grubby, magnolia painted brick corridor that was lined with posters of various burlesque acts that had given the Blue Snake its reputation as East London's premiere cabaret venue. Or so the print on a poster featuring Geraldine Driver, in a glitzy night gown, informed her.

'Yes?' the assistant deputy manager stated with a start as Julie entered the office with a peremptory knock. 'Ohh … if you're here for the auditions then you are way too early.'

'Auditions?' Julie was in no hurry to announce her official purpose and status, she found that people often engaged more fully before she did so.

'New dancers for the line up,' he informed her with an appealing smile. 'I'm Todd Barrett, by the way,' he added, standing to shake her hand. A gesture Julie found engaging, nor did she mind being mistaken for a dancer as she had a slim, well toned figure and an attractive face. She had been called a lot worse over the years, usually along the lines of 'you fucking, black, dyke cunt' or whatever other racial and gender slurs the person could think of.

'I'm Detective Sergeant Julie Lukula, I have a few questions about your headline act,' she informed him, noticing his obvious embarrassment at his mistake. He was a young man in his early twenties, she guessed, of middle height, wiry build, neatly combed brown hair, with a well defined face, a winning smile and blue eyes.

'Gerry? I'm sorry but he isn't here, I expect he's at home.' Todd's smile broadened in way of an apology.

'When would he have left?' Julie pulled out her notebook, a habit she'd never lost when questioning someone.

'Ohh … about midnight or just after I'd guess,' Todd informed her uncertainly. 'I wasn't here last night, I'm duty day manager today, making certain the cleaners get done and the place is ready for the auditions.'

'You're open every night?'

'Thursday to Sunday are cabaret nights, Monday and Tuesday it's just the compere, band and dancers, with an open-mic night on Wednesdays. Gerry's been on the bill for a couple of weeks now and he usually leaves around midnight,' he helpfully explained, though his manner was more tense than when Julie first entered the room.

'Who was in charge last night?'

'Mel, Melanie Smith, our manager.'

'We'll need to speak with her to find out exactly when Mr Driver left. You have CCTV, I take it?' Julie asked.

'Inside and out. I'm afraid Mel won't be in until later,' the apologetic version of his smile returned, 'usually not until six.'

'I doubt my inspector will wait that long so you might want to give her a call,' she informed him, the gloss of his smile having no impact on her. 'I'll also need all your CCTV footage,' Julie explained, the authority of her voice leaving no room for objection, though she was wondering when he would ask the one question she had already expected from him.

'Right,' he looked a tad perplexed, 'I'll get hold of the head of our security team first then phone Mel.' Then after a moment's hesitation added, 'The CCTV at the back, that covers the stage door and carpark beyond, is broken. It went down a couple of days ago. Thought you should be aware as Gerry would have gone out that way.'

'OK,' Julie frowned with annoyance, things had been going too smoothly, then she decided to ask, 'What will you tell her?'

'What?'

'When you phone your manager, what will you say about the police being here?' Todd looked increasingly panic-stricken, no doubt out of his depth as assistant deputy manager in dealing with the police. 'You might want to explain to her that we are investigating the death of Mr Gerald Driver.'

'Their security manager,' Julie briefed Matthew on his arrival at the club, 'arrived about fifteen minutes ago, fortunately he lives locally whereas the club's manager is coming in from Denmark Hill. The assistant deputy manager is decorative if vacuous,' Matthew raised an eyebrow at the description but Julie shrugged and simply moved on, 'but I've sent a constable to oversee his copying of the CCTV images.'

'Their security guy, he confirmed that Driver left between midnight and quarter past?' Matthew reiterated what Julie had already told him, mulling over the timings.

'He also said that when he first met *Geraldine* she was wearing a smart little business number, by which I discovered he meant a navy-blue pencil skirt and jacket. He said that Geraldine, as Gerry invariably introduced himself, was the sexiest woman he'd met in a long time. Apparently though, so the security guy says, the word is that Gerry wasn't gay but straight and happily married, which apparently isn't that unusual for those in his line of work.'

'I could walk from here to Pier Head in about half an hour,' Matthew pointed out, he'd only been half-listening to Julie but she wasn't offended having grown used to his tendency to focus on more than one thing at once. 'So either he drove to Tench Street and then met up with his attacker, or the attacker met him somewhere and dumped the car there afterwards.'

'It's a ten minute drive so there is easily an hour unaccounted for,' Julie agreed, 'more if time of death is determined as closer to two thirty than one thirty.'

'Given we know he started from here and his car ended up in Tench Street, it shouldn't be hard to track the car's movements on CCTV. Just how many new silver Skoda Kodiaqs can there be out there at that time of night?' They both smiled at the thought of all the evidence coming together. 'I'll get Ray onto it, Hayden is going to pick up Harry and come here to take over. She said the forensics team haven't turned up anything else along the beach or at Pier Head. Harry's also reported in to say the SOCOs found Gerry's handbag in his car, with his purse containing credit cards and photo licence. The car's being taken in so they can give it a thorough going over but they said they have already bagged a couple of significant items, including some nylon rope and a couple of sex toys, of all things. Plus, there's blood and shit in the back, so it's possible he was attacked in the car.'

'So it isn't adding up to a robbery gone wrong then?' Julie mused, adding, 'Although it could have been an attempted car jacking'.

'Let's not speculate. We'd better get over to speak with the wife. I'll need to get back and prepare for the press statement later this afternoon, and I'm starving so we can stop for sandwiches on the way,' Matthew said, not expecting Julie to object to a lunch stop.

'The manager will be here by then, so we could fit speaking to her on the way back or do you want Hayden to do it?'

'We both can,' Matthew said, pausing for Julie to unlock her car, 'and then compare notes just to see if there are any discrepancies. I don't know why but I feel this all started here at the club.'

The two police constables, who had called on Mrs Driver earlier, were waiting in their marked car for the detectives outside the Driver's house.

'She said she had gone to bed at about eleven last night, read for a bit then went to sleep,' one of the constables told them as they stood at the end of the driveway. 'She didn't miss her husband until she woke up at half eight. She said she often slept through his coming home but it was unlike him not to be back much after two, unless he was working away. She phoned his agent after nine this morning, who told her not to worry and he'd track Gerry down.'

'We haven't mentioned Driver being found,' the second officer informed them.

# Chapter Three

Stephanie Marie Driver was forty-two, dark haired, with a pleasant round face and black, rather sultry eyes which did nothing to alleviate her languid expression. She was on the short side, thick set and was wearing an expensive two piece when she answered the door.

'What's happened, where is Gerry?' Stephanie Driver asked, worry and tension showing in every aspect of her demeanour and voice, as she ushered her uninvited guests into the sitting room. The house was spotless, immaculate and tastefully decorated as befitted a *villa* on the outskirts of Epping, 'I've been worried sick. I expect Vic has been in touch with you.'

'Vic?' Matthew asked, putting off the bad news he had come to deliver for a moment.

'Victor Thorsson, Gerry's agent,' Mrs Driver managed to add a puzzled frown to her worried expression.

'No,' Matthew decided he could dissemble no longer. 'I'm sorry, Mrs Driver, to inform you that a body has been found in the Thames by Wapping Old Stairs and we have every reason to believe it is your husband.'

'There is some mistake …' Mrs Driver responded, puzzled denial now completely replacing her previously worried frown. 'I'm sorry but it can't be my husband you've found, he is absolutely terrified of the water and can't swim. There is no way he would go in the Thames.'

'We don't believe he got into the river voluntarily, Mrs Driver,' Matthew did his best to sound both professionally detached, while clarifying his explanation, without sounding patronising but he wasn't entirely certain he was achieving either, 'we are treating his death as suspicious …'

'Suspicious?' Stephanie Driver prided herself at being an acute bridge player and crossword puzzler, but she seemed to be having trouble grasping what the police inspector was saying. If only he could be more direct so she could point out the flaw in his thinking given the impossibility of her husband being dead.

'Yes, preliminary evidence points to him having been attacked and probably killed before he was put in the river,' Matthew paused, waiting for his words to percolate through the walls the woman's mind had put up to protect her from the shock. Then continued, 'We are sorry for your loss and understand the shock this must be for you. Is there anyone we can contact who can come here to be with you?'

'What, ohh … yes, Gerry's brother, Grahame, I must phone him,' Stephanie, Steph to her bridge partners and friends, started to get up and then sat down again. 'I've only just phoned him, to see if he'd heard from Gerry.'

'I'll contact him for you, if you give me his number,' Julie volunteered, knowing how difficult a task she was letting herself in for.

Matthew offered to make tea and he and Julie buzzed in and out of the room for a few minutes drip feeding the newly widowed woman information about how a family liaison officer would be allocated and would visit before the end of the day, what she could expect from the police and the steps that would be taken next. Steph gave them the name and number of a friend, a near neighbour, she would also like to have with her and, again, Julie was on the phone maintaining a professional tone as she imparted the terrible news, consoling the bereaved and making arrangements for them to visit as soon as they were able to do so. The brother-in-law, a black cab driver, saying he would be an hour or so, while the neighbour was only minutes away. Julie then let the uniforms outside know who to let in and who to keep at bay, as the press and curiosity seekers would not be far behind as social media was now lighting up.

'If you are feeling up to it I have a few questions,' Matthew ventured, the cup of tea he'd made her untouched in front of Steph and still no sign of the neighbour, some thirty minutes after she'd been called, 'it would be of great value.'

Steph nodded, as Julie took her cue to check on the friend's whereabouts and took a quick tour of the house before the SOCOs arrived.

'Mr Driver was performing at the Blue Snake club in Wapping last night,' Matthew began noticing that Mrs Driver seemed somewhat listless and inattentive but otherwise appeared calm, 'was he a regular at that venue?'

'Yes,' Steph cleared her throat, looking at the untouched tea but not fancying it, 'he was there for two or three weeks a couple of times each year. He did a lot of London clubs and venues but also others up and down the country. He spoke German and is … was very popular over there as well, particularly in Berlin, Munich and Hamburg.'

'Something of a success then?' Matthew ventured, noticing a little colour returning to Mrs Driver's face as she spoke of her husband.

'Yes, very much so, he's always in demand and has no end of work,' a hint of pride creeping into the widow's voice, 'though I always insist we have a break together, here and there, so he doesn't … that is, didn't burn out, you understand,' she almost smiled as she recollected. 'Although it was often while he toured either in Germany or the UK.'

'His act, he was a female impersonator?' Matthew moved the topic on.

'He has a fantastic singing voice,' the tense she used telling Matthew that Mrs Driver was still struggling to absorb his news, 'and a very graceful dancer. That is how he began, as a song and dance act with a partner. Then one day, Victor, who was to become his agent, noticed how Gerry could sing both the female and male parts of a song. His voice has a fantastic range and he is able to modulate the tone and pitch, such a voice as I'd never heard before.' She trailed off absorbed by the memory, forgetting her company.

'How did you meet?' Julie asked, having rejoined them.

'I worked for Victor at his agency, when he first started it up,' she explained, reaching for another tissue to dab her eyes which she felt should have been full of tears yet seemed to be dry. 'Gerry was worried about the act as his partner had left him in the lurch, she'd gotten herself pregnant and had gone off. He could impersonate a number of the top female singers as well as males and Victor suggested he dress the part, two halves to the act, one male and one female. Gerry wasn't keen at first, but Victor had me go shopping with him to help him pick clothes and, well, one thing led to another.'

'So he wasn't gay?' Matthew asked gently, mindful he may be treading on sensitive ground for the wife.

'No, it's a common error people make,' a brief smile flittered across her lips, suggesting the question held no difficulties for her, 'but we have … had a loving relationship. It would be twelve years next January.'

'No children?' Julie asked, having already judged the house too clean and uncluttered by toys or evidence of children living there.

'No, at first it was the lack of financial security that put us off but then, well you reach an age when you realise that too much time has passed,' she explained, still numbed from the news her voice remained monotone, 'but he would have made a good father.'

'Had he had any problems recently?' Matthew asked. 'Any financial worries, hate mail, professional jealousies, over-zealous fans or anything that may have made someone want to hurt him?' Steph shook her head in response to each part of his question.

'He had a growing number of fans,' she told them, 'they follow his blog, his Twitter and Instagram. He would show me some of the comments he received, from men and women, they are full of compliments and praise.'

'We will need to take his computer and other devices,' Julie explained. 'He has a study upstairs,' she'd already noticed it when she had poked around, 'we'll have to search that as well, to see if anyone has been causing him problems, you understand.'

'Things were looking up,' Steph informed them, 'he was working on a new act and had signed a contract to take the lead in a play, there was even talk of TV work.' Again the fleeting smile at the memory and pride she had for her husband's success.

'Did he normally wear female attire when not on stage?' Matthew asked as the doorbell rang, Julie jumping up to answer it.

'All the time, it was how he developed the act in order to get comfortable with the shoes and clothing, to be as natural looking as possible. He also switched to being billed only as *Geraldine Driver, Songstress and Impersonator*. Outside of this house, when he was working, he was Geraldine …' At that moment she broke off as a squat man in his late forties entered the room and Steph jumped up to embrace her brother-in-law, then broke down in tears.

For a while things became chaotic, once the tears started they were hard to stop. Grahame Driver tried to comfort his sister-in-law while also trying to converse with Matthew and Julie, then gave up as he also began to cry uncontrollably. Then Steph's friend finally turned up and immediately broke down herself. Matthew and Julie exchanged looks to suggest to each other they should withdraw, when the bell went once again heralding two SOCOs, to help search Gerry's office, and then shortly followed by the family liaison officer.

The brother, it turned out, added little to what they had learned from Steph. He was proud of his brother's success and couldn't name anyone who had a bad word to say about him. When gently pushed the brother admitted that in the early days of his solo act, Gerry had received some abusive emails and letters about his dressing as a woman.

'He ignored it all,' Grahame stated philosophically, still wiping his eyes, 'he never saw himself as doing anything different from what a lot of comedy actors do. I mean, look at Les Dawson or the Two Ronnies. It died away after a while, I mean, look at what you see on the TV these days.'

'Though it was also down to his perfecting the act,' Steph chipped in, between sobs as her own tears continued to flow. 'He wasn't Gerry on stage, he would come home saying how people applauded him as Geraldine for the accuracy of *her* male impersonations.'

'He was so good,' Steph's friend sniffed, 'we often went to see him when he was in London, it was uncanny, like looking at his twin sister.'

'The odd thing was it was that gay lot that caused him most headaches,' Grahame snorted derisively, then anticipating the inspector's next question qualified his statement by adding, 'Nothing serious mind, I mean, just comments on his blog and those tweet things, when he didn't support their cause.'

'How's that exactly?' Matthew wanted to know, not fully understanding.

'Oh, he was all for gays and lezzies and those bi's,' Grahame reassured them. 'I mean, a lot of them were his fans but some of them wanted more from him, for him to speak out on some cause or other, but he wasn't into politics or anything like that.'

'The new act was going to be more cutting edge,' Steph proudly informed them. 'There was going to be more satire and Geraldine was going to point out the hypocrisies of both sides of any debate. Gerry was so enthusiastic about it all, he worked so hard.' Again the tears began to flow.

The inspector and sergeant finally got away, much later than they had hoped, leaving the SOCOs to bag and label everything that they had indicated and telling the grieving widow and brother they would keep them informed and how the FLO would act as their main liaison.

'You didn't mention that you and your lezzie friends were keen Geraldine fans,' Matthew stated as they pulled away, heading for Wapping through the early rush hour traffic.

'Along with them gays and bi's you mean.' Julie, finally free of the professional demeanour required when dealing with the victim's family, suddenly burst into laughter and struggled to control the car. 'Shit, the Telegraph and Mail have such a lot to answer for.'

'Seriously,' Matthew wanted to know, 'do you get much stick?'

'More for the colour of my skin and frizzy hair than my sexual preferences,' Julie explained, she considered herself to have a thick skin, and being in the job had added a few layers, but there had been times when it had gotten to her. When she had been sixteen she had slapped a woman who had spat at her after Julie had kissed a girlfriend in the street, another time she'd floored a particularly obnoxious army private and, on one memorable occasion when on leave, she had given two men a good kicking who had rounded on her in a pub. 'What others can't accept is their problem not mine, what about you?'

'How's that?' Matthew was surprised at her question. 'Outside of being a copper I'm a white, middle-aged man, isn't that the standard against which everything else is judged?'

'Yes, I get that,' Julie responded, straight-faced, 'you are exactly the template for the type of prick that would refer to me as a lezzie.'

'Aren't I just, Sergeant,' Matthew smiled broadly, 'aren't I just.'

Matthew had let Hayden know they were going straight to Wapping nick as they drove down Wapping Lane and that he'd call back at the Blue Snake club after his statement to the media. Inspector Graves had done them proud, even the man from the press office agreed that the setting was a splendid one. Despite the weak sun, gathering gloom of the early evening and chill wind, Graves had arranged for the conference to be held in Waterside

Gardens which stood between the Marine Unit museum and police station. This afforded great views of the Thames and the police moorings and given it was open air the representatives of the media wouldn't want to hang around for too long.

Under the watchful eye of a press officer the two inspectors read out their prearranged statements. Graves giving a brief overview of how and when the victim was found and Matthew explained it was being treated as a suspicious death and asking for witnesses who may have seen either the victim or his car after midnight. While the media officer distributed packs with copies of the statements, relevant photographs and contact details. Matthew then asked for questions and a drably besuited, middle-aged man, who was obviously well versed in attending such events, not only held his hand up as everyone else did but began speaking before being acknowledged.

'Carter, NDS,' he began formulaically with his name and the news syndication group he worked for, his voice clear and cutting across those of the other journalists present, his eyes unwaveringly on Matthew, his mobile thrust forward to catch and record the response to his question. 'Inspector Merry, you will be aware of the series of hate crime attacks that have recently been perpetuated across East London, are you treating this as yet another attack in the series?'

'At the moment,' Matthew responded, he had no need to raise his voice given the silence that had descended on the jurno pack, which sensed that a meaty question had been asked, 'we are following a number of leads and not confining ourselves to any particular line of inquiry. Although we are not ruling this out as being a hate crime nor are we, as yet, ruling it in.' Matthew made a grimace of a smile and asked for the next question.

'So, a gay man is strangled and dumped in the Thames and you don't consider it a hate crime?' Carter again cut across the other jurnos.

'We did ask that you all restrict yourselves to one question each so that a wider range of questions could be addressed,' Matthew stated, his face unresponsive though his tone mildly reproving. 'However, in order to clarify the situation for you all, Mr Driver's family has stated that he was not gay and that in practice he had no links with the LGBTI community.'

A young man standing at the front snorted laughter at this, loudly declaring, 'But he was found wearing a dress!'

Matthew did not respond, though fixed the youngster with a disdainful glare, before continuing, 'As I said in the statement made, we have yet to ascertain a motive for the killing and we are not ruling anything in or out at this time.'

A young female reporter now jumped on the bandwagon with what she considered a relevant question, 'Can you release details of what resources are being deployed to solve the series of hate crimes?'

'I'm not in a position to answer your question,' Matthew pointed out, a response that didn't seem to surprise anyone other than the reporter who'd asked the question.

'In the light of all the budget cuts the police are having to deal with, is hate crime being put on a back burner?' the young man who had been disbelieving that Driver was not gay, now asked.

'Are there any more questions about this particular case, that either Inspector Merry or Inspector Graves can assist you with?' the media officer suddenly cut in, deciding Matthew needed rescuing from the snare that had entrapped him. 'If not I believe Inspector Graves is happy to take those interested on a brief tour of the Marine Policing Unit museum.'

A number of the reporters obviously thought this would provide an interesting angle to the story and began to move as if the press conference was over, when a woman standing at the rear of the media pack and holding up a digital camcorder asked, 'Just one last question, is it true that Mr Driver had recently signed a lucrative contract to appear in a new play and pilot for a television show?'

Everyone paused, looking at Matthew as he pondered his response, the inspector was much more puzzled at the direction of this question than he had been of the previous ones, 'At the present time I can only say that Mr Driver's career has been described to me as being very much on an upward trajectory, but I'm not able to confirm the specifics as yet.'

The conference quickly broke up and the majority of reporters followed Graves to the museum, while the three camera crews that had attended dismantled their gear and a few photographers took shots of the views along the Thames. Matthew caught up with the female journalist as she was exiting the gardens. She was a large black woman in a tight coat, her slight accent denoted a childhood spent in South Africa, her expression and carriage indicated a degree of weariness while her eyes shone with sharp intelligence.

'Excuse me!' Matthew hailed her. 'Your question back there, might I ask what prompted it?'

'Is it important?' she countered. 'You seemed to discount it as unconnected to your lines of inquiry.'

'To be honest,' Matthew saw no reason to prevaricate under such a keen and piercing gaze, 'it isn't uppermost in the investigation currently but that could change.'

'I see, it is early days yet and you do not want to commit yourself. However, with equal honesty, Mr Driver's career move was not central to my own investigation,' she explained, believing in Matthew's open demeanour, 'I have been looking into the links between Greenspace Media and RightOn Entertainment Services for a freelance piece I have been writing. Mr Driver's name and his "upward trajectory", as you described it, happened to have been mentioned in passing, though not as anything significant. Having heard of his murder this morning I thought it worth asking, admittedly a speculative question on my part as there is no obvious link with his being killed.'

'I'll keep it in mind,' Matthew responded, feeling there was something evasive in her answer, 'but as I said earlier we have no views on motive as yet.'

'Very well,' she rummaged in her bag and pulled out a card to give him, 'but if you find a motive and want to talk further, you can reach me on those numbers.'

# Chapter Four

'I've known Geraldine, that is Gerry, since I started here, two and a half years ago,' Melanie Smith, the manager of the Blue Snake club, confirmed for Matthew and Julie; as the three sat in her small office on the first floor, at the back, overlooking the carpark. 'He was one of our best acts, drew in a crowd from across all demographics.'

'How's that?' Matthew puzzled, he was finding the up-beat, black woman, who looked younger than her thirty-five years, at odds with his idea of a night club manager – although he had little to judge this by.

'People came to hear her sing and dance, that attracted all ages and generally couples: either hetro or gay/lesbian,' Melanie explained with a broad smile that hardly ever seemed to leave her face. She was proud of her knowledge of club management and how she used box office data, as well as her own intuition, to judge what acts would work at the club. 'Some of the dance numbers, especially with the chorus girls, are raunchy. Especially her signature *Hey Big Spender* number, would get the guys and girls of all ages hot under the collar. We also have a good comedian booked as well, which helps, and a magician who does a rather eccentric striptease as part of her magic act and a comedy juggling duo. It's classic, modern burlesque.'

'How did he get on with the other acts?' Julie wanted to know, assuming that 'modern burlesque' was code for 'artistically sleazy'.

'Fine, Geraldine wasn't a prima donna and understood the concept of a balanced show, the audience might come here to see *Geraldine Driver* but she knew that if the supporting acts did well then she was all the better received,' Melanie explained. 'She would exchange a joke with the compere as they came and went on stage, make remarks about the other acts in her pieces. Always boosting them mind, and often self-depreciating, so the audience and the other acts liked her all the more for it.'

'What about the audiences, anyone cause a fuss or problems?' Matthew asked, trying not to be distracted by the unwavering smile.

'Not as a rule, most of the audience took *him* for a female and appreciated *her* male impersonations all the more for it but Geraldine always hinted at the truth, he liked to leave them a little uncertain,' the smile broadened even more as she explained, her eyes fluttering as she had rather taken a fancy to the large, sombre looking inspector. 'He'd had a number specially written for him that he usually finished on, he called it *Life's a Drag*. It sends up the traditional drag act a bit and features a couple of quick changes in the wings,' Mel paused, pondering for a brief moment. 'I don't think this is anything important but last week some of Geraldine's agency friends came down to see the act, all comps of course, and things got a little rowdy at one point.'

'Rowdy?' Julie cut in, as much to remind the pair she was still present, annoyed with her boss who seemed to be enjoying the manager's flirtatious manner, his normally stern and professional visage taking on a rather inappropriately leering smile. Could she have done so without being seen she'd have kicked him as a reminder they were there investigating a murder.

'A couple of the group started to heckle, shouting out "Gerry, Gerry ..." like that American TV show that used to be so popular. Heckling isn't that common and Gerry can usually deal with it, but on this occasion one of our security personnel had to step in with a warning and they quietened down. Just a bit too much booze, that's all. Although one of Geraldine's more enthusiastic fans had a go at them in the interval, nothing more than "handbags at dawn" as Mike, our security manager, put it. In the end I think they were all asked to leave, after the interval Geraldine came back on doing *Hey Big Spender* and it was all forgotten.'

'Were any names taken?' Matthew asked, wondering why Julie was looking so annoyed.

'Mike would be able to tell you. The fan is well known to us, can be a bit of a creep, hangs around the stage door for Geraldine, sends flowers to her dressing room with notes saying "with my undying love". Geraldine laughs it off. He gets … got stuff like that all the time but this guy was a bit persistent for my thinking,' Melanie gave the inspector a knowing look and Matthew responded with an equally knowing 'Ahh, yes, of course' and a wink.

'You were the last person to see Mr Driver leave the club, is that correct?' Julie asked, adding, 'Sorry!' as she managed to catch Matthew on his ankle with her boot as she shifted position in her chair.

'Yes, we spoke as he was leaving, little more than goodnight really,' Melanie explained, pulling a sympathetic expression as Matthew rubbed his ankle and looked aggrieved. 'Mike was in the security office, which is by the rear door, and he shouted out his usual *Goodnight Sweetheart;* Geraldine always sang it back to him, you know the number from the TV show. I asked him if he wanted the band in early today, as he had been rehearsing some new numbers with them, and we had auditions lined up for this afternoon, but he said not, he was looking forward to a lay in,' Melanie sniffed, her smile gone as sadness suddenly overwhelmed her as she realised Geraldine would never be back. 'It's so tragic, he was so well liked and his career was really taking off. It's beyond belief.'

'Yes, our condolences,' Julie said automatically and with little feeling. 'We will be speaking with your security manager next but if you think of anything else, no matter how irrelevant it might seem, then please let us know; you have the number to ring.'

'One last question,' Matthew said, causing Julie to hesitate, half out of her chair and praying he wasn't going to make some inanely inappropriate remark to the manager. 'You are the manager here, obviously, but who actually owns the club?'

'It's Greenspace Media, they own a number of clubs in London and down the Thames corridor to Southend,' Melanie responded, her broad smile returning.

'His agent is Victor Thorsson isn't it, at the Blue Bird Agency?'

'Yes, I can get you his contact details if you like.'

'That's OK, thanks, we already have them,' Julie glared at Matthew as she pushed past him as he rose from his seat to leave the office. 'Thank you for your assistance.'

Apart from his shaved head, Mike Stennard did not particularly look like someone whose job was club security: he was in his late twenties, wearing a light grey suit, blue shirt, no tie and had the physique more of a sprinter than a bodybuilder. He lounged back in the swivel chair in the security office, trying to look at ease in front of the detectives but failing to do so.

'How can I help you pair?' he began, his face cheery though his eyes and voice denoted how tired and stressed he was by the day's events. 'Your other two colleagues have already taken the CCTV recordings and list of customers and staff we had in last night, but if there is anything else I can do …'

'I'm DI Merry and this is DS Lukula,' Matthew introduced them, glancing around the small office that had a bank of four TV screens – each showing four images from the CCTV inside and outside the club – there was only one spare seat besides the one Stennard occupied.

'I already met Sergeant Lukula this afternoon, heard that plonker Barrett thought you were a dancer,' Stennard tried too hard to inject a note of camaraderie in his voice but neither of the detectives joined him in a smile. 'There's only the one chair, I'm afraid, but I can make you both a brew if you want,' he motioned to the tea making things on the shelf behind them.

'Thanks, but no, we won't take up much of your time,' Matthew made no move to take the seat, his ingrained manners making him glance at Julie out of the corner of his eye but she studiously ignored him. She might like the thought of his rather traditional manners and she readily gave up her seat for the infirm and elderly but didn't need anyone to do so for her. So the pair stood throughout the interview. 'You were one of the last to see Mr Driver when he left last night.'

'Yes, me and Mel,' Mike looked genuinely sad at the recollection, giving a slight shrug as if trying to rid himself of the emotion. 'Geraldine always left with a cheery wave and a smile and came back the next day the same.'

'You got on well?'

'She got on with everyone, never a bad word about her or from her,' Mike told them gloomily. 'You know, at the end of each week she left a small tip in an envelope for the dressing room cleaner. Never known anyone else do that. I know it was part of the act, Geraldine was always bright and breezy, always thinking of others but it was so natural, so much part of what made her *real*, you know.'

'You say it was part of the act,' Matthew asked, 'so Gerry wasn't really like that?'

'Dun know, never met Gerry,' Mike said with a shrug and sudden smile, 'I know Geraldine was Gerry but even now I can't think of her as anything other than a girl, as Geraldine.'

'So why say it was an act? Why do you think Gerry wasn't like that in real life?' Julie wanted to know, pressing for an understanding of Driver's dual personality.

'I don't know,' Mike shrugged, lost for words to explain how he felt. 'His other impersonations were spot on, the voice and gestures, everything was perfect but they were still impersonations.

Whereas Geraldine was *just Geraldine* and Gerry didn't exist as far as I was concerned,' again he shrugged and looked embarrassed, unable to explain just how complete and perfect Gerry's main impersonation was.

'When did you leave?' Matthew asked, changing the subject seeing that Mike's confusion was misleading them.

'Just after two, only the night duty guy was left but he saw me go,' Mike shrugged yet again the uneasy, rather nervous expression returning to his face. 'I don't live far, just up by Aldgate East tube in Shearsmith House, so I use a bike.'

'The club shuts about one?' Julie asked.

'The show finishes at midnight and the band stops forty-five minutes later, people have a final drink and we hope to have the place empty by one thirty. And no,' Mike went on, anticipating their next question based on what Constable Hayden had already asked him earlier, 'we don't record who leaves or when, though it'll be on the tape from the door camera. Geraldine's act finished just after eleven thirty but, after she'd changed, she always spent ten minutes saying goodbye and thank you to her fans in the bar area, so usually only got away between twelve and half past.'

'What about last night?' Matthew hoped to get an exact time.

'She signed out at quarter past, but it could have been five minutes either side, though I think the clock was pretty close on the quarter hour, as I remember,' Mike glanced up at the clock as he spoke, both the inspector and sergeant noted it was running five minutes fast.

'Any thoughts about who might have killed him, anyone he had a problem with, anything untoward happened recently, that you can think of?' Matthew asked, as Mike once again shrugged and this time bit his lip nervously, perhaps he knew something or, like many people, perhaps he was just nervous talking to the police, most people felt guilty about something.

'No, sorry, nothing I can think of,' he shook his head, adding a final shrug for good measure.

'What about an incident last week?' Julie asked, like Matthew she suspected that the security manager was holding back on something, whether it was relevant or not was a different matter. 'The one involving a couple of hecklers and a fan.'

'Ohh … that,' a dismissive shrug to indicate that Mike thought it of no importance, 'a couple of drunks got a bit noisy but they shut up when I asked them to. The guy they was with, so Mel said, was Geraldine's agent, there was six of them on a table right up front, all of them comp'd so they'd gone a bit mad on the drinks. Only time I've seen Geraldine annoyed, actually shouted at her agent afterwards when he went backstage. Still it was nothing but a storm in a tea cup, that's all.'

'Didn't someone else get involved, a fan, what about him?' Matthew prompted.

'Started in on one of the drunks in the bar during the interval, just words at first then the other heckler joined in and there was some pushing and a slap or two. Handbags at dawn, know what I mean, it stopped the second one of my guys got to them. He got them back to their seats and hovered about for a while and it all stayed very quiet after that.'

'The fan had he been trouble before? Julie asked, sensing there was a lead to be followed.

'Ohh yer, I say, bit of a whack job but harmless,' Mike shrugged this time adding a wry smile to the mix, 'I gave his details to the policewoman here earlier,' Matthew and Julie exchanged glances realising Hayden had beaten them to it, 'but I told them he ain't the sort, mincing about all of a flutter and demanding to see *his* Geraldine but nothing more than a pest. Very polite but annoying, never took the hint that he was getting in the way or others might want to see Geraldine as well.'

'How does the security team here work exactly?' Matthew changed tack, knowing Hayden would be tracking down the overly enthusiastic fan.

'Much the same as most places we work at,' Mike shrugged again, swivelling his chair round to the screens and back as he spoke, 'me or my deputy are in here monitoring the screens and directing the others. Two guys on the door, two inside, plus me and my deputy on relief and as back-up,' there was something in Mike's voice that was trying to make it sound almost like a military operation.

'You work at other places?' Julie asked before Matthew, who was pondering the blank space in the corner of one of the screens, could think to do so.

'We all work for GR Security, they have the contract for this place and a number of clubs and pubs,' Mike explained, this time without any shrugging, perhaps feeling on safer ground with the topic. 'Most of the other guys rotate round different clubs and the money can be better up the West End, you know, tips and that. However, I got made up to supervisory officer and, as head of a security team, you are expected to stay at one place. I opted for here as it's quiet and near home. Plus it's a good team under Mel, nice lady manager, know what I mean.'

'What about the broken CCTV camera?' Matthew wanted to know, nodding at the blank square on one of the screens. 'Does that happen often?'

'Ohh … that,' Mike looked abashed, shrugging as he spoke. 'No, not often, not for some time. A while back we had a spate of cars broken into and the camera was regularly put out of action, but I had a couple of guys out there in a van and they caught 'em.'

'What about this time?' Matthew persisted.

'It went out the day before yesterday,' the shrugs were now coming thick and fast, like some exaggerated nervous tick, 'I'd had one of the guys out there from time to time, mainly as the punters arrived and left but nothing happened.'

'How did it happen?'

'Spray paint over the lens,' Mike gave a half-hearted shrug, 'someone's idea of a joke I guess, though how they got up to reach it I can't work out. The carpark's lit up at night so I can't see it'd make any difference, do you?'

'When's it scheduled for repair?' Matthew continued to push with the questioning, half-guessing what was making Mike so nervous.

'Soon, I think,' Mike stated with another shrug, then breathed a sighed 'Fuck' as he gave in, resigned at being cornered, 'I forgot to put the order in, didn't I,' another sighed 'Fuck' as he looked at his feet dejectedly. 'I'll do it today but I just forgot, been busy, but we have a contract for twenty-four hour maintenance, so it could have been fixed straight away. I can lose my seniority over this, you know. GR Security is about *total security*, no fuckups, you understand.'

'OK, thanks, for the honesty Mike,' Matthew sympathised.

'Shit,' Mike stated with a philosophical shrug, 'just my luck it happened now, normally no one would have noticed. It's plain bad luck something had to happen to put the spotlight on it.' Perhaps the coincidence of Geraldine's bad luck happening when his own poor judgement occurred didn't strike Mike, he certainly didn't seem to appreciate the vastly different extent of their relative degree of bad luck. Although neither Matthew nor Julie bothered to point it out as they left the club, mainly as neither believed in coincidences.

'We'll have a full briefing tomorrow afternoon,' Matthew confirmed as he, Julie, Ray, Hayden and Harry quickly caught up over a coffee in the incident room thirty minutes after he'd left the club. 'I'll confirm an exact time with the governor and let you all know. Ray, I'll need an update on the background checks on all the people at the club yesterday and a summary of anything of interest from the house to house and the press appeal,' Ray nodded, his team was already focused on the task but he understood that Matthew still had to confirm it was being done. 'Hayden, if you can work with the team looking at CCTV, get as much footage of the car, the victim and any possible or actual attackers that you can.'

'If we get a clear, full face shot of the attacker do you want it straight away or wait for the briefing?' Hayden was both old enough and experienced enough to get away with a touch of sarcasm at her superior's expense, even at the end of a long day.

'If you do, perhaps consult with Harry and let me know what you decide,' Matthew took it in good stead, laughing with the others and noting that Harry seemed pleased to have been included in the joke as it was a sure sign he now held full team membership. 'Julie and I will interview Driver's agent tomorrow morning and track down this fan, what's his name?'

'Stickels, Jonathon Stickels,' Hayden told him, 'has a bit of a record, various offences in the past: possession of drugs, defacing property, restraining order from a well known celeb. It's all in the file,' she informed Matthew, handing him a folder as she spoke.

'Well done, Hayden,' Matthew stated, almost gleeful at the thought of a lead.

'Teacher's pet,' Julie nudged the constable in admiration.

'Harry helped, sir,' Hayden stated modestly but also truthfully, despite her years in the force she was still proud of doing a good job.

'Right, on that note, let's call it a day,' Matthew clapped the folder on the desk in front of him as if bringing a gavel down to indicate the meeting was over, they all felt they'd made good progress. 'Everyone get a good night's sleep, we all need alert minds and an early start tomorrow.'

# Chapter Five

Matthew had delayed himself from getting home and his much needed dinner by stopping off at the MIT's base in Barking. He had not intended to stop, just pick up a couple of files he needed for two impending court appearances he had scheduled. He had once, not so very long ago, nearly derailed a case in court by being underprepared and was now paranoid about having his notes to hand so he could regularly check through and memorise them. Then, on his way out, he stupidly picked up a ringing phone. It was a message for Sergeant Lukula from the Birmingham force, a suspect she was after for a stabbing had gone to ground amongst relatives in the Birmingham area, the call was to say the youth had been sighted twice that day but had evaded capture and was still at large. Matthew thanked them for the information and stopped to text Julie the news.

'Shit,' Julie commented on Matthew's text, she was sitting on a sofa in Yvette's living room, wrapped in a towel and drying her hair with another towel.

'What's that?' Yvette called from the kitchen, absorbed in preparing their meal. Yvette, being a vegetarian, was doing her best to cook a meal for herself and Julie, who was anything but a vegetarian. Yvette was torn between not wanting to impose her own dietary beliefs on her girlfriend while, at the same time, was loath to contaminate her kitchen with non-vegetarian produce. Worse, she was well aware that Julie didn't even begin to appreciate her efforts or the inner turmoil this conundrum caused her; so long as the food was hot and filling was all Julie was concerned about.

'Nothing, just a text about a little shit who stabbed another teenager to death and has gone on the run,' Julie called back. She had four witnesses, CCTV footage of the stabbing and a clear ID of the perpetrator, all she needed was the youngster himself: Craig Warren.

'Oh, good,' Yvette called back, not really listening and not noticing that Julie was now stood in the doorway, minus both towels, her nakedness emphasised by the black ink design tattoos on various parts of her body.

'Smells nice,' Julie purred, waiting for her girlfriend to notice her. She had met Yvette a few months before, she was the dance instructor at a salsa club that Julie had decided to try. A spur of the moment thing to get herself out of the gloom of a prior bad relationship and the death of her mother.

They hadn't really hit it off at first. Yvette, as Julie was eventually to discover, had been in an abusive relationship some years previous and was still hesitant about building a relationship with anyone new. She was a dancer but only got the occasional stage job and earned her living mainly from her dance lessons and costume design work at two off-West End theatres. Her work, by its nature requiring her to be gregarious and keep odd hours, had played its part in fuelling her previous partner's jealous suspicions. The arguments had turned violent and Yvette had ended up in A&E a number of times until, eventually, a nurse and female police officer together persuaded her to seek out a women's shelter. The fact that her abuser was another woman had left her rather isolated in the shelter and, to make matters worse, CPS didn't pursue the prosecution. However, Yvette had gathered sufficient resolve to leave and start afresh. Unfortunately the ex-partner refused to accept Yvette's decision and kept turning up, on the last occasion to one of the dance classes and Julie had stepped in. Julie didn't take crap from anyone.

At first Yvette had found Julie's attitude somewhat intimidating so had been slow in letting herself fall for the police sergeant. But now, as she turned from the sauce she was stirring to see Julie in the doorway naked and fresh from the shower, she knew what she felt was love. Not simply lust, though that was part of the mix – Julie's well toned, slim body and pretty face was highly desirable – but it was the look in Julie's eyes that stirred Yvette's heart. The fact that Julie was so enjoying just watching Yvette and the domestic scene, said it all: they were at peace with themselves and each other. Comfortable in their relationship in a way that only lovers could be. Their passion for each other's physical touch was icing on a deep and rich cake.

'Surprised to see you here,' Swift said earnestly, catching sight of Matthew as he was leaving the office. 'How's the day gone?'

'Made a fair bit of progress,' Matthew told his governor, trying not to look annoyed at being further delayed, only to find himself trailing behind Swift back to the superintendent's office as he quickly updated him and agreed a time for the briefing tomorrow.

Matthew had finally gotten away from Swift. He wondered what was going on with his governor who seemed to be putting in some very long hours at the office, even for someone new in post. It was almost as if Swift was avoiding going home despite his partner being a very pleasant, warm-hearted, up-and-coming barrister. So why Swift was avoiding her company Matthew couldn't fathom. He made a mental note to ask Hayden, who seemed to know what was going on in the lives of most of her colleagues, but then promptly forgot as he focused on looking out for the speed cameras as he drove along Alfreds Way to the A13 and home.

It was long after dinnertime as he let himself into his house, he expected his daughters to be in bed and his wife, in all likelihood, sipping a wine while engrossed in an Ofsted document or some TV documentary. She was a serious soul at heart he reflected. He was, therefore, surprised to hear a man's laughter coming from the dining room.

'Hi,' Matthew said peering around the door, taking in the stranger sat at the table, on which there was a MacBook and various piles of paper, while his wife, smiling across at the unknown man, was pouring the last of a bottle of wine into their glasses.

'Hi, this is Lance, the consultant I was telling you about,' Kathy explained, her tone guilt free which made Matthew more suspicious rather than less. 'I invited him to dinner so we could work on things away from the "maelstrom of the ranch",' she turned her smile back to her guest, obviously repeating a phrase he had previously used with her.

'Hi,' said Lance, standing to offer his hand to Matthew, which Matthew briefly shook, noticing that Lance was lean and tall, wore jeans, a light, cloth jacket and open neck shirt with his sand coloured hair brushed back over his ears. His only redeeming feature, Matthew thought, was a decidedly Romanesque nose in an otherwise narrow and nondescript face. 'We saw you on the TV earlier, thought you came over rather well.'

'Well?' Matthew puzzled, he was hardly concerned about the ratings so long as the message about their need for information came across clearly.

'Although you could learn to smile a bit,' Kathy teased hoping to keep things light, she could see Matthew was tired and hungry and in no mood to be sociable.

'Though that's not a bad thing for a police officer,' Lance pointed out, 'the public want to know you are taking things seriously, after all.' Lance and Kathy exchanged smiles, no doubt having made a few jokes earlier at Matthew's expense about dour looking cops.

'Dinner is in the oven, only chicken casserole ...' Kathy started to inform Matthew.

'A million times better than anything served at the hotel where I'm staying,' Lance grinned in appreciation. 'I'm already feeling a bit of a fraud,' he went on, unsympathetic to Matthew's growling stomach, 'Kathy is doing a great job in the acting headteacher post and she hardly needs my help.'

'That's actually not true,' Kathy reassured him, 'I've been swamped since Carole was taken ill and you really helped keep things on a steady course last week.'

'Great, are the girls still up?' Matthew wanted to know, too tired to listen any longer.

'Lizzy was soundo from the moment I put her down but Becky is up. She's writing a story for homework, on the theme of greed, and I think she was hoping to be able to read it to you.'

'OK, I'll go up first and eat later,' Matthew backed out of the room, leaving his cap and coat over the back of a chair. 'Nice seeing you, Lance, no doubt you'll be going so I'll say goodnight now.'

'It's about a dog who won't share his bone,' Becky explained as she settled down to read her story to her dad, she was nine and had a serious soul like her mother, while her little sister was seven and had a tendency to be bad tempered, a trait Matthew was at a loss to explain the precedence of.

'Do dogs share bones?' Matthew asked philosophically.

'Good dogs do,' Becky was completely clear on that point, 'but Bonzo is a big, bad, ugly dog with long smelly fur, who doesn't share and is greedy.'

'Bonzo, that's an odd name for a dog,' Matthew pointed out. 'If he's ugly and smelly perhaps you should call him Lance.'

'Lance isn't a dog's name,' Becky laughed, pleased that her dad was making silly jokes. Matthew, however, hearing more laughter from downstairs was wondering otherwise.

'You're in a bad mood,' Julie observed as she drove Matthew to the carpark in Bell Wharf Lane, from where they could walk to St Swithin's Lane in which the Blue Bird Talent Management Agency had its office, 'did you miss breakfast again?'

'What?' Matthew was well fed but tired from a restless night, his mind too full of the previous day's events to find peace enough for slumber.

'I said you're in a bad mood.'

'No I'm not.'

'You bloody well sound it,' Julie stated feeling aggrieved at her boss. 'No hello this morning, just "get the car, you can drive me to the agency",' she mimicked his grumpy voice.

'I'm just preoccupied,' Matthew explained. 'Besides I didn't realise you were that needy.'

'Sod you, Mr Grumpy.'

'Sounds like you are the one in a bad mood,' Matthew pointed out – thinking of Lizzy's tantrum earlier: she'd wanted a different breakfast cereal, which they didn't have, and a different selection for her packed lunch, which they didn't have either.

'I would just appreciate a little respect in front of the others on the team, I'm not your chauffeur you know,' in practice she wasn't that put out but she wanted Matthew to snap out of his mood or the day was going to grind on more than it needed to.

'OK, fair point,' Matthew conceded. In the car their relative ranks were always put aside for plain speaking, a habit they'd acquired which allowed them to both accommodate each other's ego as well as move on with a case when things got stuck. 'Good morning, Sergeant, how are things with you?'

'Great, and you?'

'Great.'

The pair lapsed into silence as Julie negotiated the heavy, early morning traffic around Tower Hill.

# Chapter Six

St Swithin's Lane is one of the many medieval streets which still haunt London's street plan. Originally it would have sloped down to the muddy river edge but Victorian Bazalgette's civic engineering corseted the blue snake's winding path and added a few acres of prime building land between the lane's current termination at Cannon Street and the embankment at Hanseatic Walk. The street is narrow and in medieval times the houses would have vaulted out over it, virtually cutting out the sky and shutting in the stink of the open drain that still runs down its modern day centre. However, the Great Fire, the Blitz and modern planning have done their work in creating a hotchpotch of architectural design down either side of the lane, although most of the buildings are still confined within the old medieval boundaries.

The street is home to a smattering of enterprises: pubs, restaurants, shops, headquarters of illustrious organisations and even a boutique hotel. The Blue Bird Talent Management Agency can only be identified by a small sign fixed to a blue painted door which opens onto steep, narrow stairs. The agency occupies the whole first floor, of a two storey building, and comprises a modern reception area and three cramped offices beyond, the stairs continuing up to the large attic room which doubles as the agency's meeting space.

Matthew had phoned ahead to check that Victor Thorsson would be present and he and Julie were quickly ushered into the larger of the three offices. Thorsson was a big man in his fifties, broad shouldered, square faced with wavy brown hair, green eyes, thin lips and large nose. His all too masculine appearance was at odds with the eye shadow he wore and his manicured, bright green painted nails. He stood to welcome the detectives, his thin smile revealing perfectly even and brilliantly white teeth, no doubt the work of a very expensive dentist who had learned his trade in Hollywood, California.

'Terrible news, terrible …' Thorsson's voice, the result of years of training and control, was light and at odds with his bulky frame, his expression melancholy and his eyes red rimmed and brimming as if on the point of tears. 'I had already cleared my scheduled meetings as soon as I heard yesterday,' he babbled, motioning the pair to sit, after they had both gratefully accepted the receptionist's offer of coffee. 'Grahame, Gerry's older brother, phoned yesterday afternoon to give me the news, terrible …' he collapsed heavily back into his chair, waving his hand before his face to fight back the tears. There was something almost comic about the performance but it held a poignant sadness that only a natural clown could achieve.

The receptionist, a rather simpering, camp young man, brought in the coffees and asked Thorsson if he required anything else, then retreated as Thorsson, still unable to find his voice, waved him out. Thorsson's desk was cluttered with papers, two phones, keyboard and a computer screen. The leather and steel chairs that the inspector and sergeant sat on were comfortable, if worn, and in the corner was a tall, battered metal cupboard. In addition, the small office had a large window made up of smaller wooden edged panes that looked out onto the narrow street and the shuttered windows of the office opposite. The limited wall space was dominated by three large framed posters, one of Geraldine Driver and two of Vicky Delight: Thorsson in his performing heyday. There was no comparison, Vicky Delight – in platinum blond wig, heavy makeup, glitzy dress, excessively high heels and large, obviously false breasts – was a man in drag, while Geraldine was the epitome of a stylish chanteuse.

'You used to perform yourself?' Matthew asked, as always looking to ease into his questioning, coming at the core of what he wanted to know from a side angle.

'Yes, but in those days burlesque was marginal, just smutty comedians and strippers performing in pubs and working men's clubs,' Thorsson sighed, easily distracted from his grief, 'I did a comedy drag act, mother-in-law jokes between the strippers, gave everyone time to get the next round in. It was a living but I spent a lot of time finding work and that's how the agency began.'

'How did the name come about?' Matthew's curiosity getting the better of him as Julie fidgeted with her cup, wondering when he'd get to the point.

'A tattoo, I'd show you but it would mean I would have to get up,' Thorsson smirked. 'It was part of my act, I'd sing *Blue Bird to Happiness* and give them a flash. Gays would always get it first and knowing how many were in the audience told me how to pitch the act.'

'Clever,' Julie said, intrigued by the idea.

'Tricks of the trade, dear.'

'You met Gerald Driver early in his career?' Matthew moved on.

'Yes, his mother saw him as another Engelbert Humperdinck or Tommy Steele, stars from her youth. However, it hadn't come off nor had fronting a band either, then he joined up with a girl as a song and dance act,' Thorsson explained. 'The partner was good although she was lightweight in comparison to Gerry, but they scraped a living. Our paths crossed once or twice, I'd seen the act and saw his potential but with the mother as his manager I kept my views to myself. Then one day he turned up out of the blue,' Thorsson paused for a second, organising his thoughts but also at the memory of all that potential being cut short and dumped in the Thames. 'I worked from home then, a two-up-two-down in North London, still working the boards as well as trying to expand the agency. Steph, Mrs Driver to be, was my new secretary.'

'That's how the pair met?' Julie asked, trying to speed things up.

'Yes, he'd come to me in a panic,' Thorsson went on unhurriedly, recognising Matthew was a listener and happy to hear the entire tale in its fullest form, 'his partner had left him a note, she was pregnant and going back to mum and dad. His mother had charged off in a blue funk and he, left to his own devices and not knowing which way to turn, came to me.'

'Where he found marriage and fame,' Julie summarised, hoping to jump to the present day.

'My initial advice, having had him signed to the agency first, was to continue as a solo act as his talent was more than enough to compensate the loss of his partner. I then began to work on him, suggesting he try out the idea of being a fully fledged female impersonator,' Thorsson sighed at the memory. 'He had the perfect build and bone structure for it.'

'He wasn't keen on the idea, I take it?' Despite her natural inclination for brevity Julie was being drawn into the details of the victim's history.

'For many, like myself,' Thorsson, who had never been particularly guarded and certainly not ashamed about his lifestyle, explained, 'wearing female attire is a way of life. I have always been happier and more comfortable in a dress. It isn't a sexual thing, not exactly you understand. Although being gay has helped, somehow making it more understandable and acceptable to others. It's the texture and colours, the very *performance* of dressing-up.'

'Like kids with a box of old clothes,' Matthew suggested.

'Yes,' Thorsson was surprised, the rather heavyweight, male detective had hit the nail on the head with such clarity, he'd have put money on the aggressively, bright-eyed female sergeant getting it first. *Life is full of such insightful surprises*, he thought, 'exactly, it transports you to another world, a different personality, one that is more real to you than the one you were forced to adopt from birth.'

'Though not Gerald,' Julie assumed, not in the least surprised at her boss's insight, she was used to him seeing the reality behind the smokescreen most people put over their inner lives, not that Thorsson was the type to keep much back, 'he took persuading?'

'Yes, very dyed in the wool and straight-laced in his views,' Thorsson grinned at the memory. 'However, I could see the gleam in Steph's eyes when he came in so I enlisted her help and the rest is history. There was the odd tantrum but generally it was plain sailing from then on. Fortunately his mother was well out of the picture by then, replaced by the more open-minded Steph. Once Gerry understood it was a performance, an impersonation that he had to perfect, then there was no stopping him.'

'So he was a bit of a perfectionist, could be demanding?' Matthew picked up, opening up a way to a possible motive for the performer's killing.

'On no one more than himself,' Thorsson qualified, 'he could upset people but they all recognised how hard he drove himself. His act quickly morphed from *Gerry Driver, Female Impersonator*, through a couple of intermediary steps to just billing as *Geraldine Driver – Songstress and Impersonator*. It was a full on performance that went beyond the stage, he lived the part while he was working and only became Gerry when at home with Steph or during their occasional times off. Nowadays, his fans and audiences only see him as Geraldine.'

'Did that cause any problems or animosity when people found out?' Julie puzzled at the performer's lifestyle.

'Not as such,' Thorsson ruminated, searching his mind for anything that might help, 'he got the odd comment on his blog, the occasional heckling, but nothing OTT.'

'Talking of heckling I believe you went to see Gerry's act recently,' Matthew asked, his team were going through Gerry's fan base, blog and emails to see if anything stood out but so far the heckling incident was the only significant thing of note.

'Yes, he was trying out some new material and I wanted a couple of people to see it,' Thorsson shifted in his seat, his voice for once losing it lightness, from his embarrassment. 'The agency was footing the bill, of course, unfortunately my guests rather over-indulged in the free drinks and got a little boisterous.'

'They heckled Gerry, disrupted his performance, got into a fight at the bar and were then thrown out.' Julie listed the sequence of events.

'I won't make excuses, their behaviour was inexcusable,' Thorsson said, the lightness of his voice returning and his face neutral, he obviously thought it all inconsequential, 'the fight was little more than a hissy fit and the bouncers intervened. The pair involved were told they would have to leave if they didn't quieten down, but they did so and they weren't actually thrown out.' It then suddenly dawned on Thorsson why the police were so interested in the small-scale drama, 'If you are thinking they were somehow involved in poor Gerry's death, the idea is somewhat far-fetched.' Matthew said nothing, just gave the agent his long, undertaker's stare, allowing the other man to fill the silence with his own words.

'They are a couple of young entrepreneurs,' Thorsson continued to make his point, 'new on the scene, no more than a couple of college kids, but they are doing well with a string of pop-up entertainment venues which I thought might suit Gerry's new act. The pair were just up themselves a bit, flouncing around.'

'We've been told that Gerry wasn't happy,' Matthew stated.

'No,' Thorsson admitted, 'refused to see them after his act, got angry with me when I said it might be a good thing. He said he didn't need that type of work anymore.'

'His wife said his career was on the up,' Julie commented. 'What's that about?'

'His big break,' the sadness returned to Thorsson's face, perhaps as much for the loss it entailed to himself and his agency as the thought that Gerry was taken at such a moment in his life.

'One of our main backers had seen the same potential in him I had seen, they wanted him for the lead role in a musical, off-West End at first then, assuming it did well, moving to the West End. It was linked with a pilot for a new TV show, a sort of variety cum chat show that he'd host, as Geraldine of course.'

'Who is this backer?' Matthew asked.

'Just a media production company. One of the many that are out there, some being more temporary than others.' Thorsson evaded giving a direct answer.

'What is your involvement?' Julie asked, unwittingly diverting Thorsson away from Matthew's line of questioning. 'You seemed to suggest they'd gone to Gerry direct.'

'The initial contact was directly to him, yes, though nothing unusual in that,' Thorsson smilingly agreed, although not with sufficient confidence to completely allay Julie's thinking he had somehow been marginalised in the deal.

'These backers,' Matthew returned to his question, now having put two and two together and was looking for confirmation that the answer he already had in mind was definitely a four, 'would that have been Greenspace Media?'

'Well, yes,' Thorsson managed to look both confused at how they had arrived at this point, and surprised at how the detective knew.

'From the sign on your door, this agency is a wholly owned subsidiary of RightOn Entertainment Services?' Matthew asked, while Thorsson looked increasingly agitated and Julie wondered what the relevance of this was, she'd seen the company name in small print below the agency logo on the door but hadn't given it any thought.

'It's simply a financial arrangement,' Thorsson literally tried waving the idea away, his right hand giving a dismissive gesture as he spoke. 'Nothing more than a device to achieve a cash injection into the agency, I am a shareholder and remain manager of the firm, along with my two junior partners. RightOn leave us to do what we do best, you understand,' he was almost patronising at the end, as if the financial dealings of the agency would be beyond the detectives.

'So, who is the major shareholder of RightOn Entertainments?' Matthew quietly persisted, not entirely clear how this was relevant to his case but realising he'd struck on something and wasn't about to let go.

'Just another holding company, I expect,' Thorsson said dismissively.

'Wouldn't be Greenspace Media would it?'

'No, not that I'm aware,' Thorsson seemed happier with this turn in the questioning.

'What else do they do? What other pies do they have fingers in?'

'I really don't know anything about RightOn's other lines of business, and even less about Greenspace, they are both reputable companies,' Thorsson's agitation was rapidly declining, suggesting Matthew's questioning had gone cold. 'I just focus on the work here at the agency.'

'So, you don't know who actually runs either company?' Matthew asked, seeing Thorsson's agitation return as the man shook his head in response.

'You've known Mr Driver for much of his professional life and certainly for all of his married life,' Julie said, as the pause lengthened, Matthew's quiet stare eating into Thorsson's growing unease but the agent seemed equally determined not to speak, 'given how well you knew him, can you shed any light as to who may have killed him?'

'None, it's an act of madness,' Thorsson responded, his relief at the switch in the questioning only too evident to both the detectives.

'Any domestic or home life problems?'

'Not in the least,' Victor obviously considered the very idea of this to be ludicrous, 'Steph worshipped him and he called her his perfect ideal of a wife. They probably had spats like any couple but I never knew them to have a cross word.'

'Any enemies, jealous or aggrieved co-workers? Did he owe money?' Thorsson shook his head in response to each of Julie's suggestions. 'Any involvement with drugs?'

'No, Gerry was well liked, and certainly not into drugs.'

'Could he have seen something at the club? Something he shouldn't have seen,' Julie persisted.

'No, Gerry would have said. He had spoken to me about a fan who was getting a bit obsessive. A guy by the name of Stickels, an odd name that stuck in my mind. Gerry only mentioned it because the emails were getting obscene, he wasn't that worried but I told him to keep them and we'd seek legal advice. The emails were unappealing but nothing hateful not even that perverted, nothing that might suggest violence was intended,' Thorsson explained, still shaking his head, still unable to fathom why or who had killed Gerry. 'I think he tended to protect Steph from anything unpleasant, their marriage worked because he could mould her into a sort of mother figure – his own mother died just before their wedding. Steph was someone who could provide a well ordered and quiet home life, a refuge from the strain of perfecting his act. Any professional problems he brought to me and anything personal he took to his brother, despite their outward differences they were very close.'

'Who owns the club where he was working, the Blue Snake?' Matthew asked, returning to his line of questioning.

'I have no …' Thorsson began, his voice suddenly deep, taken off guard.

'Wouldn't be Greenspace Media would it? If they were signing Gerry up you'd have to know wouldn't you?'

'Yes, now you have said it, it jogged my memory,' Thorsson tried, but failed, to sound calm. 'Yes, it is Greenspace, that's how they heard of him I expect.'

'What's with all the questions about these companies?' Julie demanded of her boss as they weaved down St Swithin's Lane, dodging other pedestrians in its narrow confines as they returned to their car.

'Fuck if I know,' Matthew admitted, as much puzzled by what had emerged from the interview as Julie was. 'The deceased doesn't appear to have had an enemy in the world and the only thing that seems to upset his agent, who has known Gerry for more than a dozen years, are questions about these two companies. There is something there but for the life of me I can't see what.'

'We need to reinterview the wife, brother and club manager,' Julie concluded, equally frustrated by their lack of success at identifying a motive, 'shake the tree a bit and see what falls out.'

'Agreed, but let's see what Gerry's number one fan has to say first.'

# Chapter Seven

Jonathon Stickels resided in a small flat just round the corner from the Geffrye Museum and five minutes' walk from Hoxton station, four stops north of Wapping. The flat was one of a pair on the first floor of a three floor converted Georgian townhouse. The entrance way had a security camera, with the name of the firm that installed and maintained it underneath, Julie was on the phone to them as they walked up. Jonathon was as pathetic an individual as Matthew and Julie had guessed he would be. Short, overweight, dressed in an ill fitting black suit to denote he was in mourning, his round face and small eyes were an exact match for a sad face emoji.

'Just a few questions, Mr Stickels,' Matthew explained after introducing himself and Julie, and explaining the reason for their visit.

'Of course, anything,' Stickels gave a mildly dramatic flourish of his head, causing his thin hair to flap. Grief was written large across his doughy face, each word he spoke was punctuated by a sniff and he held a clean hanky to regularly dab his dry eyes, in the vague hope of a tear.

'How did you know Mr Driver?' Matthew began, glancing round the small flat. They were in the living room, which looked out over the front of the house, the door into the small kitchen at the side was open, another door, closed, next to the kitchen was, Matthew guessed, the bathroom. A third door, also closed, opened into the bedroom at the rear and the fourth door was the one they had entered by, off the hallway and stairs. A number of framed and autographed pictures of Geraldine adorned what little wall space remained between windows and doors.

'I am … was Geraldine's greatest fan,' Stickels told them, his voice a hushed whisper, his eyes turning to an A4 framed portrait photo standing on a small side table between two lit candles. 'I went to all her performances, at least those in London, and followed her career with enthusiasm, we exchanged emails all the time. She was a great performer and her tragic death is a loss to the stage.'

'We are aware of your past history, Mr Stickels,' Matthew pointed out. As Julie, who hadn't sat down, studied each of the autographed photos and noticed that most were standard publicity shots or blown up from pictures taken at a distance. While the autographs looked either like those stamped on publicity pictures or poor copies of them.

'My history is an open book,' Stickels pointed out trying to sound dignified.

'Yes, Mr Stickels, it is,' Matthew agreed, pulling out his notebook to remind himself of the details. 'An arrest for possession of drugs …'

'Purely medicinal,' Stickels assured him, 'just some Ganja when I get depressed, life isn't all roses and cake.'

'Causing an affray, damage to private property …'

'It was self-defence, that man had come between me and my friend, someone I adored and who adored me until that person came between us,' Stickels stated, firmly but in a relatively calm voice.

'The police report says that you stood outside your *friend's* house shouting obscenities at his civil partner, when your *friend* came out to remonstrate with you, you threw dog dirt at him,' Matthew read from his notes, as Stickels looked on – his expression that of injured innocence. 'On another occasion, captured on CCTV, you painted obscenities on your *friend's* husband's car. In the application for a restraining order to be placed on you, your *friend* stated that although you had written to, emailed and tweeted about him on innumerable occasions and regularly stood outside his house he had never actually spoken to you – other than on the occasion you had thrown dog dirt at him.'

'Sir, I think you should see this,' Julie, standing by the bedroom door she had stealthily opened, had timed her interruption to allow the inspector to finish without giving Stickels a chance to respond.

'How dare you, that's private,' Stickels jumped up with a shout from his chair.

'Sit,' Matthew spoke without raising his voice but with such force that Jonathon dropped straight back into his seat, eyes staring ahead, like a scolded child or pet dog.

Every inch of the bedroom's wall space, even the ceiling, was covered with pictures of Geraldine. Some were full size posters, others small head shots, many of those concentrated near the bed were shots captured from the internet of naked men and women with pictures of Geraldine's face superimposed over theirs.

'Right, Mr Stickels, where exactly were you between midnight and three in the morning the night before last?' Matthew demanded of Stickels, who still sat bolt upright and facing away from the bedroom door.

'Here, I was here!' Jonathon Stickels glanced guiltily over his shoulder at the two officers. 'I left the Blue Snake as soon as Geraldine finished her act, to catch my train, I got back here at about midnight. If I'd stayed, spoken to her and got chatting then it would have held her up and she'd still be …' but Stickels got no further bursting into uncontrollable sobs at the thought he had failed to save his idol.

Matthew didn't feel particularly prepared for the team briefing. He'd had a chance to speak with Ray Rosen who had summarised things for him and he realised that in some respects they had made great leaps forward, while in other areas they were none the wiser.

'Basically we seem to already have a detailed understanding about how the murder was committed but very little information about the perpetrator or his motives,' Matthew informed the team as the chatting died down. 'You'll understand why I believe the perpetrator is male as I go over what we have so far. As you know the CCTV at the rear of the club was deliberately put out of action but we have been lucky, at least Hayden's efforts have brought us some luck,' Matthew was desperately trying to look at ease and as if he were confident about the material but the fact was that if anyone had offered to take over he'd have jumped at the chance. 'She discovered a camera positioned to cover the rear of the apartments behind the club which picked up our attacker.' He nodded to Ray to run the short clip.

'As you can see,' Matthew pointed to the TV screen, 'our man is picked up scrambling over the wall at the rear of the club's carpark behind the rubbish bins. Note the dashing black ensemble he is wearing,' Matthew paused for the briefest moment to see if he'd raised any smiles but everyone in the room was intent on peering at the screen, which had frozen with the man laid length-wise along the top of the wall. 'Dark trainers, backpack, trousers and top with a hoody, wearing gloves and nothing of his face showing. SOCOs have now been all over the club's carpark and found fibres from the top of the wall that match those found in Driver's car. One of the technicians has done a calculation and the assailant's height is estimated at five eight, give or take an inch. The ratio of width between the shoulders, waist and hips suggests a male.'

'When exactly was this taken?' Julie Lukula asked, causing Matthew to scowl at his failure at not having mentioned the time.

'Five minutes to midnight,' Matthew confirmed, checking his notes, 'I'll arrange for everyone to have a copy of the timeline at the end of the meeting. We know that Gerry Driver left the club at approximately twelve ten, still dressed as Geraldine. We don't know exactly what happened, but at twelve eighteen Gerry's car is seen leaving and passing the front of the club, this from witnesses and the door CCTV. No one took much notice and the best description we have is of a dark figure driving that everyone assumed was Geraldine. The PM, however, has revealed a lump on the back of Gerry's head and, from the amount of swelling, it happened at least an hour before his death. So it's likely his attacker hit him from behind and bundled him into his car, probably tied him up, using plastic ties, then drove off.'

'It sounds well planned.' Julie muttered to Hayden, who sat next to her, but loud enough for the others to hear.

'That's exactly what everything points to,' Matthew confirmed, before continuing, 'Driver's SUV is caught on camera at various points and it appears to have been driven directly to Pennington Road, where it is parked up at twelve thirty-two. Now,' Matthew almost sighed the word, frustrated by what he had to say, 'the road is well lit, the SUV is in shot from three cameras and we even have two witnesses that saw it parked there. But,' the word came out loud and hard, 'we have no idea of exactly what happened inside the car during the time it remains there until one eighteen.'

'Witnesses?' Harry Bainbridge asked, he had no doubt that the question wasn't necessary but was taking every opportunity to make himself seen and heard.

'A man out walking his dog and a woman returning home from work, both are on CCTV but came forward voluntarily to say they'd seen the car. The guy crossed over to walk past the car, whereas the woman passed on the other side, neither thought it was occupied. The road is empty at this time of night, with construction work to new buildings on one side and offices and shops on the other.'

'Can't any of the CCTV images be further enhanced to see inside the vehicle?' Harry asked, squinting at the screen, not noticing Julie rolling her eyes.

'No,' Matthew stated, giving an indulgent smile at the young officer, 'our best guess at what happened over the next fifty minutes comes from forensics and the preliminary PM. Gerry was bound, using plastic ties, in the rear of the SUV, in a kneeling position. It's likely the seats were already down as he seems to have used it more as a van than a car. A ball-gag was inserted into his mouth and an old, rough piece of nylon rope was tied around his neck and fixed in such a way that the more he struggled the more it would have strangled him. His underwear was cut away, and a large, ridged dildo was, without lubricant, repeatedly thrust into his anus. The PM report describes the rape as being particularly brutal, and would have been very painful. The injuries sustained were significant and would have required hospital treatment. It is extremely unlikely that Gerry would have consented to being sodomised in this way.

'In addition to the anal injuries there was also considerable bruising to the testicles, one of which had been ruptured, probably from being punched or kneed as kicking Driver within the confines of the car would have been difficult. The ball-gag, dildo, rope and plastic ties were all left in the car. There were a number of smeared blood stains and, at some point, Gerry soiled himself. Traces of the blood, human faeces and urine would be on the attacker's clothing, assuming he hasn't destroyed them.'

Matthew paused to glance round at the team, surveying the blank, stern faces of men and women determined not to allow any emotion or reaction to what they had just heard show on their faces; aiming to remain detached and professional.

'Did he die in the car?' Hayden broke the silence. 'You said the rope was strangling him.'

'No,' Matthew went on, realising that his own face registered the same blank expression as all the others, it was his job to find who killed the victim not empathise with the agony of his death, 'the post-mortem couldn't determine exactly what state Driver was in at this stage, but suggests that his injuries were enough that he may only have been semi-conscious, certainly in a great deal of pain and probably unable to walk.'

'So a sado-sexual angle to the attack?' Julie puzzled, there was something not adding up in what she was hearing but she couldn't think what.

'No semen was found in or on Gerry Driver nor in the car, apart from the dildo there wasn't evidence of any other form of penetration though it can't be ruled out given the physical damage done,' Matthew explained, then paused waiting for any further questions, which weren't forthcoming. He surreptitiously checked his notes before continuing, 'The plastic ties used to bind the victim are very common so we aren't expecting to trace them. Same with the ball-gag and dildo, they are sold through a large number of online outlets and shops so it's a long shot. There are a number of fingerprints in the car, which aren't Drivers or his wife's, that we are still looking to identify but remember the attacker was wearing gloves so the prints aren't likely to be his. The nylon rope, though, does offer up possibilities. As you can see from the picture it is an orange colour, obviously worn from use with a jagged cut at each end, it has oil stains, suggesting it might have been stored or used in a garage or shed or used in some type of industrial setting. Look out for anything like it when looking at any suspect. It also has traces of human skin buried in its fibres so we are hoping, expecting, DNA from it.'

Again Matthew paused, he had given a brief smile at the thought of a key clue emerging from this and understood the muted ripple of excitement that went through the room at his words. 'At one eighteen the car drives off,' Matthew raised his voice to regain order, his tone now confident and relaxed as he had settled into the familiar routine of a briefing, 'and is picked up at various points on its brief journey to Pier Head, where it arrived at one twenty-seven. Driver's car is reversed down the short, narrow street, and one of the residents thought they heard a car but paid no attention to it as they assumed it was a neighbour. The passenger side rear is caught on the security cam of the end house, you can make out the attacker's legs and the tail gate being lifted and closed again three minutes later. SOCOs found drag marks across the small piece of grass between the end of the road and the bank side wall, one of Geraldine's shoes was found under a bush, the other one ended up in the river with the deceased, a small piece of her dress was found caught on the river wall. The ease with which Driver is moved and dumped also points to the attacker being male.'

'Was Gerry dead when he was put into the water?' Julie asked, remembering what his wife had told them about the performer's fear of water.

'No, he drowned,' Matthew matter-of-factly explained, 'the water was cold and is likely to have revived him. Time of death is given at being between one thirty and one forty. The end of the pier head itself not only gives the easiest and best access to the river from a car for some way but the end of the pier head, that is actually in the water, causes an eddy which tends to trap anything dropped into it. Driver's dying struggles in the water are likely to have pushed him free of this and the outgoing tide caused him to drift a few yards downstream to Old Stairs. His injuries and his terrified struggles at being in the water would have resulted in a quick drowning.'

'So the attacker must have known him,' Hayden concluded, stating what was on everyone's mind, 'known he wasn't a swimmer and scared of the water.'

'A swimmer might have been able, even with the injuries he had, to have gotten himself to Old Stairs and out of the water. The only reason I can see why anyone would risk dumping Driver alive in the river was as a final act of sadism. Which suggests the killer knew about Driver's aquaphobia,' Matthew agreed, he could see a number of officers had questions about this but decided to continue rather than get into a discussion on motives and possible suspects at this stage. 'The attacker then drives to the Turks Head in Tench Street and parks the car on yellow lines. We now realise this was deliberate as all of the bays just further up are overseen by CCTV from the sports centre opposite. We then lose track of the attacker in the backstreets but ten minutes later we pick up a figure, dressed in black, in the street behind the Blue Snake carpark, just twenty yards from where he first climbed over the wall. We can't be certain it is the same guy, he's on a motorbike and is wearing a helmet; however, to be certain Ray's team tried to trace the number plate and it turns out to be false.'

'It turned out to be the number of a moped up for sale in Birmingham,' Ray chimed in, 'details are online so could have been easily picked up. The false plates look realistic so suggest a degree of skill in making them, so we are going to canvas local traders, especially those with a rep for making up illegal plates.'

'The killing appears to have been well planned and undertaken with, what I'd describe as, cold calculation,' Matthew resumed. 'The killer also seems to have a knowledge of Driver's routines and knows about his fear of water; he also seems to know the local area very well. The attack itself was brutal with overtones of sado-sexual violence, although there is no current evidence to suggest the attacker had any immediate sexual gratification from the attack. Ray has had an analyst looking back through the records to see if he can find any match or similar cases recently but nothing has come up, which seems improbable given that to go from nothing to this level of violence is unusual. So, Ray is going to widen the search parameters to see if anything can be found.'

'Given the attacker's knowledge of Driver this seems personal and suggests a real hatred of Gerry,' Julie theorised, 'but that seems at odds with what we have been hearing about him, he seemed well liked.'

'It might not be someone close to him, just someone who has found out these things about him. Certainly Driver's alter ego, Geraldine, might have caused confusion in someone's mind – perhaps struck at the attacker's own sexuality. Driver may not have been gay but his ability to convincingly present himself as a female may have made him a target for any number of reasons. However, I agree there's certainly a lot of hate at the centre of this.'

The briefing momentarily stalled at this point as Matthew went silent, reflecting on his own words, before Ray spoke up, 'Duncan has been cross-checking all the statements taken so far, from customers, staff and taxi drivers, and correlating them with CCTV evidence from the surrounding area.'

'Sounds like a lot of effort,' Matthew stated, nodding towards the analyst, Duncan. He was a large, young man with a thick beard wearing a scruffy tee shirt and jeans whose left hand seemed welded to a large coffee mug.

'Not all me,' Duncan acknowledged, looking round, with a big grin cutting through his hair covered face, 'lots of help from those taking statements, checking CCTV and chasing up any gaps that appear. However, as things stand most of the customers and staff at the Blue Snake can account for their whereabouts. We have also been able to confirm Stickels's leaving Hoxton station just before midnight but we are waiting on confirmation of his arrival at his home from his entryway CCTV; although his alibi is checking out so far.'

'No real surprise there,' Julie confirmed for everyone, 'weird he might be but Stickels is about three inches shorter and five stone heavier than the figure we saw climbing over the wall.'

'A man after my own heart,' Duncan stated, patting his own growing beer gut, 'though hopefully without the weirdness.' Everyone laughed at the comment but Hayden and Julie exchanged glances that suggested their slight reservations about the weirdness angle. If anyone spent too much time on his own with a computer resulting in a somewhat warped ability to socialise it was Duncan.

'So no obvious suspect popping up?' Matthew checked, wanting to wind up the briefing.

''Fraid not,' Duncan confirmed, suddenly serious under the inspector's deadpan gaze. 'The only person who has an iffy background so far is Micheal Stennard, the Blue Snake's security manager, but he was seen by half a dozen people between twelve and half past and was with the club's manager between one and half past.'

'What's his "iffy background"?' Matthew wanted to know.

'As a teenager he was involved with some white supremacist biker gang. He got done for assault and criminal damage a couple of times and ended up with a short stretch but nothing since he was twenty-two.'

'OK, Julie will go over Stennard's alibi and any likely looking associates with a fine comb as a precaution. If you can keep me and Julie updated on anything significant emerging that will be great,' Matthew told the analyst, though with one eye on Ray, then turned his attention back to the meeting as a whole. 'Driver's agent, Victor Thorsson, is going to supply us with details of his more recent gigs, that will give us a much larger group of suspects to look into. Ray, can you do some prioritisation and allocation so statements can be taken from any likely suspects or leads that emerge. Also, the picture of the suspect clambering over the wall and a generalised description will be released for the breakfast news tomorrow, it might bring in a few leads if we are lucky. Hayden you'll liaise on that.'

Matthew realised there was going to be a massive amount of work being generated with little hope of it producing anything useful but they couldn't afford to miss the needle in the haystack, 'Julie and myself will be speaking again with his wife, brother and agent tomorrow, although we don't think they are directly involved it's possible they know the killer but don't realise it. Someone out there really hated Gerry or Geraldine to the extent that it should have been noticed. Finally, keep that nylon rope in mind, it's a type widely used, especially in work places, if you notice it then call it in and get the SOCOs out. I'd rather a dozen false calls than miss the one piece that nets us the killer.'

Matthew paused momentarily for his words to sink in before finishing with, 'Well done for where we are so far, lot of hard work and good results, keep the momentum going, keep pushing and eventually one response will turn up positive and we'll have the bugger.' He hadn't meant it as a joke but there was a smattering of laughter interspersed with a ripple of applause, the latter as much acknowledging their own efforts as Matthew's attempt at a motivational ending.

# Chapter Eight

Matthew was doing his best not to sound irritated by Swift's comments but the more he tried the less he succeeded. 'Driver's death is undoubtedly a hate filled crime but I'm just not convinced that there are sufficient links to suggest it is part of a pattern of hate crimes,' Matthew explained. He'd stopped off at the MIT East's main office in Barking, so Julie and he could go to the deceased's widow in Epping together, and had taken the opportunity to update his governor.

'I understand it would currently only be a secondary line of investigation,' Swift explained for the third time, annoyance tinging his own voice. It wasn't that he and Matthew were disagreeing but neither man thought the other gave full credence to his point of view. 'However, Intel have noted that a bike of a similar make, with equally professionally made false licence plates, was used in the Driver case and three other attacks.' Then, to underline the importance of the point he was making Swift concluded with, 'Both myself and the chief think it worth taking a look at.'

'Fine,' Matthew had already conceded the point but felt his anger move up a notch now that Swift was invoking the chief superintendent, 'as I've explained I'll do the interviews I've planned for today and if nothing changes I'll review the other cases and look for connections tomorrow. Is that OK?'

'Of course, Matthew, it's your case, I'm just passing on some additional information,' Swift decided to move on, he'd felt his annoyance rising as the conversation had progressed and didn't want it bubbling over into anger. 'If you don't have time tomorrow or it gets pushed back a day I'll understand.'

Matthew managed to suppress the *Fuck that!* which sprang to mind, though it was clearly written across his face, opting instead for a more diplomatic, 'I doubt if my interview with Superintendent Harken will take that long.'

'Don't underestimate Harken, he's a straight up guy but no one's fool,' Swift hoped Matthew would understand he was simply offering some friendly advice. The chief had asked about the complaint against Matthew and Swift had unreservedly backed him, stating he was one of his most trusted officers, before explaining that the process should soon be completed.

'That's not a problem as I don't intend to try and fool him,' Matthew informed his governor. He'd hoped that with his promotion Swift would be less engaged in his investigations than before, in practice the reverse was proving to be true and it was starting to grate. Worse still Matthew was starting to resent Swift's intervention even in areas, such as the complaint against him, where Swift, as his manager, had every right to intervene.

'Of course,' Swift realised he'd failed in his approach as Matthew's tone was obviously angry, 'I have absolute belief in your innocence, but being accused of sexually assaulting the mother of a murder suspect is causing political waves.'

'I understand that and no doubt there will be a backlash even when it's shown to be without basis,' Matthew was under no illusion how low his current standing was amongst the senior ranks.

'I'm not saying that,' Swift almost sighed, Matthew's expression told him that the inspector wasn't prepared to listen to any advice, 'but given your history, your previous involvement with a woman who was subsequently jailed, doesn't put your judgement in such matters in a good light.'

'Probably not, when put like that,' Matthew couldn't help thinking that it had been his work that had broken the case alluded to but it was Swift who had gotten the promotion, 'it always surprises me how readily the full facts seem to get forgotten. Still if Harken is really no one's fool then maybe he'll actually weigh the evidence rather than go by hearsay.'

After Matthew had left the office Swift sat, staring out the window at the drab view of the Barking industrial estate in which the MIT East's offices were located, reflecting on how his promotion seemed to be coming at a heavy price. He'd made the transition to chief inspector without a care, hardly noticing the additional responsibilities and extra authority, but since becoming superintendent he had started to struggle. His relationships both professional and personal were suffering. His work colleagues, and Matthew in particular, were finding the new politically astute Superintendent Swift was much less to their liking than the old pragmatic, job focused Chief Inspector Swift.

Somehow his new role had, it seemed, also finished off the long term relationship he had with his partner, as their plans to sell up their separate properties and move in together now seemed to be on permanent hold and they were increasingly reverting back to their single lives. Swift had no doubt that this was all a price worth paying, he was now on a path to where he could have a real influence on the future of policing. What he couldn't understand was why others didn't seem to grasp this as a good thing and accept that he was growing into his new job.

Julie had given up trying to engage with Matthew as she drove him to Epping, she had informed him that Stickels was now definitely out of the picture and she had also made time the previous evening to double-check Stennard's, the Blue Snake's security manager, alibi. He was also definitely in the clear, having been seen by half a dozen people, including the club's manager.

'It's suspicious about the CCTV being vandalised and not being fixed but coincidences do happen I suppose,' she concluded, only to realise that Matthew wasn't listening. Then after a pause, knowing about the complaint and impending interview, she decided it might help to get Matthew thinking about something else, 'Any advice about the inspectors exam?'

'Hmm,' Matthew wrenched his attention back, he'd been thinking about yesterday's interview with Thorsson and what the female journalist had said after the press briefing. 'No, you'll be alright, you'll ace it. Have you given any thought about applying for any roles in particular?'

'Not really,' Julie said, knowing that Matthew's own stalled career was hardly a model to follow. 'The governor said he would keep me in an acting-up role until something came up but he suggested my best move, given the current situation, would be to try for counter-terrorism. Although I can't say I have ever thought about moving to CTC.'

'The governor would know,' Matthew told her, his mind drifting back to his own thoughts, while Julie's thoughts remained on her own future but had switched to how things were with her and Yvette and how close they had become.

'Gerry didn't confide much in Steph,' Grahame Driver, Gerry's older brother, informed Matthew. Julie and the female family liaison officer had remained indoors with Stephanie Driver, while Matthew and Grahame had gravitated out into the large garden for a stroll amongst the autumnal flower beds. Just why they had split along such stereotypical gender lines Matthew couldn't say. However, it'd been obvious that Grahame had wanted to speak away from his sister-in-law and Matthew had readily accompanied the brother out into Gerry's pride and joy: the garden he had lavished so much of his free time on.

'I mean, it was just like Gerry,' Grahame continued in the same vein as he'd started, working himself up to tell the inspector what was on his mind about his brother's killing, 'once he started something it became the focus of his life, and it had to be perfect. Same with his act and his marriage.'

'How's that?' Matthew asked.

'When they married, I mean, it was all about creating a happy home and the perfect marriage,' Grahame glanced back over his shoulder, checking they were far enough away that they couldn't be overheard. A completely unnecessary gesture that told Matthew that Grahame thought he was about to break confidences over his brother and sister-in-law's life together. 'Steph's role was to be the undemanding, compliant wife: part servant and part companion. I don't think having kids was ever really on the table. I mean, when he came home he wanted to put Geraldine behind him and simply be Gerry: the loving, contented husband and amateur gardener.'

They stopped their sauntering at the edge of a large pond feature, twenty odd feet across, at the end of the garden.

'This was a good example,' Grahame nodded at the pond, 'Steph had hoped for a pool or a summer house with a jacuzzi but Gerry was fixated on a pond and spent most of his spare time over a few months building it. Then, just after it was filled, with plants and fish, it sprang a leak. He was just about to go on tour to Germany and he was like a maniac trying to fix it. He spent one whole night out here, floodlights set up, trying to locate the leak and fix it. In the end the plants and fish ended up in a skip, and the whole thing was relined and newly stocked, all done in seventy-two hours. How he managed with hardly any sleep just prior to his tour I don't know, but finishing it before he went off meant more to him than anything else.'

'He was obsessive then?'

'Not exactly in the way of that illness, what you call it …'

'OCD?' Matthew prompted.

'That's it,' Grahame acknowledged, 'I mean, he didn't have to turn light switches on and off a certain number of times but everything had to be in its place and just as he wanted it or he'd be upset.'

'So he could be difficult?' Matthew wasn't seeing how this linked with the impersonator's death.

'Yes, and then some. Believe me I loved my brother and I'd pop in here all the time, but I wouldn't want to stay the night. He'd drive me nuts by following me round putting everything back,' as if to emphasise his resentment at the memory, Grahame kicked one of the small stones that lined the pond edge into the water, smirked and turned back to the house. 'Thing is, I mean, since he started on his new act and all that stuff, well, he started to change.'

'You mean the theatre and TV deal?'

'That's it,' Grahame confirmed, stopping by a bed of rose bushes so as to delay getting back to the house. 'Well, it was almost as if Geraldine had started to take over. He was spending more time away from home and, when he was here, he was starting to dress as Geraldine. I mean, he'd always practice his routines up in his study but I'd never known him dress and act as Geraldine around the house. However, a couple of times recently I'd pop in and there she was.'

'Are you saying he was having some sort of breakdown?' Matthew wondered.

'No, nothing like that,' Grahame seemed horrified at the inference, 'I mean, it was more like a mid-life crisis type of thing. I just think he was starting to feel happier as Geraldine, more comfortable *being* her rather than just *acting* as her.'

Matthew pondered this for a moment, he'd heard of actors whose lives had been taken over by playing a certain role, but this didn't seem of the same order. Then the penny dropped, as he watched Grahame looking nervously around, a sheepish grin flicking on and off the brother's face as his embarrassment at what he was saying grew.

'You think he was becoming comfortable with being a woman, perhaps accepting he was gay or a transvestite?' Matthew was surprised that the brother was finding it so hard to express what he meant but, then, for many people such thoughts were something they usually avoided putting into words.

'It never used to cross my mind,' Grahame summoned up the strength to say what he believed, 'then recently I began to wonder.

I mean, at first I thought he might be seeing someone, a woman. He had that … what yer call it? *A spring in his step*, that was it, like he was so full of himself, but only when he was Geraldine. Then it struck me it might not be a woman he was seeing.'

Matthew hadn't noticed how cold it had been in the garden until he re-entered the house, the central heating seemingly set at full blast.

'Mrs Driver was just telling us about a recent visitor she has had,' Julie informed Matthew as he slipped off his coat before taking a seat, every nuance of her body language telling him she had unearthed a real gem of a piece of information, 'a lawyer from Greenspace Media.'

'Yes,' Mrs Driver took her cue, 'he phoned before coming, he said it was about Gerry's contract, although he referred to Gerry as Geraldine,' Steph gave a little smile at the thought, no doubt pleased that her husband's impersonation could fool someone as astute as a corporate lawyer. 'It seems that when Gerry signed the contract he was automatically insured. He said it was worth a quarter of a million.'

Steph seemed overwhelmed by her own words, feeling pleased and guilty at being pleased at the same time. While Grahame looked stunned and hurt that Steph hadn't already told him this. Matthew's response was more muted, trying to fit this piece of the puzzle with the others that floated through his mind.

'When exactly did the lawyer tell you this?' he finally asked.

'He left just before Grahame and yourselves arrived. Such a nice man, offering condolences on behalf of the firm, the producer and …' then seeing Grahame and the look of hurt and anger on his face she turned to him to explain. 'It's been so much to take in, I could hardly believe what he told me. It was only as I spoke with Sergeant Lukula that it all came out. I know how it must look, poor Gerry dying then all this insurance money …'

'Don't be daft,' Grahame blurted out, giving Steph a hard look then glancing at the three officers, wondering what they made of all this, 'I mean, I can't imagine anyone suspecting you being involved.'

Matthew and Julie exchanged glances, something the FLO didn't miss, none of the officers could believe that Steph Driver had anything to do with her husband's death. She seemed incapable of even taking in the fact he had been murdered and still seemed to think of the event as if he had died in some sort of freak accident.

'Of course not,' Steph seemed close to tears. When Gerry had been alive life had been clear cut to Steph, now her husband was gone everything seemed so complicated and confusing. She just couldn't find solid, stable ground to rest on. 'The lawyer said not to worry, he'd been instructed by the producer, the man who owns the company, to assist me in any way needed. He also said the company would foot the bill for the funeral, he would make the arrangements if I let him know what was wanted.' Steph paused, to sniff and dab at her eyes in a vain attempt to hold back the tears, before continuing, 'He also said the producer would want to attend himself along with others from the company, those who had been working with Geraldine.'

'That would be Mr Towers, I take it?' Matthew asked, as Julie glowered at him, her expected bombshell turning into a damp squib as Matthew already seemed to know about Towers's involvement, while Steph nodded in agreement unable to speak as her sobbing took away her breath.

'So when did you start to suspect Ricky Towers was involved?' Julie demanded as they drove to reinterview Victor Thorsson, Driver's agent.

'I don't know that he is,' Matthew explained, 'I was vaguely aware that one of the companies he owns is Greenspace Media. It rang a bell and I asked Ray to do some digging. He phoned me as I was on my way in this morning and confirmed Greenspace is owned by the Towers family, with Ricky holding a controlling interest. He also dug up the link with RightOn Entertainments, which Ricky owns outright, the company that owns Thorsson's Blue Bird Agency. You're the first I've told about this, so there's no need to sulk. Fact is I'm not at all certain this isn't just a coincidence.'

'Coincidence! Links between a murder and the UK's worst gangland family just a coincidence?' Julie had adopted the hushed, urgent tones of a news anchor reading out the day's shock/horror headlines, 'And I'm not sulking, just making a mental note of how not to treat my sergeant when I'm finally promoted to inspector.'

Matthew smiled for the first time since his talk with Swift earlier in the day. He had to admit that he thought he and Julie made a good team. Neither stood much on ceremony and didn't take anything the other said personally, they cared but not too much for it to be a problem. So it'd be a pity when the inevitable happened and she moved on to a much deserved promotion.

'Ricky's father made the family fortune through sex, drugs and extortion,' Matthew began, only for Julie to interrupt.

'You knew Ricky when you were at school,' Julie stated, remembering what little he'd told her of these things.

'Yes. For some reason, probably to rub Ricky's nose in the contempt the old guy had for his son, the father rather liked me and thought I was a wonderful kid, unlike Ricky,' Matthew skirted over the memories before returning to his theme. 'Ricky wasn't like his dad at all, tried to be but just wasn't cut out to be a brutal thug. He left as much as he could of that part of the business to his uncle and focused on building up the business side: nightclubs, pubs, massage parlours, online girls and gaming. He was soon netting a hundred times what his father had made.'

'He is still a violent thug,' Julie didn't want to rain on Matthew's nostalgic parade, but knew that Ricky Towers was thought to be responsible for a dozen or so unsolved murders and disappearances.

'True, but if you'd known the father you'd know what I mean,' Matthew agreed with a smile, thinking that everything was relative, although, he had to admit, the loss of a loved one was as heart rending no matter how it had occurred. 'If you got on the wrong side of the father then you ended up looking as if a train had run over you, and he did that with his own fists. Ricky's opponents simply disappear, latest theory is they are dropped out of an aircraft over the sea or end up the victim of a hit and run. Anyway, more to the point Ricky and his younger brother, who runs GR Security and which he operates like a small private army, control all the entertainment side, legitimate or not, including any associated sex and drugs. While the uncle and cousins run the guns and money laundering side.'

'Wow!' Julie knew about the family's extensive criminal activity, every copper in the Met knew parts of the story, but hearing Matthew's summary stated in bland, everyday tones somehow made it seem much worse than she had realised. 'You're making them sound like a fact of life, something above the law that is inevitable.'

'Like Hydra you cut off one head and two grow,' Matthew explained, trying not to over dramatise. 'What gives Ricky control over so much criminal activity is his ownership of all those clubs and pubs, etc. If you want to sell drugs, guns, sex or launder money then you have to go through Ricky's entertainment empire. He's a bit like OPEC controlling the supply and price of oil.'

'I suppose it's GR Security that stops someone from invading and taking over the empire?' Julie completed the metaphor as Matthew nodded in agreement.

# Chapter Nine

'Gerry was not gay and not a transvestite,' Victor, Vicky, Thorsson tapped his manicured and painted nails on his desk to emphasise each word as he spoke, a sign of his impatience and his annoyance at the police's apparent inability to dissociate Gerry's act as a female impersonator from his sexuality. 'Dressing up as a woman is a common stage practice for many male performers, the fact that Gerry did so with considerable aplomb was not the result of his sexual preferences.'

'When was the last time you actually spoke with Mr Driver?' Matthew asked, unconcerned about Thorsson's tone but wondering how his emphatic statement fitted with Grahame Driver's recent views about his brother.

'At the Blue Snake, after the show when the agency guests caused a scene,' Thorsson stated, trying, without much success, to look calm and unconcerned about the questioning.

'The time when he lost his temper with you.' Julie clarified, but received no response from Thorsson.

'What about before that?' Matthew asked, starting to put two and two together.

'A week or two, I suppose,' Thorsson stated, off-handedly. 'Look, I'm still very upset about Gerry, is it possible …'

'When exactly?' Matthew persisted, cutting across Thorsson's plea.

'I'm not entirely certain …' Thorsson prevaricated, then seeing Matthew's scowl deepen and realising there was little point in stalling, went on, 'It was more than a month ago, five or six weeks.'

'You didn't speak to him at all in that time?' Julie picked up on how strange this was. 'Wasn't the contract for his theatre and TV deal being finalised then?'

'Yes, but it was down to the small print, legal stuff, nothing Gerry needed to worry about,' Thorsson pointed out.

'Did that include negotiations over insurances, details like that?' Matthew asked.

'Insurances?' Thorsson puzzled. 'Not as such, there were some standard guarantees about compensation if the contract was broken by either party, Acts of God, that sort of thing.'

'So, Gerry's life wasn't insured as part of the deal?' Julie wasn't surprised at Thorsson's response but wanted absolute clarity over what the agent knew and the terms of the contract.

'Not that I'm aware, it wouldn't be part of a normal theatrical contract,' Thorsson seemed confused by the line of questioning, wondering what the police were actually after.

'It might be easier if you just gave us a copy of the contract,' Matthew stated.

'It will be on file, assuming Gerry returned it after he signed it, I'll have to check,' Thorsson flustered, again feeling pushed into a corner. 'Actually, now I think of it Gerry hadn't returned it. I'll contact Steph to get a copy made.'

'There's no need,' Matthew told him, 'it will be with the papers that were in his office and we'll already have it,' Matthew glanced at Julie who nodded, she was already ahead of Matthew on that score. 'To be honest it doesn't sound as if you were particularly involved in dealing with the contract? Was Gerry leaving the agency?'

'No,' Thorsson's concern and worry at the suggestion was all too clearly shown in his expression. 'Gerry had gotten carried away at the offer and signed the contract without referring any of it to me. He told me it was a done deal when we last met.'

'This was at the Blue Snake?' Julie sought clarification.

'No, when I met him before that, in September,' Thorsson sighed, deciding to come clean and air his own concerns. 'The meeting didn't go well and Gerry, so unlike him, became annoyed and wouldn't listen to reason. I'd suggested we review the contract and look to negotiate, even if it only produced a marginal improvement there was no need to rush. However, he wouldn't listen, he'd been meeting with Mr …' Thorsson's momentary hesitation didn't go unnoticed by either detective, 'the producer, who was very keen for the whole project to get underway.'

'The producer?' Julie again pushed for an exact answer, 'That would be Mr Towers?'

'Yes, I believe so?' Thorsson's worried look deepened. Then, summoning up his acting skills, he took a breath and his face cleared, his posture shifting so he appeared at ease.

'The same Mr Towers who is head of Greenspace Media,' Thorsson gave a slight nod to confirm this as Matthew spoke, 'and who owns RightOn Entertainments, who are the owners of this business.' Thorsson didn't nod, but raised his eyebrows as if to indicate this was the first he was hearing of it. 'In practice that would make Towers your boss, wouldn't it?'

Thorsson cleared his throat and moved the computer keyboard, giving him a moment to compose his thoughts before saying, 'As I explained previously, RightOn Entertainments gives me full control in running the agency. Our accountant simply reports to their board on profits, and informs me of any response.'

'Have you ever met Mr Towers?' Matthew's tone was deeply suspicious.

'Only briefly, when the deal to take over the agency was being concluded,' Thorsson stated with complete honesty, he'd heard the rumours about Towers and had wanted as little direct contact as possible. 'He seemed a very affable man, to the point and business like, very savvy about the entertainment world.'

'So you didn't feel coerced into the deal?' Julie probed.

'Not in the least, I was very pleased,' again the response didn't seem a lie.

'What about Gerry, do you think he was being pushed or forced into signing?' Julie persisted.

'He gave no indication of it, quite the reverse,' Thorsson couldn't help but show his disdain for what he thought of as Gerry's naivety, 'he was over the moon in his adulation for Mr Towers, whom he called the greatest producer in the UK. It was always the same with Gerry, once he had an idea fixed in his mind he had to see it through until it was completed in all its perfection.'

'It fits with what Grahame was saying,' Matthew told Julie as they walked back to the parked car, his mind still partly on the pretty, long legged, blond sat in Thorsson's reception. She was a tad too young for his taste, seemingly in her early twenties, but something about her disturbed him and it was only now he began to realise that the attractive young woman might be a man. He just couldn't be certain and made a mental note that the case was starting to get to him. 'Gerry was obsessive and had a spring in his step, as his brother described it, signing the contract could have done that.'

'So not his suddenly turning to the dark side?' Julie smirked, pulling out of the carpark, she didn't believe in people suddenly turning gay, it might have been well hidden, buried even, before coming out, but in her mind people just didn't turn gay.

'Who knows,' Matthew ignored the quip, 'perhaps he was starting to accept the reality of his situation.' Then changing the topic as they accelerated eastwards, 'Drop me at the incident room, I want to catch up with Ray, you can go home and revise as I've someone to see a bit later.'

Kathy Merry put her phone down, it was the end of a long day and she had rushed to complete everything so she could get home on time for once. Now Matthew had phoned her to say he'd be late and would have to miss the special dinner they'd agreed to cook and eat together. She tried not to feel annoyed, she understood the nature of his work was unpredictable, but they'd agreed on the dinner having realised how little free time they had together on their own, without the kids or work getting in the way.

'Hi, ohh … I can see you are leaving,' Lance intruded, his upper body poking past the door after the minimalist of knocks to maintain a semblance of the social niceties. 'No problem, we can go over my observation findings tomorrow.' Then, noticing Kathy's icy look, asked, 'Is everything alright?'

'Yes, thanks,' Kathy's face brightened as the thought struck her she could turn the disappointment into something of an opportunity. 'I'm going home to cook, would you like to join me, then you can tell me just how bad things are in the Maths and Science department.'

'Great, anything's better than the hotel food,' Lance grinned, stepping fully into the office and moving to help Kathy with her bags. 'Actually things aren't all bad, with a couple of tweaks they could almost be good.' His hand, which had landed on hers as he went to take her large briefcase, remained in contact for a moment longer than needed – long enough for his grin to widen further.

Matthew spotted Michaela Naidoo the moment he entered the bar, she was already sitting at a table with a rum and coke and her MacBook open before her, 'Hi, you beat me here I see, can I get you another?'

'Why not,' she responded with a ready smile, 'what journalist ever turned down a drink? I aimed to get here early to finish off some notes.' Michaela's slight accent, a memory of her South African homeland, added to her exotic nature. She wore brightly coloured clothes to complement her large frame, the fact that her ample bosom, waist and hips were in proportion to each other tended to result in her being described as curvaceous, while her round and usually smiling face encouraged those she met to underestimate her. Only her eyes, which missed little, told the reality of her intelligent and assertive nature.

'Thanks for coming,' Matthew stated, ordering another rum and coke and his beer; as he pocketed his cap and shrugged out of his coat before settling into his seat. He'd little doubted that she would come even at short notice, after all what journalist would miss the opportunity of an off the record chat with a police inspector. 'Do you fancy anything to eat? The place is filling up and it might be best to order first.'

Michaela glanced around, the Oyster Shed looked like an up-market pub with large windows and tables overlooking the Thames with views of London Bridge, the Shard and the Howard Kennedy building. As her husband was away and the alternative was to eat on her own, the offer of food was an attractive one. They both opted for a starter and mains, the selection of fresh fish appealing to both.

'How's your case going? I assume from your call you've run into a link with Greenspace and RightOn,' Michaela cut to the quick, as they waited for their order.

'Gerry Driver seems to have signed a lucrative contract with them recently,' Matthew stated taking a sip of his beer, 'but I can't say that there is any link between that and his death.'

'So, what do you want to know?'

'Basically why you turned up at the press conference?' Matthew decided to put his cards on the table, 'I don't buy your turning up on the off chance that it would be useful for your story.'

'I could probably list every club, pub, massage parlour, escort service and so on, that are owned by both companies.' Michaela explained, still smiling but determined not to show her hand at this stage, 'I could also list evidence of how they control the drugs and sex trade in and around each venue. However, sex and drugs in the media and entertainment industry is hardly news, it's never out of the headlines but it isn't news. I was just fishing for a different angle.'

'I can't see a link between Gerry's death and these companies,' Matthew repeated, munching through his fresh shrimp and prawn starter, 'so if you want a different angle you need to show me what that link might be.'

The sparring between the pair, over who would first bring Ricky Towers into the conversation and why Gerry's newly signed contract was of relevance, continued through another round of drinks and the main course of seared fish. It was only over coffee that Matthew decided to concede a point to move the game on.

'The only thing I can see that is unusual is that Ricky Towers seems to have had a personal hand in signing up Gerry Driver,' Matthew stated, wondering if a whisky might be too much on top of what he'd already had. 'Have your sources made any mention of that?'

'It's true that he was personally very invested in Geraldine's future career,' Michaela smirked, ignoring for the third time Matthew's comment about her sources, 'which is unusual. Towers normally signs off on all new projects and keeps up to date on progress but he expects his managers to actually run things. If anything is less than satisfactory managers are removed and projects shut down – he's ruthless in a Lord Sugar type way.'

'Really, what do your sources tell you about those people who try to muscle in on him or cause him real problems,' Matthew snorted, now convinced that the evening had been a waste of time and wishing he'd gone home as he'd promised his wife, 'I can't see Lord Sugar having a failed apprentice dropped off the back of a ferry mid-Channel, as much as the TV audience might like to see that.'

Michaela's face lost its smile and hardened, matching the intensity of her piercing eyes, 'Look, I have no intention of giving up any of my sources, so stop mentioning them,' she stated in no uncertain terms, she was annoyed at how often the inspector's eyes slipped to scan her cleavage as she talked, wondering if the rumours about him were true. 'I know what's said about Towers and his family but I can't find anything concrete about their involvement in money laundering or guns. The uncle seems to spend a lot of time cruising around the Med, and the eldest cousin, Bobby, seems intent on building a link with the neo-Nazi biker gangs of Northern Europe, but I have no idea how Driver's murder would fit with any of that.'

Matthew leaned forward, trying not to allow Michaela's cleavage to distract him, 'Neo-Nazis?'

'Yes, Bobby Towers is something of a fantasist and fanatic,' Michaela pointedly adjusted her jacket so as to cover herself better, 'loves Trump and Farage, thinks Hitler did more for Germany than make the trains run on time. It'd be a joke if Bobby didn't have access to money and weapons. He's been busy, setting up business links with various biker gangs in Sweden, Norway and North Germany, a sort of loose affiliation of the far-right. Most of these gangs make Genghis Khan look like a liberal and they have increasing control of areas of major crime, from drugs to extortion and human trafficking, their support for extremist politicians and their promotion of hate crimes is increasingly destabilising local communities.'

Matthew almost said *check mate* out loud as he finally broke through the journalist's wall of obfuscation, settling instead for, 'So that's the angle of your story. Links between crime and the far-right.'

'I've spent nearly six months, on and off, traipsing around Northern Europe tracking down stories, researching various gangs, talking to people in law enforcement and on the fringes of crime trying to put together what Bobby Towers is up to,' Michaela gave way, realising she had said too much and wondering just how much the stereotypical thick-as-shit, sexist, male copper attitude Matthew had portrayed was an act to lure her in. 'I have few provable facts and a great deal of rumour which doesn't add up to a complete story as yet,' she conceded with an exasperated smile.

'All things considered that's quite an achievement,' Matthew congratulated her, 'you would hardly have had a low profile in such circles.'

'No, though sometimes simply walking into the lion's den with a smile and a wave, confuses them long enough for you to pass through unscathed. My cover was that I was, somewhat ineptly, doing a story on immigration.' Michaela informed him, thinking it was getting late and she should be going.

'How do you see Gerry Driver fitting into this?' Matthew asked.

'I honestly don't know, Bobby has been out of the country for a few weeks now, his father and brother are in the Med, somewhere off Gibraltar partying with a Russian oligarch,' she admitted, 'but I've picked up good leads from longer shots in the past.'

'So really just fishing?' Matthew saw the dead end looming up, though wondered where exactly Michaela was getting her information about the Towers family from.

Michaela nodded, giving a small grin as an apology in recognition of them both having wasted time. However, hoping to retrieve something from the evening, she asked, 'Don't suppose you'd give me the heads up, an exclusive even, if you do break anything on the Driver case?' Seeing Matthew's surprised look, she added laughingly, 'I have to make ends meet until my big story breaks.'

'I'll see what I can do,' Matthew told her as way of a consolation prize, then sat ruminating on what she had told him, and her possible sources, while he watched her curves slide between tables as she made her way out.

Kathy was scraping the remains of the meal into the bin and loading the dishes into the machine, deep in thought about the conversation she'd had with Lance over the food and wine, about how to improve the Maths and Science department's lesson observation grades. She smiled at the thought of some of Lance's witty remarks, how well they worked together as a team and the buoyant mood the consultant seemed to be in. The sudden sensation of a hand flitting across her buttocks and an arm encircling her waist caused her to jerk upright with an, 'Oh'. Lance's mouth managing to nip at her ear lobe, his lips brushing across her cheek as she turned, both his arms now encircling her. One arm pulling her close, his other hand grasped her right buttock.

*This*, she thought, *is how a fish must feel in the grasp of an octopus.* The speed and unexpected nature of the embrace had caught her off guard and, for the briefest of moments, caused her body to respond with an ever so slight wriggle of excitement. Then her brain kicked in and she pushed him away, 'Get off me! What do you think you are doing?' Her words were firm and clear, her body tensing, readying for the attack, Matthew's disembodied voice telling her 'eyes, balls, nails and bite.'

However, her assailant had already caved in, crumpling in defeat, 'God forgive me, I … I don't know what … I'm sorry,' then with tears starting in his eyes he fled.

She followed him back into the dining room, her heart racing and knowing she should be telling him to get out but Lance was collapsed on a dining chair, his head in his hands, a picture of embarrassment and misery.

'I'm sorry, I'll go, I just need to collect my things,' he gabbled, though made no sign of moving. 'This is terrible, so foolish of me.' He turned towards her, though unable to look her in the eyes, 'I've never done anything like this before, I am so sorry, I have no excuses.'

Kathy was almost too shocked to be angry but she'd told enough girls that being friendly and nice to a male didn't mean they were allowing open access to their body. 'Just get the fuck out of my house,' her voice angry and insistent, the swear word substituting for the slap she felt he deserved.

'Of course,' he stood up, not attempting to even hint he had any dignity left. 'I realise I have destroyed any professional regard, even friendship, that you have shown towards me. I'll resign first thing, no doubt you'll want to report this to your chair of governors.' He stopped speaking, collecting his things, hesitating at the door only to apologise one last time.

'Just what on earth were you thinking?' she demanded as he started to pull the door handle open.

'I wasn't,' he freely admitted, still unable to look at her. 'You're intelligent, desirable and I'm lonely and an idiot.'

'That still doesn't give you any right to …' the words of her own advice to hundreds of girls over the years – about not allowing themselves to think that any unwanted advances were really a compliment or that they should mitigate any infringement upon themselves as being even remotely their fault – still rang in her ears. 'I thought you were one of the nice ones and not just another *hands-on pig!*'

'I know,' he looked genuinely perplexed by his own behaviour.

'However, that doesn't mean I think you should lose your job,' she conceded, feeling calmer though still very angry, she was doing her best to fit the crime to the punishment. 'The work you've been doing and the support you've provided has been of a high standard, I'd like to see that continue.'

'I … Thank you. I'd appreciate a chance to put this behind me and make a new start.'

'We'll take it a day at a time and work out a few ground rules but from now on all meetings between us will be in school and with another person present.'

'Of course,' Lance's tone was thankful though his body language still showed his misery, 'I can't thank you enough.'

'Ok, we'll speak tomorrow, now go,' she almost added *get back to class*, without thinking she'd slipped back into headteacher mode and scolded him like an errant school boy.

# Chapter Ten

Matthew was decidedly uncomfortable being on the 'other side' of the interview table and felt himself cowed by Superintendent Walter Harken's sharp and insistent questioning. The formalities over, the superintendent had focused on Matthew's written response to the allegations made against him in the complaint.

'Initial sightings had suggested that Wellend had first gone to his mother's flat but had then fled on seeing police arrive at the scene,' Matthew's tone was almost robotic, repeating the facts exactly as he had memorised them, from both his notes and his written statement.

'The uniformed officers accompanying you searched the area, while you and Sergeant Lukula proceeded to the flat?' Harken asked, he had already interviewed Mrs Wellend and the various witnesses to the complaint. He'd found the appealing, middle-aged woman, who had no prior police record, to be intelligent and articulate, calm when questioned and, as she herself stated, determined to see justice done. Unlike Inspector Matthew Merry who seemed ill at ease.

'I sent the uniformed officers to assist those who were searching the estate where the suspect lived,' Matthew cleared his throat and paused to take a sip of water. 'When we got to the flat Mrs Wellend was slow to allow us entry and, when she finally answered the door wearing a bathrobe, we heard a noise from the living room. Sergeant Lukula was ahead of me and shouted at Luke Wellend to stop, then proceeded to follow him out of the window.'

'The flat was on the second floor?' Harken sounded mildly incredulous.

'Yes, but there was a ledge below the window, then a drop onto a garage roof and then onto grass at the rear. I shouted to the sergeant to take care, somewhat unnecessarily as she is very fit and athletic, she made it to the safety of the ground with ease and gave chase.'

'You didn't follow, to back up the sergeant?' Harken's tone remained tinged with incredulity.

'No, I did not,' Matthew restrained a smile at the thought of his clambering after Julie like some overweight Batman to her agile Catwoman. 'Wellend was running to the front of the building and Sergeant Lukula was close behind, I believed my best course of action was to head to the front myself. When I turned I discovered Mrs Wellend had closed the living room door and was barring my way.'

'How exactly?'

'She had flung her arms and legs apart, with her back to the door,' Matthew hesitated at the memory, the woman was undoubtedly good-looking and her gesture had pulled open her bathrobe and showed her naked body. The sight had stopped him in his tracks, partly as he struggled to think of his best course of action in the situation and partly as he took in the sight of her shaven mons pubis, firm breasts and erect nipples. 'Her actions had allowed her bathrobe to come open, realising she had nothing on underneath I averted my eyes …'

'"Averted your eyes"!' Harken's surprise at the phrase was understandable enough, 'Mrs Wellend claims you pushed past her to leave by the *open* living room door, effectively pulling the robe off of her. You then stopped, turned on her, saying what a great body she has and attempted to grope her.'

'No, I only spoke to tell her to get out of the way,' Matthew made every effort to keep his tone neutral and his words factual, he knew that any heated denials or emotive pleas of innocence would only make him look suspicious. 'I then proceeded to pull the door open, in doing so the door moved Mrs Wellend out of the way.'

'You didn't touch her, not even to move her out of the way?' It was a reasonable enough question.

'No, I was strong enough to open the door even with her in front of it trying to hold it closed,' Matthew explained. 'She is approximately five three and a light build.'

'Though an attractive woman,' Harken adopted a *we're all men here* smirk, 'she was naked, you were alone. It must have been a tempting situation.'

'Perhaps for some, but not to me, not at that moment. I was focused on trying to get out to assist Sergeant Lukula. I didn't even register the fact she had removed her bathrobe completely until she grabbed my arm as I was heading down the hall to the front door.' It wasn't true, she had had her shoulder against the door and was hitting him with her left fist while keeping up a barge of profanities, running through an entire dictionary of swear words and curses. He'd deliberately pulled her bathrobe down, both to entangle her arms and to pull her away from the door, then he'd pushed her away, his hand on her breast to do so. Even now he could feel the memory of her hard nipple on the flesh of the palm of his hand.

'She claims you pinned her arms to her sides and you offered to get her son off if she had sex with you,' Harken reiterated the line from Mrs Wellend's statement, the same wording she'd used in her verbal answer to his questioning. 'She then claims she managed to struggle free, pushing you away, and then she ran down the hall screaming for help. She claims that she was scared you were going to rape her. She managed to open the front door before you caught up to her and pulled her back.' Harken paused waiting for a reaction but getting nothing from Matthew other than a blank, hard stare, continued, 'These actions, the screams and your tussle with the naked Mrs Wellend in the doorway, were witnessed by no less than nine of her neighbours.'

'Once I had the living room door open, I headed straight for the front door, she followed me, gripping my arm and screaming' It was true enough, though he'd attempted to free himself and had in the process touched her more than once. 'Once I was out of the door, realising that Mrs Wellend had lost her bathrobe, I did push her back inside and pulled the door shut behind me. I then pushed through the crowd and went to assist Sergeant Lukula. Though the differences between my account and that of Mrs Wellend's are slight they are significant and I believe the majority of the statements taken immediately after the event bear out my account.'

'Though a number have since changed their statements in support of the complainant,' Harken pointed out.

'By the time I arrived at the front of the flats Sergeant Lukula had handcuffed and arrested Luke Wellend. He was subsequently charged with the murder of the young man he had stabbed and the attempted murder of his ex-girlfriend, who was with the victim at the time, she is still recovering in hospital, though is out of IC,' Matthew stated, although he knew Harken would be aware of a possible motive for Mrs Wellend's bogus complaint, he thought it worth emphasising what he hoped was obvious.

'He has yet to be convicted of the crimes,' Harken rightly pointed out, 'and he claims to have acted in self-defence, the girl being injured accidentally as she intervened. The mother has conducted a high profile social media campaign to back up her claims and those of her son being innocent. There has been some media coverage and a local councillor, who happens to be a member of a Safer Neighbourhood Board, has been asking questions about the case, its handling and your actions in particular.'

'You have my sympathies for the difficult position it puts you in,' Matthew commented without a hint of sarcasm. Harken studied the officer in front of him for a moment, he'd seen many like him before: hard, blank face, determined to get a result, perhaps bending a rule or two to do so. Matthew was starting to make a good DI, by all accounts, might even rise to chief inspector but was not marked down for anything higher as he wasn't considered sufficiently strategic for higher grades, being too focused on the job in hand.

'Do you have any further statement to add?' Harken finally asked, 'Any questions you'd like to ask?'

'No,' Matthew stated, thinking it wouldn't help to mention that he'd never come across a woman with such hard nipples as Mrs Wellend before.

Sergeant Adam Crowland had agreed to meet with Julie Lukula at the incident room at Wapping nick. He arrived with two large Costa coffees, which Julie appreciated before remembering she had recently met Crowland on an Equalities and Diversity course. Crowland was in his late thirties, single and, though not socially adept, was obviously doing his best to impress. Although the full beard that masked his face and the slight nervousness that came into his voice when he was put on the spot didn't inspire those he spoke to with confidence.

Julie had asked Harry Bainbridge to join them, she thought the experience would be good for him and he was glad to be temporarily relieved from the slog of taking statements.

'Inspector Merry isn't available,' she explained to Crowland, 'but if we can go over the cases I will bring him up to speed later.'

'Is he actually taking over the cases?' Crowland asked, he'd hit a dead end on the three serious attacks, designated as hate crimes, and was hoping to pass the responsibility on.

'Only if it's determined there is an actual connection with our murder case,' Julie glowered at Harry, who was distractingly looking for a pen to use with his notebook, as she spoke. 'My understanding is that these attacks all took place at roughly ten day intervals, the last one taking place ten days before Driver was killed.'

'That's the timeline,' Adam agreed, he'd been over his notes twice the night before so was confident of the facts, 'the first was in Wood Green, a man beaten up in a carpark by two men on a motorbike, at first we thought that was racially motivated. The second was an acid attack, in Waltham Forest, two men on a motorbike threw acid at a group leaving a small club. The last was in Stratford, another club and another acid attack committed by two men on a motorbike, their victim nearly died, the doctors are hopeful but are describing his injuries as life altering.'

'What does that mean?' Harry wanted to know, his face creased with concern that he didn't really want to be given the answer he craved. '"Life altering"?'

'He's suffered significant facial burns and burns to his upper left body,' Crowland had seen, if not been able to interview, the unconscious victim. Most of the wounds had special wrappings on them but even so the detective found it more difficult to look at a badly injured living person than he did a decayed corpse. It was harder not to dwell on the suffering of the living. 'He has lost the sight in his left eye, as well as his hearing on that side, plus three fingers from the left hand, he may yet have to have his hand amputated.'

'There's been a marked escalation in the attacks,' Julie noted, again glancing at Harry, he was here to observe not to ask questions, 'but what makes you think they are linked?'

'I'm not certain the first one is,' Crowland admitted, 'I only became involved after Intel threw up a potential link to the second case that I was already investigating. All three cases involve two assailants, whose general descriptions match. The bikes used are also of the same type, in each case they had false, professionally produced number plates.'

'They were all caught on CCTV then?' Harry asked, studiously writing and ignoring Julie's disapproval.

'Yes, though it was no help with identifying the attackers,' Crowland explained with a shrug, despite what his boss thought he hadn't had much to go on to help solve the cases. 'They wore dark clothing and helmets and are of average build. That's all we have, police appeals haven't thrown up anything more. Although,' he quickly added, not wanting any suggestion that he'd been less than a hundred percent diligent, 'I've spent a lot of time interviewing people and following up even the slightest of leads.'

'But you're still not certain the crimes are linked?' Julie asked, as Harry considered his next question.

'Not really. The first victim was Charles Douglas, a black man married to a white woman. He was attacked by two men crossing a carpark on his way home from work. The constable investigating at first thought the motivation might be racial hatred. However, when questioned the man, who was hospitalised overnight, suggested it might be some guys he owed money to. That didn't check out, then a subsequent interview, at the victim's home and including his wife, revealed he was a transvestite,' Crowland couldn't help a brief smirk as he spoke. Gays he could understand, even sympathise with a bit like he might with peaceful aliens visiting his world, but transvestism was beyond his world view and just seemed comical and smutty – a seaside postcard joke.

'How did that change things?' Harry's question was even less necessary than the last, Julie gave a small, unheeded sigh but nothing more, knowing the new boy would work through this phase and learn to listen before opening his mouth.

'The wife doesn't disapprove, even encourages him,' Crowland explained, 'and it is an open secret that they attend get-togethers with *like-minded* couples,' Adam emphasised 'like-minded' as if he were talking about some clandestine and subversive group. 'So when the next attack happened, what with the bike and all, the case was kicked over to me.'

'You were already investigating the second attack?' Julie asked, unclear about the timeline.

'Only just, they were linked the morning after,' noticing that Harry looked as if he was about to ask yet another question Crowland pushed on. 'A group of four people were leaving a gay club, just a small place where you can drink and dance. The group was four guys but two were dressed as women, Lionel Wong and Perry Cheung, both UK nationals but of Asian/American descent. As they were walking to the station to get home a motorbike passed them, slowing down so the passenger could throw the acid at them. It was all caught on CCTV. Lionel, the youngest, was on the outside and caught the brunt of it, the other three had minor burns.'

'Were the injuries life changing?' Harry wanted to know, obviously hooked on a theme.

'Not as bad as the third attack,' Crowland related, 'Lionel was lucky in that there were two firemen present, who'd followed them out of the club, and they relayed bottled water from a nearby shop until ambulance crew arrived. It seems they saved his sight but he'll be scarred for the rest of his life.' Crowland paused, shifting to ease his tense muscles which were starting to cramp from the frustration of retelling the cases on which he had spent so much time for so little result. 'We were able to track the bike for someway on CCTV until it was lost in a residential area. At one point a police car almost went after them as they jumped an amber/red light but turned back to respond to the scene of the attack, it was the only time the attackers even came close to drawing any attention to themselves.'

'Cool then, no panic,' Julie concluded.

'Yes, and planned, if the third and worst attack is anything to go by,' Crowland shrugged in resignation. 'Maximilian Dwight, fifty-eight, has lived in Stratford most of his adult life and had been out as a transvestite since leaving the navy thirty years ago. For the past fifteen years he'd run a pub frequented by gays and trannies and noted for its twice weekly drag acts. Max, or Maxine as he is known, is a big guy and despite his age is in the process of gender reassignment,' again Crowland pronounced the words as if struggling with an unknown foreign dialect. 'He was locking up at the rear of his pub, at the end of another Saturday night show, when a bike drew up beside him. One of the men called him by name, when he turned round he was struck in the face and knocked to the ground. The pair then poured acid over him, got back on the bike and drove off.'

'How did he …' Harry started to ask.

'His screams brought the door staff from the front of the pub to his aid,' Crowland anticipated, 'one of them suffered severe burns to his hands, pulling Dwight's shirt off and trying to wipe the acid away from his face. On the whole it was the speed of the ambulance response that saved Dwight and stopped this being a murder.'

As Harry asked more questions, which Crowland patiently answered, Julie Lukula reflected on the escalation of violence used in each attack, the calculated way the attackers went about their business and the evidence of forethought and planning that had gone into each attack, the choice of place and the care taken over their escape. It was far from conclusive and there were still very marked differences to the Geraldine Driver case but the sergeant's gut was telling her they were linked.

# Chapter Eleven

'So you think the attack was motivated by racism or misguided homophobia, either way a random hate crime?' Julie wasn't buying it. Adam Crowland had driven her to the Douglas's, having spent the journey inanely chattering, obviously trying to impress Julie and not in the least disheartened by her cold responses. She now sat in the couple's small lounge trying to get to the bottom of the niggling sense of disbelief she had at what they were telling her.

'Other than it being the men my husband owed money to, we can't think of any other reason,' Mrs Douglas responded still trying to sound positive, though more than aware that her husband was wilting under the female sergeant's insistent questioning. Julie Lukula was proving much tougher to convince than her male colleague who now sat looking perturbed at Julie's somewhat combative attitude.

'These men,' Julie looked directly at Charles Douglas, noticing his worried frown and how he nervously wiped his sweating palms on his trouser legs, 'didn't say anything to you? You didn't recognise either of them and could only give a very general description of them?'

'No, it happened so quickly,' Douglas confirmed, his voice soft and at odds with his broad chest and height. 'I'm sorry I can't help more.'

'My husband is the victim here,' Mrs Douglas interjected, annoyed at the female detective, the fact that Sergeant Lukula was black, though a much lighter skin than her husband, put her off hinting at a racial bias to the questions as she might have done with the sergeant's white colleague.

'Although he's not the only one,' Julie explained, her tone impatient, suggesting the pair were wasting her time, 'a number of others have been very seriously injured and a man now killed. All of these attacks committed by the men, we believe, who attacked your husband.'

'Killed?' Douglas looked stunned, it was the first time a death had been mentioned. 'I had no idea,' he glanced at his wife, who glared worriedly back. 'This is too much.'

'You will have to accompany us to the station,' Julie pushed at the gap she saw opening up, knowing the truth was about to emerge, 'to look at some photos and help build an e-fit.'

'It's no use, this is too much … I'm sorry Jan,' Douglas, looked shamefaced first at Julie, then his wife and then back. 'It was Jan's brothers that beat me up but I can't believe they're involved in anything else.'

'Damn, what a fuck up! The boss isn't going to be happy with the time wasted on this,' Julie told Crowland, who'd looked stunned at the sudden change in Douglas's story. Julie hadn't been too bothered about hearing how Jan Douglas's family had never been too happy with her taking up with a black man and how, on hearing he was also a transvestite, her brothers had decided to persuade him, with their fists and boots, to leave their sister. However, Julie had been interested to hear how the brothers owned a garage, which suggested they had the wherewithal to make up the false number plates.

'I had no idea they would lie about the attack,' Crowland could have kicked himself, this wouldn't look good when reported back to his boss and had probably killed any chance he'd had of asking Julie Lukula out for a date. His only hope now was if they could find a link between the brothers' number plate making skills and the false ones used in the other attacks. He'd keep his fingers crossed as he drove them to the brothers' garage, hoping it'd prove to be a reasonable lead.

Matthew and Harry weren't having a good time of it, they'd arrived at the hospital where Maximilian Dwight was being tended only to be told he was now stable but in an induced coma and that it was likely to be days before he was out of the ICU and could be questioned. They'd had a fleeting glance of the patient as they waited to speak with the ward sister, it made both men grimace and Harry now fully understood what life altering meant.

'His nephew was here not too long ago,' the ward sister informed them, she was looking tired at the end of a long shift but still retained a smile and sympathetic tone, 'I think he went to the cafeteria, do you want me to go with you and point him out?'

'That would be very useful,' Matthew acknowledged, and a few minutes later was surprised at the young man, built like a weight-lifter, who was pointed out to him. He barely had time to thank the sister as she turned on her heels and returned to the ward.

'It's Toby Dwight, isn't it?' Matthew asked, though completely certain he had put the right name to the face.

'Yes,' the young man in his mid-twenties looked up, glum and preoccupied, then his face creased as he tried to place Matthew's face.

'I'm Detective Inspector Merry and this is Detective Constable Bainbridge,' Matthew smiled, taking a seat without being asked, 'we came here hoping to speak with your uncle.'

'You'll be lucky,' Tobes's, as he was commonly known, expression turned angry. 'They say he's getting worse, that the acid got into his throat and damaged his vocal cords and lungs.'

'I'm sorry to hear that,' Matthew stated, trying his best to sound as if he meant it. Acid was such a nasty weapon and nobody deserved such injuries, although for Matthew it was just another in a very long line of victims he'd had to deal with.

'I know you, don't I?' Tobes's mind finally came up with the connection he'd had trouble making, 'You questioned me down at Key's Gym once, about a girl that'd been killed. I can't help you with this though. I don't know why anyone would want to do it and if I did I'd be after them myself.'

'How well did you know Mr Dwight?' Matthew asked, hoping to establish how much credence he could place on Tobes's information.

'Well enough,' Tobes stretched himself upright, taking stock of the busy hospital café for the first time since entering it, the news he'd been given by the ward sister had upset him more than he'd care to admit even to himself, 'after my dad died Max saw to it that me and mum were alright. Not that she appreciated his help, called him a fat poof, though she never refused his money. When I was old enough he let me do odd jobs around his pub, then I worked behind the bar, he was teaching me the trade,' Tobes's face brightening at the memory. 'My mum said to watch my arse but it was never like that, he was always kind and respectful.'

'People liked him?' Harry asked, receiving a nod in response.

'No enemies at all? No one he ever got on the wrong side of?' Matthew asked, putting enough doubt into his voice to suggest that it didn't seem likely anyone could be such a paragon of virtue.

'He never took any stick from anyone, if that's what you mean,' Tobes enlarged. 'He never told anyone twice to lay off and he was a big guy to cross, not fat, as my mum said, but muscle.'

'Although, he still needed door security on his pub,' Matthew pointed out.

'That was when the pub started to get busier and he'd had trouble with some bikers,' Tobes explained, then after a slight hesitation continued, 'Besides it was part of the new deal he had, he'd sold a share of the pub to a bigger firm. He did OK out of it though and, as he said, it took a lot of the worry out of running the place.'

'That company wouldn't be Greenspace Media or RightOn Entertainments, would it?' Matthew was starting to see a possible pattern emerging, as Tobes shrugged in response. 'The same firm you work for,' Matthew pointed out, causing Tobes to look even more perplexed. 'Ricky Towers owns both companies.'

Tobes seemed genuinely lost for words for a moment or two, then stated, 'I might know a few people, it pays to do so in the pub business, but I ain't ever seen Mr Towers.' He confided, and then decided to emphasise his point by adding, 'I might know a man, who knows a man who might, possibly, know a man who works for Mr Towers but we don't exactly keep in touch.' Tobes smiled at his own witticism, finding the chat with the inspector a diversion from his woes.

'So your uncle was happy with the arrangement?' Matthew asked, stopping Harry from speaking as the constable looked as if he'd found the nephew's response less than respectful.

'Yes, pretty much,' Tobes responded truthfully enough but, as Matthew continued to stare at him, qualified his comment by saying, 'He got on well with the door staff that were supplied. He had a bit of trouble with one of them early on but after that they pretty much respected him. Though he was starting to get a bit pissed with the quality of some of the acts supplied.'

'What was wrong with the acts?' Matthew was starting to feel the tell-tale *tingle* that ran down his spine whenever he thought he was onto something.

'They were a bit iffy at times,' Tobes thought back to the worst one he'd seen himself. 'As Max told the agency, if he wanted a bloke in a blond wig, singing off-key while he threw his clothes around and waggled his cock a bit then he'd get someone in off the street,' Tobes's grin grew broader as he spoke, the memory of his uncle's anger and his tirade down the phone starting to make him laugh. 'He told 'em all right, his voice all posh like when he announced the acts, sounding just like the queen. He said it was a crap act and the guy's pretty face and big cock didn't make up for it being crap, and if they couldn't find him someone better he'd stop using them. They were quick to promise a much better performer next time, one of their best acts.'

Matthew smiled in sympathy, realising that Tobes genuinely admired his uncle, asking, 'What about the door staff? You said there was a disagreement?'

'It was a while ago, one of them got into an argument with Max, can't remember what over,' Tobes struggled to think back, his mind still on the phone call and how much it tickled him. 'This guy takes a swing at my uncle and Max just picks him up and throws him straight out the door. The other door staff thought it hilarious.'

'Do you remember the guy's name?'

'No, but Morgan might, he's the bloke who was injured trying to help Max,' Tobes explained, the smile on his face dying as thoughts of the attack returned, 'his hands got burned bad.'

'What about the name of the crap act?'

'I'm not certain,' Tobes shrugged, once again too upset to care much about answering Matthew's questions. 'It could have been *Titillating Tina,* something stupid like that,' then Tobes roused himself, considering the police were trying to help for once, 'Sorry, it was only a few weeks ago, but I think the agency will remember. My uncle was really pissed at them and I doubt they'll forget his phone call.'

'That'd be the Blue Bird Agency, Victor Thorsson?'

'Yep, one and the same,' Tobes stated, not bothering to wonder how the inspector knew.

'Thanks, you've been a help,' Matthew informed Tobes, as he stood, extending his hand.

'You'll get the bastards, won't you?' Tobes quietly asked, momentarily hesitating before grasping the outstretched hand in a cumbersome if strong handshake.

Matthew nodded and muttered his well practiced inanities about 'The Met will put all its resources into finding the persons responsible' – doing his best to sound as if it meant anything.

'He didn't deserve this you know,' Tobes stated mournfully. 'All his life he'd wanted to be a woman and was talking to the doctors about the surgery, to become the person he wanted to be. That won't happen now,' Tobes paused, sucking his teeth in resignation that life had a way of kicking you in the balls. 'It'd be better if he dies, never comes round, never knows what's happened to him. The poor fucker.' Tobes turned away, not to hide tears, as there weren't any, but because he'd finished and couldn't think of any other words to express his grief fuelled anger and sorrow.

'It turns out that Jan Douglas's brothers had simply used a bike that was in the garage for repairs,' Julie wound up her summary for Matthew, 'and they temporarily switched the plates from one they were breaking up for parts.'

'Sergeant Crowland was supposed to have had the plates checked out?' Matthew was annoyed and unsympathetic to such a basic mistake.

'Yes,' Julie stated diplomatically. 'He's with me now, what do you want us to do next?'

'Knocking some fucking sense into him would be a start,' Matthew stated, glad to hear her snigger, knowing she probably wasn't happy at having to do the work that should already have been done by her colleague. 'However, you've done enough, so get off home and do some final revision for that exam you have later. That's an order,' he stated, anticipating her objection. 'Have Sergeant Crowland come and pick me up, we'll visit Cheung and Wong next. I'm sending Harry to see if he can track down the names of a couple of guys Dwight has had run-ins with, probably won't amount to anything but leave no stone unturned and all that. You won't find that pearl of wisdom in the inspectors exam,' he told Julie as a way of a goodbye.

Perry Cheung had a very pleasant Californian accent that he'd never lost. He'd moved to the UK twenty years previous with his parents and now, at thirty-eight, his slight build, oval face, dark eyes and feline grace still made him a seductive female, when dressed the part, and a handsome man, as now, when wearing slacks and a sweater. Adam Crowland, who had phoned ahead to check that Perry was in, introduced Matthew and then kept himself in the background, praying that nothing else would come to light that would further suggest his investigation had been less than diligent.

'That looks a nasty burn,' Matthew opened the questioning, as was his habit, at a tangent to what he was looking for, indicating the thick bandage on Perry's neck that disappeared but bulged under his pastel green sweater.

'It is,' Perry was grateful for the sympathy, understandably he'd not received much given Lionel's injuries far outweighed his own, 'it makes moving my head and arm painful, fortunately the painkillers the hospital prescribed are keeping the worst at bay.'

'What about Lionel?' Matthew asked, glancing around the small but artistically decorated and furnished apartment.

'Back inside,' Perry explained, deliberately referring to the hospital as if it were a prison, 'they are doing tests and things to prepare for the first skin grafts. Much of his lower face and chest are a terrible mess. It's going to be a long journey.'

'I'm sorry to hear that,' Matthew sympathised, he couldn't think of anything worse than being burned, the thought of blistered flesh sending an imperceptible shudder through him. 'Have you been together long?'

'Ten years now, we were married nearly four years ago,' Perry glanced at a photo of himself and Lionel on their wedding day. Crowland, meanwhile, sat in silence wondering where all this was going, Julie had told him that he could learn a lot from the inspector but this just seemed idle chatter.

'You make a stunning couple,' Matthew's compliment was sincere. Lionel looked very handsome, if somewhat effete, in an elegant top hat and tails while Perry in a wedding dress was really quite sexy. 'The dress really suits you, quite … stunning.' Crowland frowned, thinking that now all the inspector seemed to be doing was chatting up the queer.

'Thank you, Inspector,' Perry smiled, feeling at ease. Police officers, like the uncomfortable looking sergeant sitting to one side, were not always as sympathetic or understanding.

'The attack must be all that more devastating for you both,' Matthew concluded, 'I take it nothing more has come to mind, no more thoughts about who might have done this?'

'No, I'm sorry,' Perry said, his tone now grave, his lightened mood at the memories of a happier time quickly dissipating, 'I've done all I can not to think of it and Lionel has virtually no memory of the night at all, just a little of the club and someone screaming.'

'Sergeant Crowland has, I believe, already told you this is being treated as a hate crime and the assumption is you were targeted at random.'

Crowland cringed as he heard his name but was grateful when Perry said, 'Yes, the sergeant has been very good at keeping us informed. I can't think of anyone that would have wanted to have done this to us. Lionel was always so easy going, so loved by everyone.'

'What about yourself? Either or both of you could have been the target of the attack, and, well …' Matthew glanced back at the photo. 'Perhaps a jealous admirer, a lover scorned perhaps?'

'Perhaps a good few years ago,' Perry almost smirked, liking the inspector's rather old fashioned allusion to a possible marital infidelity, he was beginning to think he'd made a conquest of the rather portly and staid looking police officer. 'However, I have been faithful for some years since before our marriage and I'm certain Lionel has been as well. We get on very well. I've decided to give up the stage and we are planning to open a restaurant together. Lionel is a really brilliant chef and I was brought up in a restaurant, my parents had one in America and now own three across London. You could say I was born to it and Lionel has a natural and great talent as a chef.'

'You still work on the stage though?'

'A song, a dance, a little comedy and a rather suggestive balloon act,' Perry explained, he couldn't help an elegant wave of his hand, his eyes fixed on the inspector, his curiosity growing as he tried to glean what Matthew was thinking. 'I might not always top the bill but I earn a crust, more than enough to have money put aside to help start our little venture.'

'Did you ever work in a pub called the Lea Way, in Stratford?' Crowland asked, if he'd missed this link before he was determined to make up for it now.'

'It doesn't ring a bell,' Perry wasn't certain, he remembered a club in Stratford but the name meant nothing, 'my agent would have a list of everywhere I've played.'

'They are?' Crowland purposefully asked, pulling notebook and pencil out, completely unaware of Matthew's scowl that should have told him that these were the questions he should already have asked Perry.

'The Blue Bird Agency,' Perry said, much more aware of Matthew's disapproving look than Crowland was.

'Your agent would be Victor Thorsson?' Matthew surmised, stopping Crowland from unnecessarily asking for the address.

'He was once, but I recently switched to one of the younger partners,' Perry explained, wondering why all this was relevant but the inspector obviously thought it important and Perry felt he could trust the man's judgement on this. 'Thorsson is going off the boil. He's losing contacts, not negotiating the best deals and having gigs fall through. Then dearest Geraldine tipped me the wink and I moved as quick as I could.'

'Geraldine Driver?' It was now Matthew's turn to be flummoxed.

'Yes, poor Geraldine,' Perry said, another tragic event to grieve coming so hard on the heels of their own terrible events he'd hardly had time nor emotional energy to mourn the loss of a friend, albeit a distant one. 'We'd worked on the same bill a few times, he was brilliant, a great performer. He could be demanding but I always thought I upped my game whenever he was around. It is so terrible.' Then a thought struck Perry, 'You don't think there is a link do you?'

'So you have worked at the Blue Snake?

'Yes,' Perry sounded as if doing so was like working with an actual snake, a necessary if somewhat unpleasant experience, 'a nice place, good audiences and when Geraldine was on the bill never any problems. The manageress can be a bit of a cow and their security manager is a real shit, alright if you like the *hands-on* type but tell him where to get off and you might find your car getting keyed.'

# Chapter Twelve

'Everything is still moving forward at a fast pace,' Ray Rosen informed Matthew, as they both munched on sandwiches the inspector had brought to the incident room from the machine in the police canteen. 'Duncan has done a good job on summarising where we are on the interviews.' As if on cue the analyst entered the room with the three large to go cups of coffee he'd been dispatched to fetch from the café up the road. For Matthew this was a late lunch and for the other pair a pre-dinner snack.

'We've compiled a list of people from Driver's last eight gigs, although that goes back only five months and includes three from a short tour in Germany,' Duncan said, seating himself and nibbling on a sandwich, he didn't want to ruin his appetite knowing that his girlfriend would be cooking dinner that evening, 'It's added twenty-two names to the list, most simply to ask what they might know about anyone holding a grudge against Driver. We are still cross-checking statements and the like but so far the alibis we are getting are all checking out, so we don't have any real suspects in sight.'

'We are missing something, someone really hated Driver to have killed him the way they did. What about his computer?' Matthew asked, thinking he should finish up quickly and get home, it had been a long day and he'd barely seen anything of his family over the last couple of days.

'There are a couple of interesting emails and comments on his blog we have looked into. Plus, his deleted files and blocked list have revealed some unpleasant communications he obviously didn't want to engage with,' Ray said, having spoken with the technicians before Matthew's arrival back at the incident room. 'He'd blocked a few people, but two in particular stood out. Basically they were hooked on the themes of tying him up and butt fucking him.'

'And?' Matthew asked, his tone mildly aggrieved that Ray hadn't begun with this as it was highly relevant and, having dealt with Crowland's bumbling investigation, expected more from his own team.

'Nothing,' Ray went on, unconcerned as he was far too experienced to doubt his own methods. 'One sender lives in Germany and hasn't set foot out of the country, the other lives in York. I had the locals check him out and he has a cast iron alibi as he was staying with his girlfriend, they'd been out on the town with friends that night. I've asked Duncan to do an analysis of who has been in contact with Driver the most, across all social media that Driver used. I'm working on the theory that the attacker was in close contact but was keeping his hatred concealed.'

'Good thinking,' Matthew conceded, nodding an apology for his previous sharp tone. 'What about the SUV?'

'We've done well in tracing the fingerprints SOCOs pulled. His wife and brother's prints have been found in the front, Todd Barrett's in the rear and on the suitcase that Driver was bent over during the rape …'

'Barrett?' Matthew asked, selecting another sandwich from the pile of boxes on the desk between them, signalling Duncan to help himself as the analyst was still on his first half as Matthew selected his fourth.

'The assistant deputy manager of the Blue Snake, apparently he helped Driver move his gear into the club. Four cases in all, the one left in the car contained spare costumes. Barrett's fingerprints are on all of them and the manager confirmed she had asked him to help. It's possible other prints might trace back to staff at his previous gigs, we're still looking into that,' a smile broke out on Ray's face as he outlined all the work the team had been doing. He was pleased at the eliminations though he knew the inspector was only interested in anything significant that remained outstanding. 'The SUV is fairly new so we have checked back to where he bought it and have eliminated two of their customer service people. Currently we have six other sets of prints we are trying to trace, they come from all over the car but, keeping in mind the perpetrator wore gloves, I'm not hopeful for a result.'

'OK, well done,' Matthew tried to sound as if he meant the praise, despite it feeling like a lot of effort just to stand still. 'Anything on what was found inside?'

'The blood, shit and urine all came from Driver,' Ray resumed his summary, munching on a BLT. 'There are trace fibres that match the ones found on the club's carpark wall, where the attacker climbed in, but with no suspect to check them against they aren't presently any use. Not much luck on the ball-gag and dildo either, they are fairly common types and are sold in a number of shops across London as well as a good few online retailers. To be honest we aren't getting very far with tracing them.'

'Why's that?'

'The shops often deal in cash sales so no record of the customer who made the purchase, while the online shops are proving difficult to pin down,' Ray looked less than pleased to say this but he knew the team were doing all that could be done. 'The main problem is that if the items were bought separately and from different vendors then narrowing down to a single purchaser is proving a slow, if not impossible, task.'

'I'm feeding all the data we are getting on the purchases into a programme,' Duncan explained, putting his half-eaten sandwich back into an empty box, 'but if one of them was bought using cash it won't produce anything useful. Our best chance is if a credit card was used for both then we might get a real lead.'

'It's a long shot, although, like the fabric trace, we might get something to use in narrowing down the suspect list. Of course we need a list of viable suspects first,' Ray shrugged, starting to collect the empty boxes to put in the bin. 'Our best hope is DNA from the rope but that's still being worked on and isn't likely to be ready for a few days yet. However, once they have eliminated Driver's DNA, let's hope it'll lead us to our killer.'

'Julie thinks the two hate crimes, the acid attacks, are linked to Driver's killing,' Matthew told them, finishing his coffee and adding the empty to go cup to the pile waiting to be binned. 'She sees a pattern in the escalation of violence used. So, she's going to focus on finding the bike and plates used; in all fairness it's currently our best line of inquiry,' Matthew could have added that it would also keep Swift off his back but thought it would sound petty. 'I've told Crowland to wind up the Douglas assault case, he can deal with the arrests and charges on that, while we take over the other two cases as part of our investigations.'

Ray and Matthew waited, digesting their food, watching Duncan pour the coffee from his to go cup into his own ever present mug. Had the analyst told them the mug was a present from his girlfriend, the first woman he'd ever actually slept with, then they might have understood his attachment to it. As things stood Duncan's coffee mug was the centre of much speculation amongst the team, who took occasional delight in hiding it during the rare moments he took his eyes off it.

'I assume from your tone you don't agree with Julie's view,' Ray said as soon as Duncan had returned to his desk and was out of earshot.

'I don't disagree with it,' Matthew told him, 'I'm just not convinced.' Matthew paused but, realising Ray was too old a hand not to guess what he was thinking, went on, 'Towers keeps cropping up too frequently in this. His links, through his companies, with the Blue Bird Agency, the Blue Snake and Driver. Now it turns out he owns the Lea Way, Dwight's pub, and Perry Cheung's agent used to be Thorsson. And Thorsson seems to be doing his best to avoid mentioning Towers by name but who also seems to be losing all his clients, including Driver.'

'Driver's killing hardly sounds gangland style, though the acid attacks could be. Although, just how maiming and killing drag artists hurts or helps Towers I've no idea, I just can't see the connection,' Ray disagreed. Then, guessing what his boss's next move was likely to be, he decided to remind Matthew that, 'You do remember there has been a memo circulated about the Towers family? The one telling everyone that they should seek permission before speaking with any of the Towers clan.'

'It's actually phrased to say we need permission if we want to speak with any of the family whom we suspect of a crime, not as a witness,' Matthew pointed out, having already re-read the memo on his way back to the incident room.

'That's a moot point if the governor finds out,' Ray warned, he rather liked his boss and hoped Matthew would think carefully about his next step, knowing Matthew could be too focused on his own investigation and miss, as more senior officers would put it, the bigger picture.

'The fate of the world teeters on the spike of if,' Matthew said with a smile, thinking he might call on an old friend on his way home. After all, at this hour, another delay wouldn't matter.

'How did it go?' Yvette wanted to know, she'd been on tenterhooks all day and only delayed asking Julie long enough to give her a heartfelt welcome home kiss.

'I reckon I've aced it,' Julie stated confidently, she wasn't a natural student. Matthew was the type to read a book from cover to cover and commit it to memory, Julie dipped in and out, linking what she read to practical applications before she could understand and learn the work. However, in all other respects she was confident and once she understood a concept she never forgot it, 'but the result won't be confirmed for a couple of days at least. What about you?'

'The director and producer still can't agree on the final designs but I think we are getting there, at least I've started to order the extra material I think we need.'

'Looks like you've been busy,' Julie observed, seeing the table fully laid, including candles, and noticing the aroma coming from the kitchen that caused her stomach to rumble hungrily.

'I thought we'd have a proper meal for once,' Yvette's own stomach flipped at the thought of what she had planned for the evening, 'you know, a little treat for ourselves. You get showered and put on something nice and I'll finish up in the kitchen.'

'God, I do love coming home to you,' Julie told her. She was finding domestic life with Yvette decidedly to her liking, somehow it calmed her and gave her a better outlook on life, more so than anything she'd experienced previously.

As she stripped in preparation for her shower her mobile rang and, though she was tempted to ignore it, seeing it was from Malcolm Swift she thought it wise to take the call. And was glad to have done so as it proved good news.

'More good news,' she shouted out to Yvette, 'Craig Warren has been picked up and arrested in Birmingham.'

'What?' Yvette called back, not catching what Julie said, 'Who?'

'Just someone I was after,' Julie sang out, thinking she'd put on a slinky number after her shower, her up-beat mood increasing at the thought that the rabidly unpleasant Warren was now under lock and key and she could get another case closed.

Lance was still babbling, something about plans for academy status that he needed urgently to speak with Kathy about. Kathy knew she would now miss her daughters' bedtime, but at least her sister, Wanda, was staying overnight and the girls loved their aunt. The finance sub-committee meeting had gone on longer than expected, mainly because Lance had sung her praises over her handling of the budget at every opportunity. She had found his fawning tedious. She then gave him five minutes to talk about his 'urgent news', as he had breathlessly phrased it, as she packed her case to head home; her office and the school were quiet as everyone else had left.

She could barely contain a yawn as the consultant droned on, well past his allotted five minutes, she'd slumped into her chair to patiently wait for him to finish. Impolite or not she decided she could listen to Lance's tortuous and monotone discourse with her eyes closed. Worse still she was now wanting to use the toilet, the result of the final cup of tea Lance had handed her at the very end of the finance meeting. Kathy opened her eyes, feeling relaxed, sprawled on the floor naked, Lance standing over her. What puzzled her was why or even if they were having sex. At least Lance looked pleased with himself, she thought as her eyes closed again, with his beaming smile and proud erection.

Matthew had not needed to go far out of his way home to find Donald Key, locating him as expected at the Black Horse pub in Lehman Street. Donald was a six foot six wall of muscle and stood out in any crowd, but he sat ignored in his usual place in a quiet corner of the pub.

'Hello, Inspector,' Donald hailed Matthew as the inspector put two pints down on the table, 'you back at Lehman Street nick then? Thought the place was closed.'

'No, I came looking for you,' Matthew informed the man mountain, they hadn't seen much of each other over the intervening years but they had been friends at school and, for a short while, Ricky Towers had been their Athos to Donald's Porthos and Matthew's Aramis. The unlikely trio had shared a bond in being shunned by their classmates. Donald's size being both a source of fear and mockery, Matthew had been the class nerd and Ricky was Bobby *The Beast* Towers's eldest son. And if a man went round claiming the title *The Beast* that was reason enough to avoid his son, although in reality Bobby Towers was far worse than any animal especially when it came to his own son.

'I'm flattered,' Donald stated, hefting the pint Matthew had bought for him, the only acceptable compensation they would both agree on for the favour Matthew was about to ask, 'That's twice in just over a year.'

'I need you to pass on a message to a mutual friend,' Matthew began, grinning at the thought of what he was about to say.

Julie couldn't sleep, she thought it unlikely that she ever would again, while Yvette slumbered, with charmingly noisy breathing, beside her. Julie had gone from stunned to ecstatic in a nanosecond when Yvette had proposed marriage at the end of the meal. Their love-making that followed had been a cliché of earth shattering intensity. Now, if she could only relax her jaw aching smile she might fall asleep.

The house was quiet by the time Matthew got home, Kathy's things were uncharacteristically dumped in the hallway, the girls and his sister-in-law were soundly asleep, but his wife wasn't upstairs. He found Kathy slumped on the sofa downstairs, still fully dressed and in a deep sleep, almost as if she had collapsed when first entering the house, overwhelmed by tiredness. Matthew watched her for a short while, unwilling to disturb her, wondering what their marriage had come to. She exhausted from overwork and he spending long hours on the job, both relying on various friends and family to look after the girls in their joint absence.

Matthew could smell another man on Kathy as he manhandled her up the stairs. She didn't wake up but repeatedly muttered 'get off' in her sleep, as he clumsily manoeuvred her onto their bed. Like a silent fart, the stink of recent sex was released when he removed her underwear. He sat at the end of the bed looking at his almost comatose wife, he couldn't blame her for seeking the affection she was denied in their too work orientated marriage, they were more like colleagues sharing the burden of parentage rather than a loving, married couple sharing a life.

*It really must stop, we must change*, he thought to himself, as she started and moaned in her sleep. He was far from blameless. He always put work first, even for the slimmest of reasons, and he'd had a number of one night stands and brief affairs, seven or eight in all, over the years. Including one, which shamed him most, with the sister-in-law who now slumbered in the adjacent room, his daughters' beloved aunt. People can change, he thought, he'd seen it happen: addicts who learned to control their addiction, criminals who went straight. Finally he fell asleep thinking of ideas for date nights, family dinners and outings, while Kathy tossed and turned, unable to wake and free herself from the nightmarish visions of rape that stalked her drug induced sleep.

# Chapter Thirteen

When Kathy Merry finally woke it was to the sound of her family making breakfast and preparing for another day of work and school. She barely recognised those sounds at first, feeling disorientated and nauseous, her only memory of the previous night and evening was the finance sub-committee and Lance's fawning praise. She couldn't even remember whether she'd had sex with Matthew. On balance she considered it unlikely, as they'd lost the habit of midweek sex and it had become a weekend routine to slate a physical rather than romantic need, yet her body told her something had happened.

She revived slightly drinking the cup of tea her eldest daughter brought her, though it was long into the day before she could rid herself of the odd taste that was in her mouth. The shower also helped revive her, at least it rid her of the stink of stale sweat that seemed to cling to her. Worse still she was sore in places she shouldn't be sore, small bruises on her body she couldn't explain.

Finally, she was ready to join the others just in time to take the girls on their school run and drop her sister at the station. Matthew, in a good and smiling mood, had left them at the gate having hugged and kissed Kathy and the girls, suggesting they should plan a family outing for the weekend. Her husband ignored her sister who happily ignored him in return, the pair liking to dislike each other. All the time Kathy feeling as if she were still dreaming and that she was somehow avoiding waking up to a reality that was so different from the one she was experiencing.

*

Matthew's briefing to the team was even more succinct than normal, though his desire to get away quickly was shanghaied by Julie's announcement that she had gotten engaged. Her rather girlish glee, both at everyone's congratulations and in showing off her ring, rather surprised Matthew. It was a side of Julie he hadn't seen before and an unexpected one. He held back long enough to make a joking remark about how his little girl was growing up.

To which Julie responded with, 'Less of the *girl* or I'll blind you with the dazzle of my ring.'

'OK, take your *precious* and get started on tracking down the bike and plate maker,' Matthew said with a chuckle, leaving her to puzzle out his reference to her ring.

In actuality he had plenty of time before his meeting but he wanted to ensure he wasn't followed. It was an unnecessary precaution he suspected, but he wanted to make certain he would have time to ponder any information he gleaned from meeting with Towers before he had to tell anyone about it. For Ricky Towers, however, taking every precaution that their meeting wouldn't be known, heard or watched was the habit of a lifetime, all part of the daily game he played.

'Good choice,' Towers said. If Matthew had found it hard to recognise Ricky Towers, in his blue suit, open necked cream shirt, manicured nails, short styled black hair and ducktail beard then his voice confirmed his identity: it still had that *I don't give a fuck* timbre that he'd possessed since early adolescence. 'Dumb arse message though. If it'd been anyone other than Donny insisting on delivering it verbally and in person they would most likely have ended up in the river.'

'It would be interesting to watch someone trying to tip Donald into the Thames,' Matthew finally made himself comfortable in the pew next to Towers, he'd fussed around deliberately, taking stock of the two dark suited men who guarded each entrance to the small church. He looked Ricky over, despite the beard and stylishly cut hair, he looked every inch like his father: five nine, thick muscular build like a wrestler.

'Why all the cloak and dagger?' Ricky got to the point, he'd been intrigued by the message to meet in St Olave's Church in Hart Street, more so when Donald Key had told him it was from Inspector Matthew Merry; Mat, as they'd both known him a lifetime ago. The reason for the meeting was much more expected.

'You're not a suspect,' Matthew cryptically explained, 'and, given all the sensitivities about meeting with you, you being on the NCA's most wanted list, I thought this might be more pleasant. Two guys reminiscing about their school days.'

'You haven't changed, a good deal fatter but still an arsehole,' Towers stated, his mind reaching back to when they were twelve and the school trip. The fat, little history teacher who told them about the church, the Great Fire and Samuel Pepys, how Matthew had known more about Pepys than the teacher and how they'd ended up at the top of the Monument, with Towers pissing through the railings on the tourists below. No more school trips for the trio after that.

'I'm not here to trade insults, I'm not a schoolchild anymore,' Matthew said, more haughtily than he'd intended, seeing the brief look of angry disdain flash across Ricky's otherwise impassive face. 'You had a vested interest in Gerry Driver and your name keeps cropping up in my investigation, so I just want to know if you know anything that might help me catch who did it.'

'I don't care for my name being bandied about in any context,' Ricky stated blandly, returning to studying the ornate church decorations, remembering being told the place had been levelled during the Blitz and then reconstructed, it intrigued him that anyone could care so much about something to bother.

Matthew sighed, 'If you are going to fuck me about, you should have brought more men,' his tone resigned, if Ricky was going to act the crook then he'd get treated like one, 'I thought I might be doing you a favour, but obviously not.'

'If you want to do me a favour then tell me what you have on Geraldine's death and I'll take it from there,' the slightest change in Ricky's tone of voice made Matthew feel as if the temperature inside the cold interior of the church had dropped a degree or two.

'It doesn't work like that,' Matthew explained, settling back in the pew, taking in the church's ornate decorations. A memory of Ricky floating into his mind. They were eleven and just going up to secondary school, Matthew was holding Ricky while he sobbed and Donald stayed in the background keeping watch. Ricky's tears weren't from the bruises and lumps he had off his dad. Not even his father's words, the insults and put downs, had any impact on him. It was simply his frustrated rage and hatred for his old man having no other outlet than tears. 'One day,' Matthew had told him, 'one day you'll get him back.' However, Ricky never had the chance, a shotgun blast to the back of his old man's head saw to that five years later. But, for a short few years, the boys had a close bond, including Donald who did nothing but keep watch and keep their secrets.

'As I said, you are not a suspect,' Matthew continued, after a pause, that left much unsaid between the pair but gave them time to think back over thirty years. 'Neither am I stupid, if you knew who is responsible then I'd be wasting my time asking and, given what you have just asked me, I can only assume that isn't the case.'

'So what do you want to know?' Ricky was getting impatient, beginning to think the meeting a mistake for the memories it was bringing back and the times he had long since buried along with his father.

'Gerry had recently signed a contract with you, your company that is, and you were personally involved in the production of a stage and TV show specifically aimed to promote his unique talents, is that correct?' Matthew had already noted that Ricky had referred to Gerry as Geraldine and wondered if that was habit with him.

'Yes, Geraldine was incredibly talented,' Ricky confirmed, 'I saw that when I first saw her perform in one of my West End clubs. Victor Thorsson said I'd be bowled over with the act and I was, when he introduced *her* as Gerry I was ... well, gob smacked.' Matthew noted Ricky's melancholy tone.

'When was this?'

'Two and a half years ago,' Ricky stated, rousing himself, looking round to check his men were still blocking the doors and still out of earshot. 'I had other projects to keep me busy, but the more I saw Geraldine the more I realised the potential.'

'You saw her regularly?' Matthew kept his voice soft and questions short, just a tap to keep the hoop spinning, the story flowing.

'Yes, on and off stage. We talked about the act, her plans and it made me realise I could focus on the production side, take the whole thing under my direct control, have some fun for once,' Ricky suddenly stopped, giving Matthew a sharp look, realising he was saying too much. 'Anyway six months ago I decided to stop thinking and start doing, things were just starting to come together and now this.' Again Towers paused, his face now more grim than melancholy, 'It's not the money I resent losing on the deal, it's pennies, but the toe-rag who did this spoilt my fun, hurt me, so if I get my hands on him he will suffer – long and slow.'

'We have Driver's copy of the contract he signed with you,' Matthew changed the subject, he could see the anger welling up inside Towers and remembered how unpredictable that made him, how they'd often end up fighting until Donald pulled them apart. Only on one occasion Donald wasn't there. 'There's no mention of any insurance but Mrs Driver tells us that ...'

'He loved his wife, respected her,' Ricky interrupted guessing at Matthew's question, 'he wouldn't want to see her going without anything because of his death.'

'You were close then, good friends and not just business acquaintances?' Matthew asked, realising Ricky wasn't going to elaborate and the money he'd arranged to be given to Mrs Driver didn't appear to be of consequence to him.

'Not with Gerry, no,' Ricky looked Matthew in the eyes, a clear message the detective should take care over what he asked next. Ricky remembered Matthew's arms round him, pulling him back and off the old pervert who'd run the small video store at the back of the arcade. The store thrived on the sale of porn and the thirteen year old boys had liked to browse, especially in the back room where they could watch extracts from the videos and look through the magazines. He hadn't minded the owner watching, talking to them, but he'd exploded when the old guy put his hands on him. Matthew had laughed at first, then got scared at Ricky's frenzied attack, pulling him off. When Ricky had turned on his friend, Matthew had reacted without thought knocking Ricky to the ground then, seeing the fury that remained in Ricky's eyes, he'd run off. After that their friendship was over and their lives went on their different courses.

'How much was Thorsson involved in this?' Matthew judged this a reasonable question, Ricky had, intentionally or not, already told him a great deal.

'That old bugger,' Ricky laughed, he held no animosity towards Matthew, the past was the past and he had moved on. 'He's had his time in the limelight, he'd topped a few bills as a drag act in his youth and has gone on to make a good go of the agency.'

'Then you took it over,' Matthew prompted, noting Towers's tone had mellowed to a more philosophical one now the questions didn't touch on him personally.

'He needed the money,' Ricky explained. 'He'd already brought in two partners, but he has a lavish lifestyle, like that guy Micawber,' the reference reminding Matthew that Towers wasn't the illiterate, muscle bound villain his old man had been, 'so it was an opportunity for both parties. Thing is he is lazy, doesn't put himself out. Geraldine was getting fed up with him and his half-hearted representation, so my coming on the scene and the new contract was a way of moving on. Thorsson will get a small pay off but Geraldine was done with him.' Ricky paused, his brow creasing at a thought, 'Do you suspect Thorsson had a part in this?'

'No, he has an alibi and he isn't the type,' Matthew ensured he smiled as he spoke. He hadn't completely ruled Thorsson out, he obviously wasn't the killer but that didn't mean he wasn't involved in some way. However, he didn't want Ricky making a preemptive strike on the old has-been. 'Just one last question, you obviously knew Gerry – Geraldine – well, do you think he was troubled by anything? Or was he involved with anyone?'

Ricky made the effort to look as if he gave his answer some thought before saying, 'I don't think so, she was occupied with the new act, the preparations and that. I don't think she had much time for anything else.' Then, deciding he'd spent enough time speaking with the inspector, he ended their tête-à-tête by saying, 'Get the bastard who did this Mat, Geraldine was a lovely woman and a great talent. I won't ask you for a name, just have the cunt put inside and I'll see to him.'

'Still as bright as ever,' Matthew sighed, getting up and heading for the exit, 'telling a detective inspector your intentions to maim and kill a man.'

'Fuck off,' Ricky stated with just enough intensity to make the man on the door wonder if he should be stopping the inspector, but seeing Matthew's grin and Ricky shrug, simply pushed the door open to allow the detective to leave.

'The techs reckon, it's a Honda X-ADV,' Harry Bainbridge informed Julie, as they looked through the various photos of the bikes used in the two acid attacks and Driver's killing, 'They are pretty certain it's the same type of bike used in the acid attacks. However, the one of the bike we think Driver's killer used to get away on, they are less certain about, as the CCTV picture quality isn't good enough, but it's a possible match.'

'Great,' Julie didn't sound confident about the task she'd set herself. All the normal searches of stolen bikes and local owners hadn't produced anything of use, or to be more accurate had highlighted many dozens of possibilities, most of which they couldn't even start to eliminate. 'There's been no abandoned vehicles found that match the general description so in all likelihood it's being kept somewhere.'

'With the false plates they could be using the bike every day and simply changing the number when they need to use it for the attacks. I checked with Duncan and none of those we've interviewed own an X-ADV, only two ride Hondas and they have alibis.' Harry was equally despondent at their chances, but was trying to think of something positive to add. 'The oil stains found on the orange rope, from the back of Driver's SUV, is motor oil, one that's commonly used on bikes.'

'As well as some cars, outboard motors and even petrol mowers,' Julie pointed out. 'No, I think our best course is to focus on firms that supply the materials to make number plates with. It will have been a small order so we might have a chance to trace someone who has bought stuff. If that doesn't produce any results, then we'll try every stockist in as wide a vicinity as we can cope with and check on thefts. Ray's having a list drawn up of places reporting a theft that remains unsolved. Right, we should get started.'

'Err … Before you do, just wanted to say congrats on the engagement,' Harry had held back congratulating Julie earlier, wanting to speak to her in person.

'Thanks, I'm more excited about it than I would have thought,' Julie admitted, she'd been so wrapped up in enjoying the *now* with Yvette, she'd never given any thought to how their future might pan out but marriage seemed a natural step for them.

'It's good you can be so open about such things,' Harry said, determined to take the opportunity.

'Getting married isn't that big a deal,' Julie laughed, 'well, mine is of course. My engagement is a life shattering revelation.' She couldn't resist flashing the ring once more, wiggling her fingers so it caught the light.

'No I mean …' Harry's resolution was faltering, his voice becoming nervous.

'What?' Julie decided that was enough teasing and it was time for mutual support and all that. 'The fact that you are gay as well. That's not much of a revelation either,' she reassured, her smile warmer for being less ecstatic. 'Come on, work beckons, we can swap stories about our love life over lunch. Of course, if you ever want to wind the boss up we can do it when he's here, he just loves to hear about his colleagues private lives, means he has to think of something of his own to say.'

It took far less time for Matthew's bending of police protocols to be discovered than he expected. He had barely returned to the incident room, after a reflective walk on a pleasant November day from St Olave's, round St Katherine's Dock and down Wapping High Street, when Swift called him for an emergency meeting with the chief superintendent and himself.

'This is Chief Superintendent Harvey and Inspector Patel from the National Crime Agency,' Chief Superintendent Amanda Green introduced the officers, as Matthew and Swift took their seats. Any bravado about what he'd done quickly ebbed away from Matthew as he listened to the clipped tones of the chief, an Oxford graduate and ex-solicitor who was known as a tough and experienced officer and who now led the Homicide and Serious Crime Command. 'And this is Superintendent Swift and Inspector Merry of MIT East.' Green paused momentarily, knowing she hadn't been able to brief Swift, she had a slight concern about how he might react but realised she would have to trust to luck on that point. From Matthew Merry she expected prevarication, perhaps even denial.

'Having received a phone call from CS Harvey earlier today, complaining about the actions of one of my officers, I have called this meeting so that you, Inspector Merry, can explain your actions of this morning. I am hoping that in this way we can avoid a more formal review of what has occurred.'

'Yes, ma'am,' Matthew responded, nodding to Harvey and Patel in way of a greeting. 'Well, as the only thing I've done today, outside of briefing my team, has been to talk with Mr Ricky Towers concerning what he knows about the death of Mr Gerry Driver, I assume it must be that which we are here to discuss?' Matthew noticed Green's mild surprise, his answer wasn't the prevarication she'd expected.

'The same Mr Towers who is the subject of a long term major investigation by the National Crime Agency,' Harvey stated, sounding very much like an accountant who had just discovered a balance sheet that didn't balance, while Patel simply scowled at Matthew.

'I believe so, sir,' Matthew calmly agreed, though he felt less than calm knowing his excuse was wafer thin, 'he's proven to be cooperative.'

'Ricky Towers?' Patel hissed in disbelief, she had spent a year leading the surveillance team that watched every move Towers took, including those of his bowel, only for him to go AWOL this morning and then, after a panicky forty-five minutes and with a great deal of luck, for him to be spotted leaving a church in the wake of Inspector Merry.

'Yes, he'd been working with Mr Driver,' Matthew explained with a polite smile, 'producing a stage and TV show that he'd hoped would have launched Mr Driver into the *big time*. He was able to clear up a few points for me regarding the contractual arrangements and how Mr Thorsson, Driver's agent, fitted into the picture.'

'Are you aware of the memo that has been circulated regarding contact with Mr Towers?' Green asked him, her experience in cross-examination all too evident from her tone.

'Yes, ma'am,' Matthew nodded, feeling himself entering a safe haven, 'the one stating we should seek permission before interviewing Mr Towers as a *suspect* in any crime, I believe it said, no matter how minor the crime.' Green and Harvey exchanged glances having noticed the slight stress Matthew put on the word 'suspect' while Patel fell for it hook, line and sinker.

'You think murder so minor a crime that you thought to ignore the memo?' Patel stated with mock disbelief, her Birmingham accent more evident than usual as a result of her annoyance.

'No,' Matthew felt a twang of remorse for Patel, who looked like she was an otherwise pleasant person. 'Nor did I consider him a suspect, he was simply helping me with my inquires.'

'I believe the meaning of the memo was perfectly clear,' Green stated, she wasn't into splitting hairs, that was why she'd given up being a lawyer. 'Did you have permission to speak with Towers?'

'No, ma'am,' although Green had been looking at Swift when she spoke it was Matthew who answered, 'as you said the memo was perfectly clear so I didn't believe it necessary. The points I wanted to clarify are relatively minor, I can't even see that I'd need to ask Mr Towers for a statement.'

The look Green gave him was enough to know he'd won the argument, although she proceeded to give him a dressing down and, in his turn, Matthew apologised if he'd misunderstood what he thought was a clear memo. Green suggested that Harvey might want to have the memo reissued, through the usual channels, but this time approving the wording himself. While Swift and Patel kept quiet, although looking at Matthew as if he was the biggest arsehole on the planet. At least Swift could console himself that he'd not been included in the dressing down and was asked to stay and discuss matters with Green and Harvey at the end of the meeting. While the mightily annoyed Patel got the unlooked for consolation prize of being told she should go with Matthew, so he could debrief her about his meeting with Towers and how he had so easily side-stepped all her surveillance measures.

# Chapter Fourteen

Kathy had never experienced a day like it before, a day of uncertainty and disorientation. She hadn't been able to focus on anything and she'd regularly found her mind drifting back to the gap in her memory. She'd even resorted to phoning her sister at work to ask if she remembered her returning home yesterday evening.

'It must have been late,' Wanda informed her, she was a pharmacist and Kathy could picture her with the mobile clamped between her shoulder and ear while she continued to make up a prescription, 'I was just dozing off when I think I heard you come in, then later there were noises on the stairs. Of course that might have been the Plod –' her name for Matthew – 'trampling over human rights on his way to bed.' Her sister continued to chat, telling Kathy about how things were not working out with her latest boyfriend and the possibility of a promotion, but Kathy wasn't listening – she was watching herself twirl around the office or perhaps the room floated around her, she wasn't certain.

Kathy felt better for walking around the school corridors, especially at lunch when she was able to engage with pupils, though she didn't eat as she had no appetite. The worst came after lunch. She had walked into her office, laid on the floor and removed all her clothing, lying there, legs and arms outstretched, gripped by a terrible sense of dread. It was only when her secretary asked her if everything was alright, as Kathy had spent the last five minutes stood in the open doorway just staring into her office, that she realised it had been a waking dream. *It must be stress and overwork,* she thought, *or a bug, that would explain the loss of appetite and nausea.* Then she wondered if she'd spoken those words out loud as her secretary told her to sit and rest for a moment while she made Kathy a cup of tea. Kathy, however, resolved that enough was enough and phoned her doctor to see if she could get an appointment.

Inspector Patel, Nisa as she told Matthew to call her once her anger had passed, proved to be a charming and insightful person. For some reason the meeting with Green and Harvey had taken place in Charing Cross Police station rather than The Yard, perhaps Green saw it as a neutral venue, so Matthew had pulled out all the stops in trying to pacify Nisa as they walked round the corner to a Costa's.

'What really galls me,' Patel stated without rancour, nibbling on the muffin Matthew had bought her along with a large americano in a to go cup, 'isn't that we lost contact with Towers but that you managed to speak with him in private. We normally have to go through a phalanx of lawyers before we can even discuss a parking fine with him, even then all we ever get is a "no comment" from some mouth piece.'

'How did you lose him?' Matthew dodged the question. He'd already given her an honest if abbreviated version of his conversation with Towers and wasn't keen to reveal his personal, if distant, connection with the villain.

'His offices, with a luxury penthouse apartment above – no less – isn't far from St Katherine's Dock and his uncle has his motor yacht moored there …'

'He's not in the Med then?' Matthew interrupted, he'd finished his sandwich and coffee and could concentrate on the conversation, wondering how out of date the journalist, Michaela Naidoo's, information was.

'Just returned,' Patel responded, puzzling at the question. 'Towers walked down to the dock with half a dozen men but somehow gave us the slip before boarding, we think he jumped into a passing car as only six men boarded the yacht. Just how did you know about his uncle having been in the Med?'

'The yacht must be a fair size.'

'A modest fifty-one metres,' Patel grinned despite herself, she hated the Towers clan with every fibre of her body but she couldn't help admiring their lifestyle, 'the asking price was seven million euros. Though their financial advisors using various off-shore banks would have reduced the amount they actually paid. We are still trying to track all the money flows involved, in case it links to money laundering, but it's a mountain of paper to follow,' she concluded, raising her eyebrows in despair.

'So not short a few bob then?' Matthew commented, thinking back to the designer jeans and trainers Ricky used to wear as a kid, though he'd still lived with his mum in a modest mid-terraced house.

'The legitimate businesses – that's all the media and entertainment concerns, the clubs, pubs and parlours plus the expanding online sex services – gross between eighty and one hundred million a year. GR Security and Investigations grosses another fifteen million,' Patel informed him, trying to sound indifferent about the figures but the scale of the enterprises still awed her. 'As for the illegal side, the drugs, guns and money laundering, then it's about twice as much again.'

'They pay taxes on the legit businesses?' Matthew asked, half joking and half in seriousness realising that he hadn't known just how big Ricky had become, it confirmed though that his investment in Geraldine and his pay off to Mrs Driver really was *mere pennies* to him.

'More so than most businesses that size, he doesn't want to leave himself vulnerable in the way Capone did by not paying his taxes. Although he has problems keeping his cousins and uncle in check, the purchase of the motor yacht being a case in point.' Patel smiled, thinking she should be getting back, a murder was a serious thing and every life counted but to compare Matthew's investigation to the litany of criminality the Towers clan were responsible for each day just didn't stack up and every minute of her day counted. 'Ricky's personal income is more in the region of twenty million rather than the eight point six he pays tax on. We just can't find any proof of the existence of that extra income, he pays his accountants a fortune to keep his books in order.'

'I can't see how Driver's death fits with the scale of operations you are talking about,' Matthew mused out loud, hoping to keep Nisa's interest for a few more questions.

'Neither can we or we would have passed the information on,' Patel pointedly stated. The NCA was always professional in its relationship with other forces something, as Matthew had proven earlier, that wasn't always returned in kind. 'But Towers was spending increasing amounts of his time on meeting with Driver about the theatre and TV project. It even had its funny side at first, it caused a few embarrassed faces as a number of the guys had been commenting on her good looks, then the background checks came back that Geraldine was a man.'

'Did they think Geraldine was Ricky's latest girlfriend?' Matthew asked, his leering grin deflecting Patel's attention as she added his name to the long list of her male colleagues whose insight suffered from an overactive libido.

'He tends to use his wife as an escort, calling on her to accompany him when needed, and when it isn't necessary for her to do so he uses a regular escort. However, he isn't the sort to have any attachments,' Patel reflected for a moment, remembering what Matthew had told her about Towers taking Driver's death personally. 'Ricky Towers likes to see himself as a media mogul and I think the Driver thing played into that. Towers is like the ageing king who has lost interest in his kingdom and lives for his own pleasures. He's delegated a great deal to a range of captains and lieutenants, but hasn't loosened his grip enough for them to be a threat, at least not yet.'

'So, who is in line to take over, his younger brother?' Matthew asked, noticing Patel glancing at her watch.

'No, Gary stays clear of the main family business and Ricky in particular,' Patel explained, thinking she should really make her excuses and leave. 'If GR Security and Investigations didn't work almost exclusively for Towers we probably wouldn't be interested in Gary at all. The uncle thinks of himself as some sort of elder statesman, but in reality does very little other than cruise about partying with anyone corrupt or corruptible enough to further the Towers family collective interests. No, the real heir to the throne is Robert Towers, that's Bobby – named after Ricky's father – the eldest cousin.'

'He's the one involved with the North European biker gangs, isn't he?' Matthew's question stopped Patel in her tracks, she'd been collecting her things and edging forward on her seat to stand, now she was still and watched him as if he were some prey animal on which she was about to pounce.

'How did you know that?' It was something few, even in the NCA, knew about, she herself had only been briefed in case the names of certain Danes and Swedes ever cropped up in the mountain of information she gathered from the various types of surveillances she had in place. The growing links with the biker gangs worried the highest echelons of the Met and NCA not only for their criminality, which was wide ranging and extreme, but specifically for the increase in hate crimes and violent attacks that grew in the wake of their expansion. Add to that an increasing concern about links between terrorists and the far-right and it became understandable why Bobby Towers's activity was of such interest.

'As you pointed out, they live and work on my ground, so you hear things,' Matthew's instincts were on high alert, Michaela might know more than was healthy for her. 'To be honest Bobby Towers is seen as a bit of a joke on the streets, like a kid playing with motorbikes and dreaming of biker gangs.' Matthew laughed, unconcerned about his lie, he needed time to fathom how, if at all, this bit of information fitted into the growing picture. A right wing motorcycle enthusiast might make a good fit into the puzzle, especially if his actions undermined his cousin Ricky's grip on the family business.

Kathy went to bed early – she'd been bad tempered with the girls and Matthew all evening – and quickly fell into a deep, heavy sleep from which she awoke unrefreshed only when the morning alarm rang.

'Take the day off,' Matthew insisted, concerned by the number of times his wife had woken him with her muttering and kicking out in her sleep, a sure sign of stress – even his daughters were concerned that their mother was not her usual self and were pitching in by preparing their own breakfasts, 'you're obviously coming down with something and they can manage for a day without you.'

'I'll leave early, Jeremy can take the staff meeting,' she relented, though not telling him about the doctor's appointment but giving him a reassuring smile, pleased at his concern.

'Have you seen anything of the boss?' Ray asked, Matthew had gone AWOL again after the morning briefing.

'No, he said he was going to see the governor, back at base,' Julie said, stretching, it'd been a long day working on the computer, making phone calls and checking on cross-references with Ray, chasing small leads until they were eliminated. 'He didn't look happy at the prospect but made no mention of where he'd be after lunch.'

'Still looking into links with Towers?' Ray speculated, he didn't like it when an officer, especially the lead of the inquiry team, went rogue, it tended to disrupt the information flow and create gaps in the net they were constructing around the, as yet unknown, killer.

'Hope he's having more luck than I am,' Julie admitted, wanting to go home, knowing Yvette would be there and they had so much to discuss and, she thought, a cuddle wouldn't go amiss. 'The suspect list is drying up and I'm getting nowhere on finding the bike.'

Five minutes later Harry Bainbridge sauntered into the incident room looking happily smug.

'What's afoot, Sherlock?' Julie teased, causing some of the office staff to smile.

'Well, Watson,' Harry was beginning to feel his feet as part of the team and was increasingly less daunted by Julie, something she thought was a good indicator for his future well-being, 'I've followed up on a couple of leads that came out of the interviews the boss and I did,' Julie made every effort to look suitably impressed, while the others in the office got on with their work, including Ray though he kept one ear on the conversation, 'and I finally got GR Security to give me the names of all the door staff who had worked at the Lea Way. Mike Stennard's name was on the list, so I called a couple of the guys who worked with him at the time and Stennard is the guy who Max Dwight humiliated by throwing him bodily out of his pub.'

'Mike Stennard, the security manager who works at the Blue Snake?' Ray checked, without looking up from his work.

'Yes, the same person that Perry Cheung described as being an arsehole,' Harry's smugness was starting to grow exponentially. 'I gave Perry another call and asked him for more details. He said that Stennard was often unpleasant to him and was not past groping the female staff. When Perry stepped in on one occasion it turned into an angry argument and then a brief fight, Perry got a black eye and Stennard got a knee in the balls, much to the delight of those who witnessed it.'

'Stennard's got a cast iron alibi for Driver's killing,' Julie pointed out, 'but we should interview him again to see what he knows about the acid attacks.'

'If he proves to have been involved in them then he may have helped set up Driver's killing,' Ray pointed out, trying but failing not to get ahead of things.

'And Stennard conveniently forgot to report the Blue Snake carpark security camera being out of action,' Julie sat up, putting two and two together. 'That's good work, Sherlock.'

'One other thing, skipper,' Harry stated, if he had a pipe and if he smoked he'd be happily puffing away on it, the epitome of smugness, 'I got chatting to one of the doormen and he said Stennard wasn't liked as he was always getting an easy ride and any cushy jobs going. Turns out he is mates with Robert Towers: that's Ricky Towers's eldest cousin, Bobby.'

'Now why would a little oik like Mike Stennard be mates with jet-setting Bobby Towers?' Ray wondered, as Julie grabbed her jacket and pulled Harry back onto his feet.

'I don't know,' she called over her shoulder as she swept out of the incident room, 'but I aim to find out.'

Matthew was having a late lunch at the Town of Ramsgate, having spent the morning being given another dressing down by Swift. It seemed that while both Swift and Green were not unhappy about putting one over on the NCA, who they thought tended to look down on the Met – which everyone knew was actually the premier force in the country – they didn't like Matthew going out on a limb. Swift was particularly aggrieved at not being told anything, not only as Matthew's manager but also personally, especially given his defence of Matthew's actions in the past, Swift thought he deserved to be treated better. Matthew didn't disagree but at the same time thought it would have put his governor in an impossible situation had he known. As things stood Swift was protected from any fallout by being able to deny any knowledge of what Matthew was up to. Unfortunately for Matthew, Amanda Green had pointed out to Swift that Matthew's undermining of his authority did nothing to enhance Swift's profile with senior staff. So Matthew kept his peace and promised in the future to err on the side of caution and keep Swift fully informed.

'It's a good lead,' Matthew agreed with Julie as she spoke with him on her car's hands free phone, as he finished his pint, 'make certain you tell Harry I said so,' knowing the constable could hear what he said. 'I'll spend this afternoon looking into Bobby Towers's right wing activities. There is no way he is Driver's killer, he's a bit of a throw-back and looks like a hairy ape with a beer gut, nothing like the guy in black we have on CCTV. However maybe there is something behind all this we haven't picked up on yet, something more subtle than a frontal assault on Ricky's position. It's good work, keep it up.'

The doctor's examination was more traumatic than Kathy had anticipated and she trembled throughout. She'd been resolute in detailing all her symptoms: the gap in her memory, her odd waking dreams, her tiredness and general inability to concentrate, her bruises, occasional nausea and the original soreness which had now developed into an uncomfortable itch she felt between her legs. She put it all down to stress and overwork as a result, she explained, of her taking up the acting headteacher post for which she was probably ill prepared. It was the suddenness with which it had come on that worried her.

'Stress can underlie many things, including reducing the immune system which might possibly explain your case of thrush,' the doctor informed her as she started to tap away on her computer, it wasn't simply a matter of recording symptoms the process also allowed her to give thought to those symptoms and what they might point to. 'You'll need to speak with your husband about that, if he is exhibiting any symptoms he'll need medication to break the cycle of reinfection.'

'Of course,' Kathy had taught health and sexual awareness long enough to cope with a dose of thrush, it was the fear of an impending breakdown that was worrying her.

'The memory loss is more of a worry though,' the doctor ruminated, aware of her patient's growing tension. 'Is it possible you have fallen over? That might explain the bruising, although there's no sign of trauma to the head that might account for you blacking out.'

'I have no memory at all, not even how I got home,' Kathy reiterated, the more she struggled to remember the events of that night the more the room swam around her.

'You say your husband found you asleep on the settee and carried you up to bed,' the doctor still peered at the screen, not that she was actually reading anything displayed on it.

'Yes, that could account for the bruises, I suppose,' Kathy sounded uncertain and far from convinced.

'Some of the disorientation and strange sensations sound very much like flashbacks, which can be the result of stress,' the doctor finally swivelled round in her chair to face her patient. She hadn't seen very much of Kathy in her surgery but she remembered her as being confident, intelligent and cooperative. It was not the same woman who sat trembling before her now. 'You also mentioned that your rectum was sore for the day after, it still shows signs of redness from an abrasion.'

'Is that significant?' Kathy asked, feeling bewildered, feeling as if she wanted to cry.

'How did you feel in the days leading up to your blackout?'

'I was fine,' Kathy stated, though she may have been deluding herself on this, 'everything was going well. I was tired, but not exhausted and drained like this, and I was very busy but I felt in control of everything, nothing getting on top of me.'

'What about at home, with your husband?'

'It hasn't been easy,' she admitted, there had been a growing anxiety they were drifting apart, 'but we have started to talk about it, even last night my husband was asking about arranging a date night or some family outing so we had time together. Although, I was too tired to think about it which isn't like me at all,' she also remembered the even more disturbing and uncharacteristic shiver that went through her each time Matthew had touched her. She held back a sob, crying wasn't like her either.

'There's something more traumatic about this than overwork; it's coming on so suddenly, the blackout, your tiredness and your flashbacks, it's almost like PTSD.' The doctor paused for her words to sink in, before continuing, 'Could something have happened to you on the way home? An accident or an attack perhaps?'

Kathy stared back at the doctor, shocked at the thought. Then she was lying naked on her office floor, a heaving weight, another body, pressing down on her, pressing into her. While the doctor comforted her sobbing patient.

# Chapter Fifteen

Michaela Naidoo was waiting for Matthew in the bar of the Tower Bridge Premier Inn Hotel, sipping a rum and coke while nibbling on bar snacks and working on her MacBook.

'Are you staying here?' Matthew asked, putting down a refill for Michaela and his own beer.

'Yes,' she looked askance at the unasked for drink then, remembering her comment about not turning down a free drink at their last meeting, nodded a thank you. 'It's more convenient when my husband is away now the children have flown the nest. You said you have some more information for me.'

'I do,' Matthew decided to get to the point, 'but first you need to come clean with me.' Michaela's initial look of surprise at Matthew's words turned into a hard scowl as he explained, 'Frankly, I don't believe you just happened to attend the press briefing in the vague hope of finding a link between Driver's death and Towers's organisation.' Matthew could not suppress a smile, there was something about the combative journalist he rather liked, not least of which was her cleavage, 'Nor do I think you got your information about Bobby Towers and his links with biker gangs in Northern Europe first hand. I have no doubt you are a fine investigative journalist, you certainly look fierce and determined enough, but I can't see anyone linked with white supremacists talking to a black, female reporter.'

'They're a breeze compared with the typical sexist, British, male copper,' she told him, raising her glass in salute, in case he was in any doubt that she included him in the description. 'I'd be much more impressed if you had turned up with some hard facts to exchange rather than just being here to ogle down my blouse.'

'You know, digging around in Bobby Towers's business could be dangerous,' Matthew changed track, embarrassed that his attraction to her ample curves was so obvious, 'but I suspect you know that.' She responded with a nod, her scowl melting into a grin as she realised her jab about his being sexist had hit home. No doubt he was sensitive about such criticism given the sexual harassment complaint, her police source had told her about, that was outstanding against him. 'The fact remains, that Bobby's actions don't seem to be widely known, so either you are better at your job than a raft of police forces, with all their resources at hand, or you have had some insider help.'

'A source is a source,' Michaela stated enigmatically, wondering just how much of what she had been told about the complaint against Matthew was accurate.

'What I think is that you got most of what you know about Bobby Towers from your source here, in London, rather than in Northern Europe and the same source is worried there might be a possible link with Driver's murder,' Matthew's thinking was more guess than deduction but Michaela's fleetingly annoyed look confirmed his conjecture to be accurate.

'If we are into discussing rumours I have a juicy one of my own,' Michaela informed him, covering herself by taking another drink from her glass.

'If you are withholding something that would help me track down Geraldine Driver's killer then I will arrest you,' Matthew's tone was flat, his eyes now locked on Michaela's, not in the least distracted by her comment about juicy rumours.

'I really am as much in the dark on that as you still seem to be,' she said, deciding to bend a little to the pressure he was applying. 'It would be a benefit to me if I could find out anything about a link,' she stated truthfully, taking another sip of her drink, 'for no other reason than being able to trade it for further information on Bobby.'

'Is that your idea or theirs?'

'Theirs,' she admitted, she had hesitated too long before answering his unexpected question to make a lie convincing. 'I had a phone call a little before the start of the press briefing alerting me to the potential.'

'Do you want another drink?' Matthew asked. Giving the journalist time to think at this point was a gamble but he knew the risk would pay off if he was able to make her believe they were actually on the same side.

Mike Stennard had been perplexed when the police sergeant and constable had turned up at his flat, informing him that they had further questions and would like him to accompany them to the station. He'd thought his best policy was to cooperate, especially as his wife was home and he didn't want to answer anything in front of her, after all he had a cast iron alibi for when Driver was abducted and killed. However, now he sat alone in the interview room at Wapping Police station he began to wonder if he should start thinking about getting a solicitor.

'You used to work at the Lea Way pub, for Maximilian Dwight?' Sergeant Lukula asked, after she'd gone through the formalities.

'Not for Dwight,' Stennard corrected, 'but I worked there as one of the door staff for GR Security, I was the deputy supervisor.'

'You were involved in an altercation with Mr Dwight,' Julie stated, noticing that Stennard seemed to be less tense than when he'd first arrived at the station.

'He became aggressive when we had a disagreement about the number of door staff the place required, then he went for me. We are trained to try and deflect any aggression,' Stennard told them pompously, feeling at his ease, 'and, as he wasn't listening to reason, under the circumstances I left. I got reassigned to the Blue Snake, you could say it did me a bit of a favour.'

‘We were told you were thrown out on your ear,’ Harry said, hoping to put Stennard on the back foot, but was disappointed with Stennard’s ‘I don’t remember that’ response.

‘Do you remember a more recent argument at the Blue Snake,’ Julie asked, still wondering why Stennard seemed so at ease, ‘with Mr Perry Cheung, one of the performers?’

‘I remember it, yes, bit of a storm in a tea cup as I recall,’ Stennard seemed almost surprised that something of so little consequence was being brought up. ‘I was joking around with some of the staff and suddenly he started shouting and pushing me. I put my hands up in defence and accidentally caught him one. It was all over in a second.’

Julie paused, looking at Stennard, his excessively relaxed manner telling her he was prepared for her questions which made her doubt the truth of what he was saying and doing more than just covering up for his injured pride. She gave him the dates and times of the acid attacks, without stating why, and asked him where he was. After a small amount of prevarication, as he appeared to struggle to remember, he explained that on each occasion he was out with Todd Barrett.

‘We had been for a drink then went to his place to watch the match,’ Stennard, smilingly, explained. ‘It’s quieter at his place, no yelling and screaming at the TV screen, his old mum has a TV in her room so we have the place to ourselves, you see.’

Harry asked him about the matches he’d watched, which he remembered in detail, and the pubs they’d been to beforehand, which he was more vague about. Although Julie increasingly wondered about his calm and detailed responses, Stennard didn’t seem in the least bit fazed, even when Harry finally warned him that ‘we’ll be checking this out’ Stennard’s response was a shrug. He didn’t seem to have any doubt his story would be confirmed, his very confidence heightening Julie’s growing suspicion that the alibi had been prearranged.

‘You drive a motorbike don’t you?’ Julie asked, changing the subject.

'Yes, a Triumph Sprint actually,' Stennard's smile didn't waiver.

'Our records show that you've only ever driven motorbikes, bit of an aficionado I take it,' Julie stated, causing Stennard to shrug unconcernedly again.

'One last thing,' Julie said, Stennard still smiling and looking as if he was going to be told he could go. 'How exactly do you know Mr Robert Towers?'

'Bobby?' Stennard, taken by surprise, sat up and for the first time since entering the interview room looked ill at ease, 'I've known him a while but not that well. He's the cousin of the guy who runs GR Security.' Stennard's explanation trailed off.

'Although he has nothing to do with the company,' Julie thought she had already worked out the link between the pair and was simply looking for confirmation of this. 'The fact is you knew him before you started at GR, before even you did your stint inside. You knew him from your gang days, isn't that correct?'

'I'm not trying to get you drunk, you know,' Matthew brightly informed Michaela, putting her third rum and coke down along with his second pint, though he still had some of his first to finish. 'In another life maybe,' he added with a wink. She might have responded in kind, as she was hoping to get something out of him about the complaint against him and the rumours she'd heard, but he moved on before she had a chance. 'Fact is, I'm happy to put my cards on the table. You're not the first journalist to get hot tips from a police source, no doubt in return for a quid-pro-quo on what info you have. Well, I'm happy to share stuff with you myself, you seem the professional sort. I'm not interested in who your source is just what they think the link is between Driver's murder and Ricky Towers.'

'Like I said, I don't know that they do believe there is a link,' Michaela shrugged, 'but, they would be interested in what you know or find out.' Matthew sipped his drink, pondering this for a second. If that were true he wondered why didn't they go through normal police channels to ask him about the case? Of course that would mean they would probably have to confide in Matthew about their own case, which might be a problem if they were using Michaela as an informer off-the-books. Or, perhaps they weren't senior enough and already knew more than they should about what Towers and his family were up to.

'I can tell you that they know Ricky Towers and Driver had been spending a lot of time together, on this theatrical project,' Michaela went on, slightly disturbed at Matthew's silent stare. She wouldn't put it past him to caution her for withholding information, just for the sake of it, so a semblance of going along with him, she thought, couldn't hurt. 'My contact doesn't think that the financial loss would upset Towers but that the murder and the way it was done might be a message of some sort. Perhaps a way of telling him that he wasn't beyond someone's reach.'

'It's possible,' Matthew conceded, it chimed with his own thinking. 'If there is a link it is the only one that makes sense. It might pay for you to ask your contact what else she knows, why she would think that.'

'I will,' Michaela said as she packed her MacBook away, not even noticing that Matthew had used 'she' to describe her contact, whom he suspected was Inspector Patel from the NCA, 'but I have to go, a dinner date.' She paused, having stood, looking down at him then, deciding she had nothing to lose, said, 'If you are serious about swapping info from time to time then keep in touch.'

'I am and I will,' he extended his hand which she took, smiling, at least their knowing that they didn't trust each other was a possible start; she had other sources she trusted less.

He watched her leave, starting on his second pint, giving her a wave as she went through the door. Then he counted to twenty and went out after her, keeping his distance as he trailed behind her. Once or twice she looked back but Matthew kept, as much as he could, to the opposite side of the street or behind other pedestrians when he couldn't. More than once he had darted after her through moving traffic at an intersection, after he'd let her cross well in front of him while the traffic was stopped. And, once, he'd waited on a corner watching both exits when she went through a store and out of a side door.

He doubted if she suspected that he would follow her. She thought him too much the unimaginative, sluggard of a copper – more interested in her cleavage than what she knew – she was just being naturally cautious. Eventually she turned down Shad Thames and entered the Blue Print café. Matthew hung back for a minute or so before risking walking past, hesitating a moment by the door as if studying the bill of fare and then walking on. It was long enough for him to recognise the blond, seated opposite Michaela and facing the door. It was unmistakably the same young woman he'd noticed at Thorsson's Blue Bird Agency, the one whose androgynous features had caused him some doubts.

'Go and find Todd Barrett,' Julie told Harry, they'd left a much less confident Stennard to stew on his own in the interview room, 'and see if he confirms Stennard's alibi, get as much detail as you can and be certain of it. Actually, take a formal statement, it'll give him cause to think that much more carefully about telling the truth. I'll stay here and do the same with Stennard.'

Julie took Stennard a cup of coffee from the station machine, which given its taste was on a scale along with water-boarding, and then laboriously went through his statement with him. Stennard insisted that he'd asked a mate with help getting him a job with GR Security and his mate had asked a mate, who happened to know Bobby Towers. However, beyond that, Stennard denied any knowledge about Towers. Although he admitted that his mate had told him that Bobby had been willing to help as he had dealings with the same biker gang that Stennard had, long before, been involved with. Stennard was at pains to stress that he'd put all that stuff behind him since doing jail time.

Julie couldn't fathom it, the connection seemed coincidental but, what with Stennard's increasingly uncertain and nervous answers and the very strangeness of the coincidence, she couldn't help be suspicious. She couldn't put her finger on it but something didn't feel right about what Stennard was telling her.

Matthew hung around in Butlers Warf, as dusk drew in and the day turned damp. He could see Tower Bridge upstream to his left and, in the gloomy light, could just make out the bend in the river downstream, to the east, where Old Stairs was on the opposite bank. Although an idle passer-by, of which there were quite a few, might have thought him absorbed in the view he always had at least one eye on the café door. Ninety minutes later, starting to feel the cold and damp from the November evening, he was rewarded by seeing the unmistakable figure of Michaela Naidoo leave the café. He'd already convinced himself this meeting could not be a coincidence and that, assuming they left separately, he was going to follow the blond.

A minute later, somewhat impatiently, he circled closer to the café entrance and had to divert to peer into a neighbouring shop window as the blond emerged, wrapping a bright red poncho around her. She didn't go far, turning down the Thames path to cross over an inlet on a narrow bridge and then go a little way down Bermondsey Wall. Shortly, she stopped at the entrance to one of the converted Victorian warehouses that overlooked the river, and used an intercom to gain entry to a building. Matthew, very much aware of the two CCTV cameras which overlooked the door she'd entered, stopped to find his handkerchief and blow his nose, barely giving himself time to glance at the small sign which did little to advertise the name of the office building's owner: GR Security and Investigations.

Matthew arrived home a little less late than normal but not as early as he had hoped. However, he was able to sit down to a family meal with his wife and daughters. The girls were enthusiastic about the idea of a family outing, perhaps the Natural History Museum or a zoo. Although his eldest asked if she could attend a sleepover on the Friday night. Matthew wasn't certain how to respond, wasn't she still a little too young at nine to spend the night at another girl's house?

'Nearly ten, Dad,' Becky reminded him, 'and all my friends are going. Jenny said you could phone her mum to check.' Then, in a tone dripping with early onset teenage angst, added, 'That is if you don't trust me.'

'Don't you trust Becky, Dad?' Lizzy, Becky's seven year old sister and agent provocateur, asked with the innocence of an angel.

Matthew looked at Kathy, hoping for some support, she was normally able to divide and conquer the pair but on this occasion simply looked blank and gave an unresponsive 'Of course' leaving the girls to finish the meal in a huff, with no plans resolved.

'What's wrong?' Matthew finally plucked up courage to ask as they prepared for bed. His wife had been acting so strangely over the past few days that he'd resolved to let her make the first move when she was ready, but now felt he couldn't put it off any longer, 'I know I've been working late too often and I missed our date night, believe me I'd rather have been here …'

'It's nothing,' she said, meaning she didn't want to discuss it, 'I'm tired and have a headache, that's all.'

'Perhaps you should see a doctor,' he reached across the bed to touch her, surprised at how she jolted away as if repulsed at his action. 'At least, have a couple of days off, to rest maybe.'

'No, I'll be fine, just let me sleep,' she stated sounding drained of emotion, turning over and ending the conversation.

The truth was she was far from fine, still thinking about the gap in her memory and the doctor's suggestion. If she went to the police what could she say? It would sound insane to say she may or may not have been in an accident. How could she ask them to investigate something she had no idea about and may not have happened? What's more it might get back to Matthew, and she couldn't bear that. She lay a long time thinking things over, finding it impossible to make any decision. Matthew also lay awake, sleepless, trying to concentrate on the case but his thoughts kept returning to his wife.

Earlier he'd phoned Julie and then his governor for an update, although he'd told neither what he'd discovered that afternoon. He told Julie he'd talked with a journalist investigating Greenspace and RightOn but had hit a dead end, nor did he correct Swift who had assumed that he'd questioned Stennard with Julie. Either way his conclusion with both was that they were not making any real progress on the case but simply generating a lot of unsubstantiated conjecture. Swift had finished the conversation by saying he'd attend the morning briefing to get a fuller picture and discuss with Matthew ways forward and resource implications.

However, the lack of progress and ambiguity around the case worried Matthew less than his wife. At first he had dismissed his own thoughts that she was having an affair, now he wasn't certain. He knew his wife well enough to know that she'd be plagued by guilt if she'd slept with another man. In her place he would easily shrug off such guilt but Kathy would endlessly dwell on it, allowing it to torment her until it affected her health. Perhaps he should turn over and simply tell her it didn't matter, they should ignore any slip and get on with their life, not let it get between them. Then he thought of her seemingly angry shudder at his touch. Did she now hate or despise him for pushing her to this? Or had her sister finally let slip about their indiscretion – as he thought of it, downplaying it in his own mind – all those years ago.

Matthew was annoyed, hurt even, that Kathy didn't want to talk things through with him. Her apparent indifference to or ignoring the problem between them, her silence on the issue as he saw it, simply made him angry. While his own reaction, which he recognised was childishly stubborn, was to clam up. So they both lay awake well into the long hours of the night, neither moving in case the other thought them awake, both locked up in their own unhappiness, both determined the other should be the first to turn over to resolve the impasse between them. The closeness and dependency of their married life had become a wall between them.

# Chapter Sixteen

Matthew arrived late at the incident room for the morning briefing he was supposed to be leading. He'd left his wife to lie in while he got his daughters ready for school but, even so, he'd departed on time only to get caught in a snarl of rush hour traffic that was slowed by road works. He wasn't, therefore, in a good mood as he rushed into the office and was taken aback when he was met by a scene of joy and merriment. Julie had announced she had passed her inspectors examination and everyone was busy congratulating her. Swift was as good as his word, announcing that Julie would be acting-up as inspector as quickly as he could get the paperwork done.

'Well done,' Matthew told the elated Julie, trying to sound enthusiastic despite his mood. 'Which reminds me, you and Eve will have to come to dinner soon, I think Kathy wants to see your ring.' It wasn't entirely true, but he thought having the couple over might help cheer Kathy up.

'Yvette,' Julie corrected him, surprised at the invite as Matthew wasn't the type to socialise much with his colleagues. 'Of course we'll come, just let me know a few dates.'

'Oh, I thought you called her Eve for short,' Matthew tried to cover his faux pas, realising he rarely talked anything but shop with Julie, or anyone else come to that, but was then distracted by Swift who seemed keen to start.

The briefing confirmed the investigation was bogging down, there was nothing new from forensics and Ray was still chasing the DNA on the orange rope used to tie and partially strangle Driver. Harry confirmed that Todd Barrett, whom he'd questioned late the previous evening at the Blue Snake, had given a detailed statement which confirmed Mike Stennard's alibi for both acid attacks. Apparently the ill-matched pair often went for a pint and to watch a match at various pubs but recently had decided to do so at Barrett's house. He'd also spoken on the phone with Todd's mother who, though confused about actual dates, confirmed they did this. And that it now seemed a regular thing with them – on the few occasions that Todd now came home – and she'd moaned about the noise they made while she was left upstairs watching her game shows.

'I also did a background check on Todd,' Harry went on, pleased to be able to tell the others about the initiative he'd taken. 'There's no history of any criminality and he has been in steady employment since leaving college. He doesn't own a car or bike, he doesn't even have a licence – never even had a provisional one – and he goes everywhere by public transport.'

'Not that unusual in London,' Matthew said glumly. Then, thinking some praise was due, more brightly added, 'But good work for checking. It seems to confirm him as a reliable witness.'

Julie confirmed she was still trying to trace the motorbike or who made the number plates, but, as with the other lines of inquiry, the odds were getting longer on turning up a positive lead. Everyone, except Matthew who was keeping his own inquiries to himself, now believed that Driver's death was part of a sequence of hate crimes which had started with the acid attacks. Unfortunately, Stennard had been the best, but now aborted, lead they'd had so far. Once again they were hitting a brick wall.

Hayden, at least, had some positive news as she had been working with the press office to prepare another media briefing. A set of stills from the CCTV footage of Driver's abduction and where he was dumped in the Thames, made into a slide show for digital release or as a story board for old fashioned newspapers.

‘It’s presented as a narrative of the events of how Gerry Driver was killed,’ she explained, having shown the twenty-five second slide show, ‘without the gory details of course, but as a story of the crime. It ends with an e-fit, that is an artist’s enhanced rendition, of the man we are looking for, obviously we have nothing of his face but it says a lot about his build.’ She stopped to circulate copies of the e-fit around the room. Matthew thought it looked like a silhouette figure that could match thirty percent of the male population in the area, but he held his tongue as they’d gotten leads from worse information.

‘The press release is going out at midday today,’ Hayden continued, ‘and we hope it’ll play over twenty-four hours in the various media. I’ll be working with Duncan to correlate any public responses, to prioritise the order in which calls are followed up.’

Ray ended the briefing with a quick reminder for everyone to keep up to date with their paperwork so it was processed. The hint had been directed at Matthew, who had gone silent on what he’d been doing recently. However, it was Harry Bainbridge whom it prompted to remember he had yet to contact the Blue Bird Agency to discover the identity of the unsatisfactory drag act that Max Dwight had complained about.

After the briefing Swift made it clear to Matthew and Julie that he was neither unhappy with the progress being made nor the direction the investigation was taking and, as such, he was prepared to continue with the same level of resourcing. Matthew made no attempt to tell his governor about the line he was pursuing, partly because he was unclear where, if anywhere, it was leading and partly as he thought Swift might close him down.

GR Security and Investigations offices along Bermondsey Wall were as low key in advertising themselves as they were high on security to get inside. The door intercom and buzzer, overlooked by security cams, was only the first hurdle the inspector had to pass through. The second was a rotating door scanner, the type used by some banks to ensure those entering carried neither guns nor explosives, manned by a guard. The next, and most formidable, was a receptionist sitting behind a blast grade laminate security window who interrogated Matthew as to the purpose of his visit.

'As I have explained,' Matthew stated with as much quiet anger and impatience as he could muster, 'both on the door intercom to you and, then again, to this person,' Matthew gave a slight nod to the door guard who stood beside him, 'and now once again to yourself, I am here to speak with the owner, Mr Gary Robert Towers, on matters concerning a murder inquiry. I've shown you my credentials. I do not need a search warrant, as I do not want to search your offices, and if Mr Towers doesn't want to help me with my inquiries then I am happy to leave and will return with a dozen uniformed officers to escort him to a police station to do so.' The receptionist, looking not the least concerned about the inspector's demands, told him to take a seat while she checked if Mr Towers was available.

Matthew sat in a functional chair, one of a pair, bolted to the floor and meditated for ten minutes in an attempt to reduce his blood pressure, before being told by the receptionist he was granted an audience. The guard escorted him up a flight of stairs where he was handed over to another guard who escorted him along an office lined corridor and up another flight of stairs to the second floor, which housed a staff break-out area and the owner's large glass walled office. Matthew waited another ten minutes, again with his guard standing over him, although in a much larger and padded leather chair than the one downstairs.

Gary Towers finally entered his office from a small lift and went straight to his desk, keeping said desk and the guard between himself and Matthew. 'I'm sorry to keep you waiting, Inspector,' Towers's tone was clipped and authoritative, not unsurprising for someone who'd been a captain in the Royal Engineers for many years. 'I'm not entirely clear how I can help you with your inquiries but I am at your disposal.'

Gary was the oddity of the Towers clan, being tall and fair haired as opposed to the dark, stocky features that ran through the rest of the family. He'd also completed his tertiary education, having gone on to study engineering at university, then had done a stint in the army. Five years previously he'd resigned his commission and set up GR Security and Investigations, primarily to reorganise Ricky Towers's chaotic and crumbling security firms into one efficient and highly profitable operation. However, at thirty-eight, he was still mainly known because he was Ricky Towers's kid brother.

'That's good of you, Gary, the wait wasn't a problem as I was enjoying the view,' Matthew said, standing to extend his hand, an act that made the guard shift anxiously and caused Gary Towers to frown. 'You won't remember me, it must be getting on for nearly thirty years, but you still have that same look in your eyes of determination and defiance you had as a kid.' Matthew waited with his arm outstretched while the puzzled Gary slowly leaned across his desk to shake his hand.

'You have me at a loss, Inspector,' Towers informed him, unsuccessfully searching his memory for a clue to Matthew's identity.

'We let you play football with us occasionally, over the park, you and Donald verses me and Ricky. Me and Ricky always won, not that that ever stopped you trying.'

Gary looked perplexed for a moment then the light dawned along with a broad grin that lit up his normally sombre face.

'What can I do to help you?' Towers finally asked, his tone cordial, having sent the guard away, 'I suspect it has to do with Geraldine?'

'She died just over the way,' Matthew informed him, pointing downstream towards Pier Head and Old Stairs on the opposite bank.

'If you are here to ask if I witnessed anything, I'm afraid I didn't,' Gary informed him, his grin fading.

'No, I'm here to ask you about Ricky's relationship with Geraldine,' Matthew explained, his own tone serious, 'and about a young woman, a blond with striking features who was wearing a red poncho when she entered your building yesterday in the early evening.'

'Perhaps you will join me for lunch?' Towers avoided answering, 'I believe you are describing Tina, my partner, she's in our apartment on the floor above.'

Kathy had started her day determined to shake off whatever it was that was troubling her, at least she hadn't had to deal with Lance who was obviously avoiding her, and a day working with pupils and staff had started to cheer her up. Staying away from her office, which only served to remind her of the stresses and worries associated with her acting headship, seemed to be working. And she decided to have lunch in the canteen so she could spend time mingling with staff and pupils. However, a fight, an angry altercation over a minor slight, broke out in the queue and, though it constituted a further distraction for her, took her back to her office. It was as she berated the two lower school boys, working up to assigning them to the restorative justice group, that once again her office began to spin. The boys shouted in alarm as their headteacher stopped speaking in mid-sentence, lurched upwards then fell sprawling to the floor.

Fortunately two of her office staff were first aiders, so a 999 call for an ambulance was avoided as Kathy quickly revived under their ministrations. Disorientated at first, she accepted tea and declined a taxi home, her staff were not going to let her drive and had decided on her behalf she needed to go home. Kathy felt herself returning to her senses, coming to the realisation that she could not sustain denial any longer. If her work was being directly affected she was determined to take back control of herself. Tea drunk and staff thanked, she accepted a lift home; then asked to be dropped off at the High Street as she could walk to her local police station from there.

*

Close up Tina was obviously a man, the timbre of his voice was the deciding factor for Matthew but the hard, angular bone structure of his face also gave lie to his otherwise feminine look. The inspector recalled studying Geraldine's face at close quarters and, even after she'd been dead a few hours, there was no sign of Gerry to give the game away. Such was the persuasiveness of Gerry's impersonation that he had tricked death into accepting him as Geraldine.

The vegan lunch, which Gary quickly prepared and served, was undoubtedly healthy but somewhat muted as the conversation failed to flow in anticipation of Matthew's unasked questions.

'I spoke with Ricky recently and he indicated how upset he was by Mr Driver's death,' Matthew finally began, sitting in an opulent green leather and mahogany armchair as he sipped the excellent coffee, though his hosts continued to drink only filtered water. 'From what he and others have told me, he seems to have grown exceptionally fond of Geraldine.'

'I really can't say,' Gary responded, 'I'm not particularly close to Ricky. I see him perhaps half a dozen times a year normally at some function and only rarely, and not for some time, in private. Though over the last year he does seem to have been increasingly accompanied by Geraldine.'

'We saw Geraldine perform, shortly after we first met her,' Tina inserted, keeping her voice soft and airy, 'and only afterwards realised he was a man.'

'Yes,' Gary agreed, a slight grin cutting his face at the memory, 'there wasn't the slightest hint from either of them beforehand as to Gerry's real identity; he had us both completely fooled.' He glanced at Tina, who sat at his side, but she made no further comment. Although her smile slipped for a second, as she studied her shapely legs. Matthew was also looking at Tina's legs but he didn't fail to notice her brief change of expression, the sudden flash of animosity that had passed over her face – jealousy perhaps?

'So, there is more than the river keeping you apart?' Matthew asked, his questions jumping from one topic to another.

'My years in the army,' Gary explained, seeing no reason to dissemble, 'changed my outlook on life and Ricky was always distant.'

'Ricky could be a bastard when he wanted,' Matthew calmly stated. 'I take it he hasn't changed?'

'Things certainly took a turn for the worse when you stopped coming round all those years ago, the only time he ever hit me was when I asked where you were. "I don't want that two-faced fucker round here anymore" was his final comment on your absence,' Gary informed him, studying the man who sat opposite, trying to see the gangly thirteen year old he'd looked up to almost as much as he did his brother, in the portly, unsmiling detective. 'Still, all water under the bridge.'

They had moved post-lunch to the roof conservatory: with its minimalistic if luxurious furnishings, surrounded on all sides by a well tended garden balcony and with stunning views in all directions. Gary, standing beside a large brass telescope on a tripod, pointed almost directly across the river to three smart – seven floor – tower blocks, explaining, 'The nearest one belongs to Ricky, the lower floors are offices for his various companies, the upper floors are where he and his live-in staff are accommodated. His wife tends to stay at their Essex place, a small mansion in the back of beyond near Rayleigh. The luxury penthouse suite is his primary residence, he has a gym, sauna and lap pool as part of the apartment. The floor below is like a games complex combined with a private club house, it is where he entertains and holds meetings. Altogether it makes this place look like a council flat.' Matthew noted that for someone who claimed to rarely visit his brother Gary knew his living arrangements in some detail.

'Did Geraldine ever stay over?' Matthew bounced back to his main theme and though Gary shrugged his face suggested that Geraldine was likely to be the only person ever invited to do so.

*

Harry Bainbridge had had a hard time getting the information he wanted out of the Blue Bird Agency but in the end, to avoid yet another visit from the police, they had relented. Harry barely had time to type up the report and forward it to Ray for the salient facts to be included onto HOLMES2, before he was told by Julie to go help Hayden and the analyst, Duncan, to deal with the flood of calls coming in following the latest press release. Hayden was looking very pleased, she'd already given priority to two calls. One, a gay couple whose neighbour was always shouting abuse at them and who rode a Honda X-ADV. And the second, a motorist who'd phoned in to say he'd had a near accident in Wapping Lane with a motorcyclist, similar in description to the one in the e-fit, just before two in the morning in question and had seen him turn into a petrol station.

Hayden let Julie, who was speaking on the phone to the owner of a small motor parts shop, know she and Harry were going to follow up on the two leads.

Julie shortly followed them out, telling Ray, 'I'm going to the Bow Street nick, as they still have the CCTV footage of a break in from a likely parts shop.'

'Time, patience and meticulous checking of details,' Ray said aloud to no one in particular, the office staff who remained were all too busy to pay attention, 'is all it takes to break a case.'

Kathy had been quickly dealt with at the police station, the moment she'd mentioned the possibility of her having been sexually assaulted she was whisked to the privacy of an interview room and was dealt with by a young and sympathetic female CID officer. Having given the constable further details, as limited and somewhat confused as they were, she was left alone for a few minutes, while the officer went to speak with someone. No doubt a more senior officer would shortly appear and, equally sympathetically, tell her to go home and stop wasting police time with such vague uncertainties.

'I've spoken with an officer from our special unit,' the young constable, her face bright but professional, told her on her return, 'and they are on their way.' Then seeing Kathy's look of dismay, quickly added, 'It will be another female officer but one very experienced in dealing with this type of case.' Again the officer paused, watching Kathy's growing anxiety. Kathy's heart was racing, doubts whirling through her mind, that she had it wrong and she'd be shown up as some sort of mental case. 'You know, you are very brave,' the constable said, retaking her seat and holding Kathy's trembling hand. 'We know what it takes to come here and report this. You have my word that we will listen to all you say, we'll go at your pace and do all we can to support you through this.'

Kathy smiled momentarily, the officer looked barely out of sixth form and the irony of the situation did not escape Kathy as it was usually she who was reassuringly comforting a panic-stricken youngster. Then she burst into tears.

# Chapter Seventeen

'How did you two meet?' Matthew asked Tina, after Gary had left them alone at the inspector's request.

'At a club, both a little drunk, our eyes met,' Tina modestly giggled, hiding her mouth with her hand, 'and it was lust at first sight.'

'What's your real name?' Matthew bluntly asked.

'It's Chris, though everyone knows me as Tina,' Tina explained. 'I'm perfectly happy and comfortable to live my life openly as a woman. Gary is equally comfortable with our life choices, though I can't say that his family approves.'

'Surname?'

'Barron,' Tina stated after a moment's hesitation, 'my mother's maiden name, she has always supported me. Unlike my father who ran off with another woman when I was eight.'

*Better than kicking the shit out of you, like Gary's dad,* Matthew thought but didn't say. Old Bobby Towers managed to kick rage and hate into his eldest son but he couldn't kick the determination out of his youngest.

'Tell me how you know Michaela Naidoo?' Matthew asked without preamble or pause.

'Michaela? Ohh … just a friend? How do you know?' Tina responded off guard.

'Are you happy to talk about meeting with her?' Matthew continued, 'I expect Gary might not be too pleased to hear that you have been discussing his family's business with a journalist.

And I seriously doubt his brother Ricky would be nor his cousin Bobby, come to that.'

'Gary knows about Michaela,' Tina was quick to reassure the inspector, 'and the business I discuss with her is purely my own.'

'Oh? That isn't what Michaela has suggested,' the shocked and disapproving scowl this produced on Tina's face told Matthew that she had, at least for a moment, wondered if the journalist had betrayed her.

'She's interested in my life story,' Tina expounded. 'My life at school, how I had to hide my real self, then how I came out in my teens. And how I now live openly as a woman and my struggles to break into the entertainment business.'

Matthew pondered this for a moment before matter-of-factly stating, 'I don't buy it, a journalist will write any story to make a buck but your life story isn't that exceptional this day and age.'

'You saw me at the agency,' Tina looked daggers at the inspector for doubting her, 'you must remember as you could not take your eyes off my legs then either. Well, I'm not having any luck with Thorsson getting me gigs so I thought that getting myself in the papers might be good publicity.'

'You'll get publicity if Ricky gets to hear of it,' Matthew pointed out, none too amicably. 'Fact is you are at one end of a two way communication pipe with the police at the other end and Michaela shuttling back and forth as go-between.' Tina's face was murderous, but her mouth was clamped shut as she looked round to see if Gary could possibly have overheard. 'Look,' Matthew continued, his voice softer and tone more conciliatory, 'I'm only interested in how Driver's death fits into all this. The almighty Ricky Towers was obviously infatuated with Geraldine, something you and Gary might not mind but would have been seen as a weakness by his kith and kin. So, is Driver's death a warning to Ricky or the start of a move against him?'

Matthew paused for Tina to take in what he was saying, her anger subsiding, although she remained tight-lipped. 'I'll let you sleep on it, to consider what you know and then you can contact me,' he handed her his card, 'either to meet for a private chat, if Gary's not in the know, or here if you prefer. However, if I don't hear I'll be telling my governor what I've discovered and things will get more public.' Matthew had no doubt Tina was the weak link in the chain he'd been following, it was a risk giving her time to think things over but one worth taking if she realised the sense in cooperating. He certainly thought he'd get more out of her that way rather than dragging her to the station now.

Matthew actually made it home before Kathy for once, his wife still looked drawn, tired and distracted but somehow calmer. He didn't dwell on it though and they ate dinner with the girls. Over dinner it was decided that Becky could go to the sleepover and they would all go shopping the day after and would eat out, a prospect that seemed to please his daughters more than the possibility of a trip to a museum. They watched TV for a bit and the girls had showers and went to bed. Kathy also went up for an early night, giving him a kiss and saying she'd arranged to take the next day off so as to have a long weekend, leaving Matthew to have a whisky and ruminate on his case.

The more convinced he became he was on the right track the less he felt certain about the rationality of his arguments. Perhaps he was simply bending the evidence, which was far from conclusive, to fit his half-baked theories? Maybe the following morning would be a good time to test his thinking out on his colleagues, at the very least both Swift and Julie had a right to know what he'd been up to.

'Did I not make it sufficiently fucking clear that you were not to approach any of the Towers family without first getting permission from me?' Swift had started before Matthew could open his mouth, both he and Julie had been summoned to the Barking office of the MIT East having been making their way separately to Wapping. An irate assistant commissioner, angered by an early morning call from a furious CS Harvey of the NCA, had phoned Chief Superintendent Green over breakfast, who in turn had angrily phoned Superintendent Swift as he'd left for the office. The shit had gathered pace and heat as it flowed downwards to finish its journey in Matthew's lap. Matthew realised his gamble on leaving Tina to stew had not paid off and, no doubt, she'd contacted Michaela who in turn had contacted Inspector Patel who had started the avalanche that now crashed, if an avalanche of shit could crash, around him.

'I'm sorry,' Matthew began, trying to sound as sincere as he could muster, 'I didn't think …'

'That is plainly evident,' Swift interrupted, he'd be the first to admit his comment was a cheap shot but he had been very embarrassed by his boss's call as Matthew's actions were making him look as if he wasn't in control of his own officers. 'You have gone against a direct instruction both from me and the chief superintendent and, by deliberately ignoring those instructions, you have potentially put a high level investigation at risk,' Swift had practiced his wording before Matthew's arrival so that he was exact in his meaning. 'Your actions not only undermine my authority they also raise questions about your judgement, your ability to actually do your job as a detective inspector effectively.'

'I understand how things look,' Matthew could see where Swift was heading and a part of him even thought he probably deserved to be suspended but he'd been certain of his gamble in giving Tina time to consider her options, so had done nothing to cover his back, 'and I understand if you believe my actions warrant my suspension.' It was Matthew's calm and measured tones that made Swift avoid any hasty decision, 'However, I didn't plan to speak with Gary Towers, I actually went to interview Tina Barron, it then transpired that she – that is *he*, Chris is actually a man – is Gary's partner.'

'Did you actually meet with Gary Towers?' Swift asked, still angry but hoping Matthew would say no, even if it were a lie, that would be enough to get them all off the hook.

'Actually, sir, I had lunch with him and Tina,' Matthew stated solemnly, which was worse for Swift's blood pressure as he had to hold his anger in check rather than vent it if Matthew had smiled. However, there wasn't even a glint of levity in Matthew's eye.

'Lunch?' Swift made the word sound like the command to fire at an execution.

'It seemed churlish to refuse as he'd been rather pleasant,' Matthew decided to skip details of the meal, though he was tempted to inform Swift that it hadn't been that great, 'and it put Tina at her ease, so she gave me most of the information I asked for.'

'Which was?' Swift was beginning to think he could see light at the end of the lengthy tunnel Matthew was leading him down.

'Basically, what Tina Barron's relationship is with Thorsson and Michaela Naidoo, a reporter I've been looking into,' Matthew explained, sticking to the facts – if not to all of them. 'To be honest, it was a long shot and proved to be a dead end.'

'Who are Naidoo and Barron, exactly?' Julie had been doing her best to keep in the background, she didn't understand why she was present and wanted no part in having to take sides, but this was the first she had heard of this pair.

'Naidoo is the journalist who spoke to me after the first press conference about Driver's killing,' Matthew explained, again being careful to edit the facts as he still wasn't ready to put forward an alternative theory to explain Driver's murder, 'I spoke to her again and she seemed suspiciously well informed about the Towers family. Tina Barron's name came up and I went to interview her – *him* – in the hope he could give me more details about Ricky Towers's relationship with Geraldine. As I said it was a long shot, but I thought Tina might know more as I assumed she – *he* – also knew Geraldine,' both Swift and Julie were staring at Matthew, hardly believing what they were being told. 'Thorsson is Tina's agent, though I got the impression that wasn't working out, and what with him – Tina that is – being a transvestite, well, I rather jumped to the conclusion that he might have some insight into any connection between Ricky and Geraldine that might have gotten Geraldine killed.'

'Are you any the wiser?' Swift wanted to know, he tried to keep abreast of all the cases his officers were working on, realistically this was often little more than an outline but he could see that Julie was as surprised as he was to be hearing these details. A fact that did not help Matthew in any way.

'No, not really, sir,' Matthew sounded genuinely put out by the fact, even more so than by the crap storm he'd created. 'Nothing concrete, just an impression that Ricky and Geraldine were *very* close. Unfortunately, nothing to suggest that Driver was killed to get at Ricky Towers, although equally nothing to rule it out.'

'The Towers name does keep cropping up, sir,' Julie admitted to Swift, her mind on rearranging the pieces of the puzzle rather than on what she said.

'In what ways?' Swift demanded, wondering just how much of a grasp he really had on the investigation into Driver's killing.

'Oh, you may recall we thought we had a lead on a suspect for the acid attacks,' Julie explained, realising she'd inadvertently wandered in front of Swift's line of fire, 'Mike Stennard, the security manager from the Blue Snake, but it turned out he has alibis for both attacks as well as Driver's killing. However, as a teenager he had got mixed up in a small way with a white supremacist biker gang, the same one Bobby Towers is involved with, and we think that Bobby may have gotten him his job. My contact in Gangs says most of the bikers work for Bobby but he seems to have gotten a couple into GR Security, perhaps to keep an eye on what is going on or simply as another way to demonstrate his patronage to fellow Aryans. Whatever the reason Stennard seems closer to Bobby Towers than he's letting on.'

Swift eased himself back in his swivel chair, rocking himself slightly from side to side as he contemplated the two officers before him. He couldn't fault their detective work, nor their intuition and hard work but Green was expecting to hear that he had suspended Matthew and, as things stood, Matthew needed to be taught a lesson in team work.

'The main problem I have with all of this, Matthew,' Swift decided on a course of action, 'is your failure to communicate, a factor that is vital in any investigation. I take it you haven't put any report in on your activities to Ray, so it's on the system?' Matthew, genuinely shame faced, shook his head, 'I can see from Julie's reaction that she knew little of what you were doing,' Matthew nodded, it was true enough and he didn't want to get Julie in trouble, 'and you certainly haven't been keeping me fully informed. As unexpected as your meeting with Gary Towers was, you should have phoned me afterwards, I would have understood and been able to tell the chief, who could have passed it on to the NCA. That would have saved everyone a lot of unnecessary angst.'

'Yes, sir, I see that,' Matthew agreed, surprised at his own growing arrogance, over the years he seemed to be more and more willing to put his own judgement before that of everyone else's.

'On balance I don't think your actions warrant suspension, but I am taking you off the case,' Swift paused. Matthew nodded his acceptance though inwardly he wanted to do the TV cop thing of jumping up and shouting *fuck you and your red tape!* then throwing his warrant card on the desk and storming out. Instead he considered his meek acceptance of the situation as nothing more than a tactical withdrawal. 'Julie, I will be confirming your acting inspector role later today but, as of this moment, you are leading the inquiry team on the Driver killing. Please ensure you keep me up to date with developments. Thank you both for coming in at short notice, that will be all.'

*

‘How did the team take it?’ Matthew wanted to know, as Julie put down the two pints she’d bought on the table and made herself comfortable at the relatively unoverlooked corner table in the crowded Town of Ramsgate pub.

‘Ecstatic,’ she stated, straight-faced, ‘they are all for a new broom and optimistic we’ll now solve the case in record time.’

‘I see, impressed with their new inspector are they?’ Matthew observed, taking a mouthful of his pint, thinking he should order some sandwiches for them both.

‘Oh yes, there’ll be no buggering around on my watch,’ she informed him, checking out the bar menu. ‘By the way Ray said “thanks for the report, better late than never”.’

‘Cheeky sod,’ Matthew finally laughed, feeling his tension ease. ‘Congratulations again by the way.’

‘I’m going to visit the families to update them and explain I am taking over, without going into the whys and wherefores,’ she reassured Matthew. ‘No one has suggested that Driver was gay, quite the opposite,’ Julie stated, going to the heart of the matter, glad her apprehension about meeting Matthew for a late lunch was proving unfounded. She hadn’t expected him to be bitter but you can never tell about these things.

‘His brother hinted at having his suspicions,’ Matthew pointed out, getting up to order a couple of club sandwiches, adding when he returned. ‘And Ricky’s marriage seems to be a bit of a sham.’

‘What exactly did Tina Barron and Gary Towers tell you?’ Julie assumed Matthew had been economical with the truth earlier.

‘Gary was at pains to explain how he rarely met with his brother and that he knows very little about him and his business affairs, though it didn’t entirely ring true. On the other hand he was quite open about his relationship with Tina. That’s her stage name by the way, she also goes by Christopher Barron, and when I phoned the Blue Bird Agency to ask about her it turned out they had already spoken to Harry about her. Tina was the act that Max

Dwight complained about. Her dream of being on the stage might prove short-lived if Dwight's assessment was correct, although the agency said they were still representing her.' Matthew paused to take a bite of his newly served sandwich, then continued as he chewed, 'However, I got the impression that Geraldine and Ricky were a real item.'

'Although nothing to confirm it?' Julie asked, though she guessed what the answer would be.

'No, but given Ricky's background it isn't something people will openly acknowledge,' Matthew pointed out. 'Homophobia is still the default setting of a lot of people in this country. It might be OK for the liberal elite and those of dubious moral character, like politicians and actors, but bastard hard criminals still have to maintain a certain standing in the community.'

Julie swallowed to avoid choking on her sandwich, Matthew might cynically make light of the matter but such prejudice was a blight to many people in all walks of life. 'Which means that even if the motive for killing Driver was in some way to get at Ricky Towers, it doesn't actually rule it out as a hate crime,' she pointed out.

'That's the path you should be following, Inspector,' Matthew said after another pull on his pint. 'We keep straying away from the question that we should be answering: why did someone hate Geraldine, or Gerry, so much that they killed him the way they did? It's a degree of hatred that is likely to come from jealously or betrayal, perhaps a mix of both.'

'That's a good point,' Julie agreed, adding with a smile, 'and it is the question I will be asking as you are now off the case.'

'You're late,' Matthew pointed out as Michaela Naidoo put her rum and coke down and sat in the chair Julie had vacated over an hour ago. On the plus side he'd had time to ponder the outcome about the complaint of sexual harassment and assault made against him by Mrs Wellend. He'd picked up the letter on his way out of the Barking office and only had time to quickly read it before heading to Wapping. The complaint was not upheld but stated that both parties had misconstrued the other's words and actions. A wording that diplomatically did not suggest the complainant was lying and, as such, it wasn't a total vindication of Matthew's conduct.

'You're lucky I came at all,' Michaela responded with a huff, 'I don't jump at your beck and call. In fact, I only came to hear your side of being suspended.'

'You see, you shouldn't trust Patel's information,' Matthew caught the slightest of puzzled expressions flit across Michaela's brows at Patel's name, 'as it is neither up to date nor accurate.'

'Really,' Michaela wasn't to be put off by Matthew's bravado as she thought his words simply a sop to his pride, 'it must be hard coming on the outcome of the complaint made against you.'

Michaela's counter blow hit home and Matthew didn't cover up his obvious confusion. His notification would have been sent so it was timed to arrive when the complainant, Mrs Wellend, got her copy. Swift, as his manager, would have also been notified. However, for Michaela to know meant that someone else in the force had also seen a copy, hot off the press, and that didn't seem likely to be a lowly inspector. A fact which confirmed he was wrong about Patel and had jumped to one conclusion too many.

So Michaela's contact must be Chief Superintendent Harvey at the NCA, the man leading the special unit set up to investigate Ricky Towers and his family. He was the only one superior enough to pull strings to get an early sneak-peek at the complaint outcome. And he wasn't the type to want to share information about his case with a Met officer, especially if he was using Michaela off-the-books. Matthew, however, forced himself to stop his mind racing ahead on what this tit-bit meant and focused on what Michaela was saying.

'Given your form on this, it must have been hard for them to exonerate you,' Michaela smiled, maliciously. It wasn't just that she sensed a story emerging out of these events she was also enjoying seeing Matthew taken down a peg or two, although she couldn't exactly say why. Perhaps it was the rather obvious way in which he tried playing her for information, and he was an arrogant bugger. 'You'll need to keep your nose clean for a time, if there are any more reports of unwanted sexual advances then they won't be able to cover up for you again.'

'I see,' Matthew made a point of seeming annoyed by her words, 'you went to the *if-you-don't-have-a-story-make-one-up* school of journalism?'

'I don't have to make it up, as far-fetched as it might seem,' she said confidently, 'it's already a matter of record that you propositioned and had intercourse with a female suspect in one of your previous cases. Now you've tried the same thing with the mother of a man you've arrested for murder, a man who claims he was acting in self-defence.'

'Michaela,' Matthew said, downing the last of his pint, hoping he sounded completely sincere, 'I enjoy these games with you but you are being played on this one.'

'So you are denying that there is any truth in either allegation?' Of course she expected him to deny it.

'Your information is simply wrong, a twisting of the facts and no more, and your source will disown you if it goes to print,' Matthew informed her standing to go, he'd had enough for one day and intended to get home early for once. 'This is only being done now to distract me from looking at any links between Driver's killing and Towers more closely. Even though I'm still not convinced that any such link is relevant to the investigation, the questions I've been asking recently are making someone very nervous. Perhaps your police source is simply worried I will spook Ricky and his family and it'll make them even more cautious than they already are – I don't know. However, I'm certain it isn't going to do you any good by getting caught in the middle.' Matthew shrugged as he finished, looking down at Michaela with a smile, for once ignoring her gaping cleavage and he maintained a steady and unfazed eye contact. Even so he didn't think she believed a word he said but that, he concluded, was her problem.

# Chapter Eighteen

Hayden was back at her desk, her excitement mounting as she re-examined the CCTV footage she'd taken from the petrol station late the day before. She'd been in such a rush to look at it again that she hadn't even stopped for a vape before dashing into the police station. The images she'd recovered from the garage were obviously of Driver's attacker, the false number plate and general description matched, and now she had two sets of HD colour images. The biker had stopped on the well lit garage forecourt not to buy anything but to adjust his machine, the bike appeared well used and the paint work, now seen clearly in colour, had some distinctive scrapes. She could also make out the distinctive heavy boots he wore, the black denims and black hoody under his helmet that shielded his face and, from what was caught on camera of his hands, he was definitely white. There was also something about the way he moved and manhandled the bike that seemed to confirm him being male, despite his slender build. However, there was still nothing of his face but the description she was compiling of the bike, its rider and the clothes he wore was now much more detailed than previously. The man might not be readily identifiable, although someone might recognise him from his clothes and general description, but the battered looking Honda could very well ring a few bells.

Kathy was trying to compose herself. She still wasn't ready to tell Matthew and the girls what had happened to her, although she had made up her mind to do so over the weekend. But for the moment she wasn't in the mood to do so as her head still whirled from everything that she had gone through that day. The extended interview with the police had exhausted her. Although, to be fair, Sergeant Gillian Raynaud – from the sexual offences unit – had proven to be sympathetic, understanding and efficient. Kathy had particularly appreciated the latter two character traits as she didn't want tea and sympathy but someone to take her seriously and get things moving. Most importantly, the sergeant was clear about being realistic of the expectations she might be raising, explaining to Kathy each step they would be taking but not overstating either the speed nor the likely outcomes these steps would produce.

'We will be interviewing everyone who was at the meeting with you. It's possible they might have witnessed something, or can give us a clue if one of them remained behind or returned after the meeting,' Raynaud explained as she read through Kathy's statement. 'We will also be looking at the school's CCTV and examining your office and car. We can't be certain where the attack took place, but it is likely they used your car to get you home.' Kathy nodded her understanding, she was certain her office was somehow key as, when she was in it, it seemed to trigger the worse flashbacks.

'We'll also be taking the clothes and coat you wore, plus your bag and phone,' Raynaud continued, she wanted to clarify all the basics before coming back to finish Kathy's statement with some questions about her family and home life, especially to put into context Lance Fulbright's groping her.

'I'm sorry but I have already washed the underwear and blouse I was wearing,' Kathy explained, each word uttered was now enlarging the guilt she felt at not coming forward earlier. Although Raynaud had reassured her a number of times that this was not uncommon and in practice she had taken the decisive step relatively quickly.

'It doesn't matter, there still might be evidence to find, they'll be put under the microscope,' Raynaud paused, she knew the physical evidence would be minimal and, given the delay in collecting it, probably of little help with a court case. 'Every little piece will play its part, help tell your story so we can make an arrest,' Raynaud was keen not to say much about what might follow this. She knew that an arrest may not lead to a court case or, even if it did, that the odds were stacked against a jury convicting the perpetrator. All they could do is take one step at a time. 'I will be speaking to your doctor as well and we will need to have various samples taken from you before you leave here, as it will help in matching or eliminating anything we find.'

'I understand,' Kathy nodded, determined to be resolute and wanting to get as much over as she could, 'whatever you need.'

'We will also have to speak with your husband and take samples from him,' Raynaud paused again, studying Kathy, a victim's reluctance to involve or notify those closest to her wasn't uncommon but it was equally common for one of them to be the actual perpetrator and for the victim, intentionally or not, to hide the fact.

'Does that have to be today?' Kathy asked, telling strangers, particularly professionals like the police or her doctor, was one thing but she wanted to protect Matthew and her daughters from the pain she knew it would bring them. To protect them from the shame, despite all she remonstrated with herself, that she so acutely felt.

'I can wait until Monday, and it would be better for him to come in voluntarily,' Raynaud conceded, understanding how difficult each step was for Kathy.

'Why do you say it like that? You can't suspect Mat surely?' Kathy was too stunned at the thought to be horrified or angry.

'No, but we have to rule him out and anyone else close to you, male friends, colleagues,' then seeing Kathy's face fall and resolution falter, Raynaud quickly went on to say, 'Only those close to you or who you feel may have been taking an unwarranted interest in you. Anyone you may have been intimate with or has pushed their attentions on you.'

'There are none of the former, not since my marriage, and only Lance has *pushed himself* on me,' Kathy stated. There had been incidents in the past, a male colleague with wandering hands and others occasionally suggesting going for a drink or meal, all easily rebuffed and stopped. There had been one brief flirtation three years ago, that might have blossomed into an affair but, fortunately for them both, circumstances had intervened and the temptation had withered.

'How do you think your husband will react to your telling him?' Raynaud asked, knowing that too many men blamed their wives or girlfriends for being the victim of a rape. And would persuade them with emotional arguments or their fists that it was better to keep it secret than risk, as he saw and feared, public humiliation.

'He's a police officer,' not even Kathy knew why that might make a difference but she'd been wanting to say it for some time, as if Matthew's job somehow automatically exonerated him or would put him beyond any hurt or recrimination her situation might bring him, 'a detective inspector in MIT East.'

'Of course,' Raynaud could have kicked herself, the surname was uncommon enough but she hadn't put it together with the dour inspector she knew. 'I've worked with him a couple of times,' Raynaud admitted, then thought to change the subject rather than starting to describe how some of her cases evolved into murder. 'He will know much of what I'm about to tell you but there are a number of support services you can call on …'

'You look glum,' Yvette stated, she'd had a day of arguments and tantrums from the director – a real bitch of a diva – who was questioning every stitch and button hole of each of the costume designs they had already agreed on, 'bad day?'

‘I’m now acting inspector and lead on the Driver case,’ Julie told her with a mix of unhappiness and underlying pride. ‘Matthew got kicked off,’ she explained, ‘he deserved it but even so he’s a good copper and I’m surprised at the governor not wanting to keep him on the case.’

‘How’s Matthew taking it?’ Yvette wondered, pouring them both a glass of wine, celebration or not they both were in need of it.

‘Ohh, the same as he does everything else, pretending he doesn’t really care while bottling it all up inside himself,’ Julie stated, happily clinking her glass with Yvette’s and taking a sip. ‘I know he is tougher and more intelligent than a lot of people give him credit for but his dispassionate and cynical world view is an act that fools no one.’

‘Really?’ Yvette had only met Matthew once, and then only briefly at a team BBQ, along with the other wives, husbands and partners or designated drivers as in reality they were. She had quickly been left to her own devices, while the team talked shop and drank heavily, but Matthew had struck her as a rather cold individual. ‘Are you certain it isn’t your own passionately felt emotions you are projecting on him?’ Julie pulled a face and held out her glass for more wine, it’d been a long day and there were other things she wanted to chat about, not least of which was the wedding ensembles her affianced was designing.

‘Hello, Paul, I need to tell you about something serious that has happened,’ Kathy had carefully thought through what she wanted to say before phoning Paul Stoppard, her chair of governors. He was a well meaning senior accountant in a mid-sized business but who had the habit of dominating any conversation he was involved in, quickly taking it down a path of his own choosing.

‘Hello, is that Kathy?’ Paul paused, not to listen but to decide which of the things he wanted to hear about he’d bring up first, ‘How are you? I hear things haven’t been going too well recently.’

‘What?’ Kathy was almost taken aback but was prepared for any ambush and ploughed on with what she had to say, ‘Things have been very difficult for me the last few days …’

‘I know, Lance has had a word with me, the stress you’re under and all that,’ Paul was glad Kathy had phoned, there were a few things he had been wanting to say to her and this gave him the opportunity to do so, ‘and I’ve been speaking to one or two of your staff to get their take on things.’

‘What, no. Paul you must listen to me, something serious has happened and it involves the police, there are things you need to do,’ she put as much authority in her voice as she could muster, desperate that he started to listen, to ensure certain safeguards were put in place.

‘There’s no need to worry, I’ve spoken to Lance and he will take over for a few days while you rest,’ then Kathy’s words finally filtered through. ‘What? Why are the police involved, what have you done?’

‘First thing Monday you must contact the school’s HR service at the LA,’ Kathy had a name and number ready to give to him but wanted to be certain he fully understood first, ‘one of the staff at the school has been accused of gross sexual misconduct, of sexually assaulting a colleague. There are safeguarding protocols in place that need to be put into action, but you have to inform HR, they will work with you to see everything is done correctly. Do you have a pen to take down this number.’

‘What, this is terrible,’ Paul was duly horrified. ‘Who has made the accusation?’ However Kathy insisted he take down the name and number before she continued.

‘I don’t see what we can do?’ Paul puzzled. ‘Surely it’s a case of innocent until proven guilty, the poor fellow has a right to continue working until he’s actually convicted surely.’

‘HR will explain the safeguarding issues and everyone’s rights to you, we are not proportioning blame it’s a matter of protecting everyone,’ Kathy struggled to remain professional, a lifetime in teaching was driving her to do this one last task correctly before she could revert to being the injured victim, putting herself and her needs first.

'Who on earth would have gone to the police?' Paul worried. 'Just think what this will do to the school, its reputation, just as things were turning round. I'll phone Lance, see what damage limitation we can put in place.'

'Paul, phone HR before you do anything,' Kathy said with a firmness tinged with anger. 'Lance is the one currently thought to be the main suspect. You *must not* contact him, Paul, the police will be in touch with you to explain everything.'

'Kathy, ill or not you should be dealing with this, not passing the buck to me,' Paul's sympathy had reached its limit.

'Paul, I won't be in next week, it is me that has made the accusation to the police. It is me that has been raped.' With that she put the phone down and took it off the hook.

'I've put a film on and left them to watch it,' Matthew told his wife, he felt singularly at a loss to know what to do, 'I still think you should let me call Wanda, get her over here.' However seeing Kathy's adamant shake of her head, changed track, 'What about your mother then?'

'God, Mat, this isn't some event I want to share with everyone,' she angrily told her husband. 'If, when I'm ready and want to, I'll let them know but for now I just want some peace.' It wasn't fair to be angry with Matthew, her blurting it all out in the car as they left the shopping centre hadn't been her intention. It had been on her mind all morning and she had decided it would be best done after dinner, taking care so as not to unduly upset her daughters – then it had all just spilled out of her as they left the carpark.

'I'm sorry,' Matthew said for the umpteenth time. On hearing, if not really taking in, Kathy's sudden outburst he'd gone into police mode: saying and doing the things he'd learned from the manuals and protocols of his job. It was only as Kathy had started to scream at him to shut up and the girls crying penetrated his mind that he realised that his sympathy and questions, though correct for an officer, were the worst thing he could have done as a husband. He'd pulled over and hugged his wife, joined by his daughters who had struggled past the seat backs.

The hugs had worked far better than any words could have and eventually they pulled apart, though remained united, and Matthew had driven his family home in silence. He'd taken the shopping and Kathy to the kitchen and then settled the girls in the living room, explaining as simply and carefully as he could what had happened to their mother and what they could do to support and comfort her. Then he returned to the kitchen, knowing it wouldn't be long before the girls found a reason to come out and be at their mother's side.

'There's nothing I can say,' he explained, taking her hands in his, 'other than I love you and if I could take your pain away I would.' The words were clichéd, he knew, but had to be said. He hadn't cried since Lizzy had been born and wasn't going to now despite the tears in his eyes. His mind running through a list of things he intended to do, starting with getting legal support and speaking with Sergeant Raynaud. He needed action to avoid dealing with the anger he felt bubbling inside himself. 'We will get through this together, you're strong enough but as a family we are stronger. We'll do whatever you want, whatever is needed, and I'll make certain nothing gets caught up in the system. We'll get the bastard, together we'll work through this.'

Kathy smiled, Matthew may be an idiot at times but he was her sweet idiot and she was glad he was here, holding her hands and looking so mournfully protective of her.

'Do you want a cup of tea, Mummy?' Becky asked from the kitchen door.

'And biscuits?' Lizzy asked, pushing in beside her sister.

*

It was much later – after cups of tea, take-away pizzas, wine, much talking, more hugs and a few tears – that Matthew was half-watching the TV that had remained on, if ignored, since their return home. Kath had spent a little time separately with each of her daughters, answering their questions and reassuring them that she and they were perfectly safe. Eventually Matthew had carried each of his sleeping daughters to their bed and then joined his wife on the couch with a bottle of whisky, she now slept curled up and huddled beside him. He was numb from the drink and the shock but thinking about what he needed to do. How he needed to act with Kathy, what he should guard against saying, how they both needed to help their daughters through this and allow them to be part of its resolution. He also thought of the phone calls he'd be making, the favours he'd pull in and everything he should do to ensure that Kathy was as fairly treated as the system would allow. A system he knew that was stacked against her.

He wasn't paying any attention to the TV, the sound turned down but his eyes were on the news banner which ran below the current affairs programme. His mind, automatically reading if not comprehending what was flashing before his eyes, suddenly switched on. Two men had been shot and killed earlier in the day, at approximately twelve fifteen in the afternoon, in the St Katherine's Dock area of East London. A massive police search, involving armed officers, was underway looking for the shooter. The police had identified and informed the families of the two men, one of whom was Richard Towers, wealthy media mogul, the other man was his driver. Matthew reached for the remote and shut the TV off as he had more important things to deal with.

# Chapter Nineteen

For the first time since joining the force Matthew didn't want to be at work, he'd rather have been at home with Kathy. Becky, his eldest daughter, wanting the reassurance of another adult, one whom she trusted, had phoned her aunt Wanda early on Sunday morning and her aunt had come straight round. Matthew had felt a little out of it as the four females conferred, reassured and hugged a great deal. Eventually Wanda had spoken to him privately, going over what he intended to do and the support she felt her sister needed. She ended, reassured that he had her sister's best care as his first priority. But saying he should continue to work as normal and send his daughters to school, as they needed to keep to a regular and familiar routine. So it was arranged that Wanda would take some time off and be with Kathy. Thereby leaving Matthew, who'd kept his mobile and landline turned off since Saturday afternoon, to return to a form of normality on Monday; although he felt nothing like his normal self.

'Obviously Chief Superintendent Harvey from the NCA wasn't happy having Towers's shooting passed to us to investigate but in practice he is running things,' Swift explained. The tiredness in his voice explaining his lack of concern that Matthew had arrived late, on top of his not having been contactable the previous day. Nor had Swift paid much attention to Matthew's excuse of a family crisis. Such a lack of concern was uncharacteristic of a man usually very people orientated. 'I'm liaison, working with him to ensure the two parallel operations work efficiently. The chief attends the briefings so she can direct the strategic direction and is working with the AC to ensure resources are available from both sides. CTC sits in on the briefings as well, their concern is with the money laundering side of Towers's operation as well as the cousin's links with various far-right groups, which means that a terrorist link can't be ruled out.

'However, terrorism isn't a part of the investigation focus, not on the evidence we have so far, not that we have much to go on as yet. Harvey believes that whoever is responsible will show their hand shortly, by starting to take over direct control of Towers's clubs and other operations, and that will point us in the right direction.' Swift wearily finished not sounding particularly convinced by Harvey's viewpoint.

'Parallel investigations?' Matthew found it difficult to sound even vaguely interested in the operational details but Swift was too tired to notice, his monotone summary being no more than a mechanical repetition of words he'd heard and said a dozen times over in as many hours.

'Julie is still running the investigation into Driver's killing and the two hate crimes, and I am leading on the hunt for Towers's killer,' Swift squeezed his eyes closed and pinched the bridge of his nose, trying unsuccessfully to ward off the dull pain of a headache. 'From the work Hayden has done on collating various images and the comparison done by forensics, no one has any doubt that the same bike and rider were involved in both killings. The same type of bike was used in the acid attacks but now, on balance, our thinking is that it's a coincidence.' Swift wearily explained, 'At least, that's the official line, although I wouldn't rule out the possibility we are looking at two or even three separate cases.'

'Why two investigations?' Matthew could sense that Swift was growing impatient, no doubt he had plenty to do and had only managed a few hours' sleep in the past thirty-six hours.

'More like two approaches aimed at achieving the same end, the NCA focus is on the impact of the murder on the Towers organisation while we are looking solely at the shooting. Harvey is convinced Towers was shot as part of a takeover, either by a rival or as a result of a family rift,' Swift patiently explained, his bland phrasing making the motives for the brutal murder sound mundane, almost an everyday occurrence. 'The issue is just who exactly is involved. Harvey seems to think that Bobby Towers, the eldest cousin, is likely to have had a hand in it – possibly supported by another organisation, one of those biker gangs he is allied to.'

Matthew gave a non-committal shrug at the suggestion and looked even more sceptical at what Swift said next. 'Gary Towers is also being looked at, given his rather cool relationship with his brother and his control of the security side, although Harvey has put him at the bottom of the suspects list. However, it is down to Julie to discover who did the actual killing. Not that anyone believes the killer will be found, he'll either be dead or already out of the country.'

'From what I've heard Ricky Towers was shot at close range, doesn't that suggest he knew his killer?' Matthew was doing his best to sound as if he cared a flying fuck but Swift could take no more as the thoughts of the mountain of work he still had to climb grew in his mind.

'You can get the details from Ray, he's working with the NCA team to ensure everything from both investigations gets tied together,' Swift told him, an edge to his voice that came from the growing pounding in his head. 'However, at the moment we don't have anything concrete to bring Bobby in for questioning and the family's cooperation has been limited. They have all decamped to the family home in Essex, surrounded by the combined ranks of heavy-set guards and even more heavily litigious lawyers. Getting FLO access hasn't been easy and the family hasn't been cooperative, especially with their lawyer present all the time. However, given they are the grieving family of our victim, we are on a bit of a back foot and don't want to push too hard – at least, not at this stage.'

'So, what's the plan?' Matthew asked, then suddenly realised what Swift was about to tell him to do.

'Seeing that you managed to speak with both Ricky and Gary recently we have decided you are the ideal man for the job,' Swift might have smiled at the irony but was in no mood to do so, 'If you can find a way into the family, avoiding the lawyers, and try to see what dynamics and tensions exist between them, what they are saying to each other or not saying, at this stage any nuance might provide a clue. The only thing we all agree on is that the family knows more than they are saying.'

A second incident room had been set up at Wapping nick, though in practice it was really no more than somewhere for the NCA officers to hang their coats. Matthew could see that Ray was fully occupied with Inspector Nisa Patel, to whom he nodded, and another officer he didn't recognise. Julie and Harry were out, following up on sightings of the bike and rider based on the last police appeal, while the office staff seemed doubly busy. A few, like Ray, were working with NCA officers ensuring everything was, as Swift put it, tied together or, like as not, tied up in red tape as Matthew ungraciously thought.

'You OK, sir?' Hayden asked noticing Matthew standing at the front of the room watching the others like some idle passer-by.

'Yes,' he stated, rallying himself, 'just a long weekend. Do you have the details of how the shooting took place.'

'If you've been watching the news, then you have it all,' Hayden told him, deciding not to press him about his weekend, he really didn't look or sound himself. 'They even have the CCTV footage, what little there was.'

'It happened just near the underpass in Nesham Street, didn't it?' Matthew had assiduously avoided the news on Sunday, only hearing a report on the radio as he drove to Wapping that morning.

'They were stationary, looking to turn right onto Vaughan Way,' Hayden confirmed. 'The bodyguard sitting in the passenger seat thought he heard a bang on the rear nearside door. In his statement he said he thought a motorcyclist had knocked into them trying to turn left, then he heard Towers opening the nearside rear window. As he turned to say that might not be a wise move there was, what he described as, an explosion and next thing he knows he's deafened and covered in Towers's brains and blood. The driver, next to him, fell forward onto the steering wheel with half his face splashed over the windscreen.'

'Nice,' Matthew was looking through the HD colour crime scene photos Hayden had handed him as she spoke, 'he was lucky not to get caught in the blast, sawn-off shotguns have a wide spread even at close range.'

'Right side of his face was peppered with shot and fragments from Towers's skull,' Hayden grimaced, 'they think they've saved the sight in his right eye though. He's under guard in a private room but, all things being equal, he is likely to be fit enough to be released tomorrow or day after.'

'Towers wouldn't have opened his window just like that,' Matthew stated, handing back the photos.

'That's what I said,' Julie informed him, bringing an extra swirl of purposeful activity with her as she entered the room with Harry close behind.

'Inspector,' Matthew welcomed her, trying not to sound cold.

'Inspector,' Julie responded brightly, wondering why Matthew looked so unhappy, was his resentment of her taking over his case now coming out as things were hotting up? It wasn't like him but who could tell? 'It was a bullet proof SUV, even at close range the glass would have deflected most of the shot, the killer must have known that.'

'If Ricky knew the shooter, recognised him even with the helmet on …'

'The only CCTV footage we have is of the motorcyclist driving away down Vaughn Way and his visor looks as if it is down, though I suppose that doesn't mean much,' Hayden informed Matthew.

'But the point is Towers must have recognised him and was unconcerned enough to wind down the window,' Julie concluded. 'Which fits with him being the same person who killed Driver, knows them both.'

'How does that fit with the acid attacks?' Matthew asked.

'Perhaps it doesn't?' Harry chimed in, obviously relishing being Julie's gofer as it kept him close to the centre of action.

'Or it's someone who had to prove himself with a prior killing?' Hayden conjectured.

'Harvey, the big cheese from NCA, doesn't seem to think the hate crimes are connected,' Julie informed them all, she had been at the late night core briefing which had included the AC, both CSs and Superintendent Swift. 'The thinking is that Towers's killer had a lot of insider knowledge, which is most likely to have been supplied by a family member either his cousin or brother.'

'Are there any other leads?' Matthew asked, feeling more as if he were going through the motions as his mind kept turning back to Kathy, thinking he should phone and check if she was OK.

'No forensics and only the one clear shot on CCTV as the shooter rode away from the scene,' Hayden informed him. 'The NCA surveillance team were the only witnesses but were too far back and only saw the motorcyclist approach. It was all over and he'd ridden away before they realised what was happening. They tried to give pursuit but lost the bike when it turned down an alley leading to Pennington Street, the killer must know the area well as we didn't pick him up on CCTV again. Just prior to the attack Towers had been to the barbers, a high class place just round the corner, it was part of Towers's routine and I suspect the surveillance had become …' there was the slightest pause as Hayden, aware of NCA officers sat within earshot, chose the most diplomatic word she could think of, 'complacent.'

'Why would a man like Ricky Towers go to a barber?' Matthew, for the first time, felt his interest peak. 'Surely he'd have someone visit him to trim his hair and beard.'

'They said it was a regular appointment,' Julie explained, she'd interviewed the manager and hairstylist herself, 'he paid to have the place to himself for a couple of hours each Saturday. Just him, while his guard sat on a sofa watching the door and the driver stayed with the car outside. Apparently, Towers liked the atmosphere and the service,' Julie hadn't been particularly surprised to be told this as salons and barbers could often be a small island of peace in a hectic schedule for many people. 'As far as anyone could tell everything went as normal, he drank tea and liked to chat about the latest fashion trends or the footie, all the usual stuff that their typical customers, the successful and wealthy, wanted to hear.'

'So you are still focused on finding the bike, then?' Matthew finally asked, something about the barber nagging at him as not fitting with everything else they knew about Ricky Towers.

'Hayden is leading on that line,' Julie told him, with a nod and a smile at Hayden. 'Myself and Harry are interviewing everyone we can find associated with Ricky Towers, having started with those who live and work in the tower block he owns at the other end of the High Street. The NCA are focusing on those people who will benefit from his death, those high up in his organisation. I understand you've been delegated to liaise with the family,' Julie smiled at the irony of this, at the same time wondering what was making Matthew even more gloomy than usual.

Matthew stood looking out across the rain sodden Thames, trying to phone his wife as he worked out how to go about the task that had been allotted him. The rest of the team were preparing to leave the dry, warm incident room to go about their own work. Kathy's phone went to voice mail, as did his sister-in-law's, they must have already left to speak with the barrister he'd arranged to give Kathy advice on how she could expect things to proceed – Matthew thought it best she was under no illusions. He left no message, she'd see he'd called and would get in touch when she was ready. He didn't want to dishearten or undermine Kathy's resolve, knowing that Sergeant Raynaud would take care to give realistic expectations, but it was better that she understood the realities of what she faced so she'd know not to let her hopes be raised without good reason.

Ironically, now that Matthew had his boss's blessing to speak with the Towers family he felt little inclination to do so. The deceased Ricky and his still living brother, Gary, might have some cause to trust Matthew but for the rest of the family he'd be just another intruding copper, unwanted and thought of as nothing better than an eavesdropper on their grief.

'Hi, Donald, it's Matthew,' there was silence at the other end of the phone, no doubt Donald was immediately suspicious of Matthew's phone call. 'Have you been to visit the family yet?'

'No,' Donald was no fool and realised what Matthew was about to ask, 'I doubt if they'd expect me to call, I'll attend the funeral of course, send flowers, but we weren't that close anymore.'

'The powers that be believe Gary or Bobby are behind Ricky's shooting,' Matthew informed him, he'd need to tell Donald what the police were thinking if he was to gain the man's willingness to act the spy.

'More fool them,' Donald stated, his tone resigned at the request Matthew was working up to ask, a request he was equally resigned to turn down. 'Gary's the last person to put his brother in harm's way. He gave up his army career to involve himself in the family business, that he'd spent his life avoiding, simply to get Ricky out of a jam. And although I wouldn't put anything past Bobby he had little to gain at this point.'

'Why's that?' Matthew turned hearing Ray call after Julie who just left the room, then watched as Ray got up and raced after her.

'Rumour had it that Ricky wanted a quiet life and to just run their legitimate businesses. There was no reason for Bobby to stir things up just when he was getting everything he wanted.' Donald explained, he kept his ear to the ground and, as no one doubted his loyalty, there were plenty who were happy to gossip in his earshot.

'What about all this biker gang stuff he's been stirring up?' Matthew asked, moving to the far end of the room away from the window and the group that had returned to the incident room.

'Bobby's like his dad, and his namesake dead uncle, unless you are white and male, part of the Aryan nation, then you are just a lower form of life and not to be trusted. So, he's been cutting the family's ties with those groups he doesn't trust and setting up links with those he does,' Donald snorted. 'As if one drug dealer is more honourable than another.'

'Look, I just want the person responsible for shooting Ricky, others can deal with the Towers crime organisation,' Matthew explained, trying not to allow Julie's loudly spoken orders to those around her intrude on his thinking. 'If you go to give your condolences, and I think his old mum might expect that, then just let me know if anything odd crops up. If you get a sense that they know who might be behind this, anyone acting strangely, that sort of thing.'

'OK, I'm not promising but I'll try,' Donald sighed, Matthew had always been the one to push them towards trouble when they were kids. It'd been him who'd bet Ricky he couldn't hit a tourist on the head by pissing from the top of the monument, a suggestion that had led to a spectacular stream of piss spraying across the crowd below and the three friends being barred from any future school trips.

'What's going on?' Matthew asked turning back to Ray as he wished Donald 'luck and God's speed' as he ended the call.

'The DNA has come in from the orange rope,' Ray informed him with a broad grin, 'and it's been matched to Mike Stennard. Julie's going to pull him in for further questioning and has sent Nisa Patel and Hayden to pick up Todd Barrett, the guy who's given Stennard an alibi for the acid attacks. Julie thinks Stennard might know who killed Ricky Towers, given his links with Bobby's biker chums and his DNA being on the rope used to tie Driver up. He may not be directly involved but it's likely he knows more than he is letting on. And Julie thinks if she can break the alibi Todd Barrett has given Stennard for the acid attacks then she can use that as leverage to get him to tell all.' Ray beamed, literally rubbing his hands with glee at the thought they were close to cracking the case.

'OK,' Matthew didn't sound particularly enthusiastic, which caused the buoyant Ray to frown, his mind was on Kathy and hoping she would phone soon as he felt a desperate need to demonstrate his unwavering support for her. 'I'm going down to the barbershop and to take a look at the crime scene.' Matthew left without further comment leaving a puzzled Ray wondering what was wrong with the inspector.

# Chapter Twenty

Mike Stennard seemed no more fazed by his being pulled in for further questioning than he had done previously. 'There's plenty of rope knocking around the Blue Snake like that,' he derisively informed Inspector Lukula, still feeling on sufficiently safe ground not to ask for legal representation.

Despite Stennard's apparent bravado, Julie could almost smell the guilt oozing from his pores and mingling with his cheap cologne. They had already searched his flat, to no avail, and had done the same to Geraldine's dressing room at the Blue Snake. She had also sent Harry to double-check the lock-up garages near Stennard's flat, to see if he leased one from a second or third party, while she questioned Stennard. Now she and Harry were heading back to the Blue Snake with another team and a warrant to search every inch of the club. Julie was on the scent and intended to leave no stone unturned.

Inspector Nisa Patel, a willing aid to Julie's team now that they seemed to be onto something, and Hayden were having even less luck at Todd Barrett's small two-up-two-down. The mother's home help was there and explained that Barrett's mother was on some heavy medication that left her drowsy and listless most evenings and that the old woman now rarely went out. As far as they could make out the son hadn't been home since Saturday.

'He's often away these days, he works you know and is often out, leaves me on my own,' the mother informed them, lucidly enough, her voice a mixture of rancour and pride. 'He lives his own life and doesn't have time for his old mum. You'll find that out soon enough,' she told the two female detectives, assuming women of their age must have children, 'daughters stay and will take care of you but sons are born to leave and make their own way in life. He's off with some girl I expect. Do you have daughters?'

'One,' Hayden informed her, smiling at the thought of her independent twelve year old daughter doing anything other than making her own way in life while her boys, despite all her attempts to train them otherwise, were much more likely to be at home until they each found a woman to cook and clean for them.

Todd's room contained a few old clothes and the usual detritus a young man might accumulate.

'It looks like he's cleared out for a few days,' Patel surmised. 'Though there's enough left behind to suggest he intends to return.' They checked the rest of the small house and the ramshackle, half-derelict shed but found nothing of interest, then phoned Julie with their limited findings.

The barbershop, which was just round the corner from Nesham Street, was decidedly up-market. It was a spacious place with a number of mauve, velvet sofas and chairs in the waiting area, immediately inside the wide glass doors that looked out onto the start of a pedestrianised street, with parking at the shop's side.

'The man with Mr Towers always sat in that chair,' the manager, a tall, slim, well groomed Asian man in his early thirties, who spoke with an accent acquired from a private education, informed Matthew with a wave of his hand. The high backed seat indicated would have given the bodyguard a view of the interior as well as the doors and approach. 'The driver remained with the car, a large, black SUV in the space closest to the door, it was kept reserved for Mr Towers.'

'Towers came every Saturday?' Matthew asked, taking in the six, well spaced, stations each with their own barber chair, basin, mirrors and equipment that formed the work area of the shop.

'*Mr Towers* came most Saturdays,' the manager stated with an emphasis that suggested he was discussing a valued customer. 'It has been a regular thing for a few months now. He was a very private man and he booked and paid for the entire shop so he was our only customer when he visited. Occasionally he'd cancel but still pay and often he would arrive late or go early but that was his privilege. He always had Martin do his hair and Aisha his manicure and neck massage. He was a man of taste and refinement who enjoyed the meditative and spiritual well-being our establishment offers. There is a spa upstairs ...'

'You don't serve tea,' Matthew observed, noticing the expensive coffee making machine with an array of Viennese biscuits and pastries on a nearby glass topped table. 'I thought you told my colleague he had tea each time he visited?'

'Yes, he ordered it specially from next door,' the manager explained. 'A rather good-looking young man, who always wore a blue suit, brought it in.'

The café next door dealt in a range of vegan snacks and speciality teas.

'No, we don't deliver, though you can get anything to take away,' the young man behind the counter told Matthew, the place was busy and he looked resentful of the time the inspector was taking up with his questions.

'Blue suit, take-away speciality chi tea every Saturday?' the young woman serving down the counter asked, as she handed change to a customer.

'Yes,' Matthew confirmed, turning to her, leaving the male assistant to serve the next person in line. 'You remember him?'

'He'd sit outside or by the window, like he was waiting for someone, drinking a ginger and lemon green tea. And would then order a speciality chi tea to take away when he spotted them. Although, I never saw who he bought it for.'

'Did he pay by cash or contactless.'

'Cash,' she stated, already taking her next order, 'but if you want to speak with him he works up at the Blue Snake, you know the club on Wapping Lane.'

'Are you certain?' Matthew was surprised to discover a link back to the club.

'Oh yes,' she continued to serve while talking, so versed in working behind the counter she didn't need to think what she did, 'I've been there a few times and recognised him, I often asked what acts were booked.'

'Todd's left,' the manageress of the Blue Snake told Julie, 'worked his notice and gone last Friday.'

'Do you know where to?' Julie asked, something didn't add up, Patel had contacted her to say it looked as if Barrett had packed up much of his clothing and gone off but if he'd worked a month's notice it was hardly a bunk, his notice would have been given about the time of the first acid attack.

'No,' the manageress wondered what the inspector wanted with the mild and inoffensive Barrett, 'I know he'd applied to work on the cruise ships some time ago, but he just said he was off to pastures new.'

'SOCOs have found various pieces of the orange coloured nylon rope and are taking samples to see if anything can be matched but on the whole it all looks too new,' Harry informed Julie, as he entered the office, somewhat breathlessly having come up from the basement below the stage.

'Is he a close friend of Mike Stennard's?' Julie asked, taking in what Harry had said but not approving the rushed manner in which he'd informed her and in front of the manageress as well, the constable needed to learn some circumspection.

'I don't think so,' the manageress seemed mildly surprised at the suggestion, 'obviously they worked together here and we all get on but Todd was a bit of a dreamer,' she almost said he was a bit of a drip, 'Mike's the opposite, down to earth, a bit of a card.'

'That's him,' the manager of the barbershop confirmed, handing back Matthew's phone. Matthew had contacted Julie with his news about the blue suit wearing employee of the Blue Snake. It wasn't a great leap of deductive power for Julie to assume it was Todd Barrett and had snapped a staff picture, framed with others on a wall, of the youthful ex-assistant deputy manager and sent it to Matthew. 'He'd bring Mr Towers's tea, always handed it to him personally, they would chat for a few minutes and he'd leave.'

'Did you ever over-hear what they spoke about?' Matthew was perplexed at this development.

'No, it was made perfectly clear that we were all to take a break, in the staff room, when the young man came in. Mr Towers's assistant would knock to let us know he'd finished.'

'It doesn't make sense,' Julie told Matthew, speaking on the hands free set as Harry drove her back to the incident room while Matthew drove his car along Nesham Street. 'Why would Barrett be having clandestine meetings with Ricky Towers, it's a bit like a CEO of a multinational having meetings with the mail boy?'

'If Barrett has done a bunk it might suggest he knows something about the shooting, his finishing working his notice could be just coincidence,' Matthew pulled out onto Vaughan Way, noting that the only evidence of the road junction being a recent crime scene was a yellow board appealing for witnesses to come forward.

'It's possible but the manageress said he bought them all a drink the day he left, doesn't sound at all like someone doing a runner,' Julie told him as Harry parked outside Wapping nick, 'she didn't think he was that close to Stennard either,' she added, sounding despondent at the conflicting and inconclusive evidence they seemed to be collecting. 'I'll be letting Stennard out on bail as we have drawn a blank so far and circulating a description of Todd

Barrett, including alerting ports, etc. Harry is going to contact the various cruise lines to see if Barrett's been signed on with any of them.'

'I don't remember seeing Barrett when I visited the Blue Snake,' Matthew said, as much to himself as to Julie, 'but his photo looked familiar.'

'You probably remember it from the staff photos up on the wall in the club,' Julie told him. 'I can't see Barrett being directly involved but we need to discover if he's lying about Stennard's alibi. Otherwise we're stuck.'

'You're convinced Stennard's involved then?' Matthew asked, although he was of the same opinion himself.

'Yes, Barrett could be as well but I tend to think he's been pressured into giving the alibi and knowing he was off to pastures new probably didn't care much either way,' Julie sighed, hating not being able to see the wood for the trees. She'd been hoping for more of a breakthrough, it being her first case as an inspector, but she had every intention of cracking the whip so the team chased down every lead late into the night. While Matthew, having been sidelined in the case, had the luxury of going home.

'Lance Fulbright remains the main suspect,' Kathy informed Matthew, they had shut themselves in the living room while her sister played with Lizzy and Becky upstairs. 'The others on the finance committee confirmed he stayed behind with me.'

'What else?' Matthew gently asked, he wanted to show his interest and concern without pushing. Noting how Kathy still spoke more as if she were an observer of events rather than as being at their centre, he judged her still to be understandably extremely fragile.

'They've taken samples from my office carpet, from which they hope to recover DNA,' she hesitated for a moment, recalling the sense of foreboding she'd recently experienced whenever she'd been in her office, but then determinedly pushed on. 'The school's

CCTV has been blanked for the entire evening and the console has been wiped clean. However, they have found his prints in my car – although none, other than mine, on the steering wheel or gear stick. My doctor has attested to the bruising she found on my body and she has passed on the detailed notes of the examination she gave me. All of which Sergeant Raynaud said was a help.'

'They've interviewed Fulbright, I take it, searched his hotel room and his home?' Matthew was trying not to sound the policeman but was concerned that everything that could be done was being done. He knew Raynaud had a good reputation and had stopped himself from checking up on her, even so his concerns remained.

'He's denied the attack and what happened in the kitchen,' Kathy hesitated. Raynaud had shared what Fulbright had told her, checking his claims against Kathy's own statement, but she couldn't bring herself to tell Matthew the man's obnoxious twisting of the facts. 'She also said they have recovered some evidence from his home but wouldn't say what as yet.' Matthew had no delusions as to what Fulbright would have said, an affair with Kathy would explain all the evidence and couldn't be disproved, although it sounded as if Raynaud had found a possible lead at Fulbright's home.

'One other thing,' Kathy stated, her brow furrowing at the thought, 'she asked me for more details about how I have been acting at school and home recently.'

'I've given details of that in my statement,' Matthew confirmed, trying to sound positive, 'your acting out of character doesn't prove you were drugged but helps suggest you were.'

'That's what she said, and that my going to the doctor when I did helps,' Kathy paused again remembering Raynaud had pressed her on how she was finding the acting post and her relationship with Fulbright. 'It's just that she seemed to be thinking this could all be down to a stress related breakdown,' Kathy paused again, looking Matthew squarely in the eye and hoping for an honest, rather than just a supportive, answer. 'That isn't possible is it, that

I'm just imagining it all? Would this really happen to me? Could I be …'

'If you say it happened then I believe you,' Matthew stated with all the sincerity he could muster, as he reached across to take her hand, although she pulled back to study him intently, assessing the degree to which he meant what he said. 'You are not the type to delude yourself and what you feel is the truth of the matter is what counts. Just keep in mind what the barrister told you: be clear about the facts, be confident, show the emotions you are feeling and don't let anyone try to *what if* you.'

'I don't doubt what has happened,' she said as much to reassure herself as her husband, 'I just keep coming back to why Lance would have done it. He's educated and seemingly well adjusted, how could he do this?'

'You can't tell by outward appearances,' Matthew stated, he almost smiled at the naivety of the question, 'people hide their true natures deep inside themselves, if they didn't my job would be a lot easier.' His smile evaporated before it was fully formed on his lips, his mind wandering back to his current case as he spoke, someone was hiding their real self and motives deeply out of sight but he couldn't see who as yet.

'What about you?' Kathy's question brought him back with a bump.

'What?' Not understanding what she asked.

'What do you hide deep down for no one to see?' There was no sign of any levity in her question, but an intense curiosity and concerned expectation mingled in her eyes that made Matthew sweat as if he sat under the gaze of some inquisitor general.

'Nothing, not from you,' his lie seemed pathetically inadequate.

'What about that complaint that was made against you?'

'What?' A flash of anger ran through Matthew that she should doubt him but he understood how vulnerable she was, how her secure, safe life had been ripped away and replaced with the chaos of doubt and suspicion. 'I'd forgotten to tell you, I've had the outcome. Here, I'll show you.' He stood to get the papers from his coat pocket that hung in the hall, his phone ringing as he returned, and handed the papers to her.

'There isn't much I can tell you,' Donald's deep voice rumbled out of the phone as Kathy read through the findings. 'Bobby was being the twat he's always been. One minute telling the others he'd make whoever did this pay, then saying he'd warned Ricky about doing business with all those Slavs: apparently they are all Muslims and devious to the core. We then got half an hour of why working with the white brotherhood would make things so much better, in the end even his dad told him to change the tune as he was upsetting his grandma.'

'Anything else?' Matthew asked, though he was more concerned at watching Kathy read than listening to Donald.

'Gary was quiet, kept to himself pretty much and only spoke to his ma,' Donald stated. 'Did you know she's in a wheelchair now, lugs round one of those small oxygen tanks and has to take a lungful of it every so often?'

'Was Gary on his own?' Matthew asked, 'No Tina with him?'

'Hardly,' Donald laughed at the thought, 'that'd be like a red rag to his uncle and cousins. They ain't exactly the tolerant sort and he only got back into the family business on Ricky's insistence, so he's even more isolated now than before. Although,' Donald added as an afterthought, 'I did hear him tell his ma that Tina's away for a while, she's got some gig up north.'

'So no suggestion anyone there knows anything concrete about who is responsible for Ricky's death, no discreet hatching of plots for retribution?' Matthew checked, though Donald was already confirming what he'd suspected.

'Not that I could tell,' Donald told him, no doubt in his voice. 'Like I said, I can't see what Gary would get from it and he seemed at a loss, really upset he was. As for Bobby, the more he said the more obvious it was he hadn't a clue. I left when the sound of his voice had me wanting to do him assault and battery. However, I'm glad I went, said my piece to Ricky's old ma, she was always a kind woman.'

'Thanks, Donald, I owe you,' Matthew stated.

'Yep, and it'll be a double,' Donald informed him more than half seriously.

'We should get together sometime soon, recount a few childhood memories,' Matthew agreed.

'The rose tinted past,' Donald laughed, signing off.

'This doesn't exactly say you are blameless,' Kathy said without emotion the second he put his phone down, before he'd even regained his seat next to her.

'It never would have,' he explained with a shrug, 'basically it is her word against mine. In the end they had to take into account circumstances and my past record,' her face fell in doubt as he spoke. 'In the end the only right course of action I could have taken was to have followed Julie out to the window but it wasn't reasonable to have expected I do that.'

Kathy folded the paper up and handed it back to him without saying anything.

'Do you think I am capable of crossing that line?' He asked, not angry but curious to know what she wanted from him. Her response was a shrug, not certain what words to use to convey what she wanted to say.

'You know I love you don't you,' he said, speaking as if of the sun rising and setting – an irrefutable fact – without emotion or challenge. 'I know at times I take you for granted, I put the job first and I should do more to show you how I feel. But I do love you, you are my rock.'

'That's just it,' she said, suddenly latching onto his words and realising what she had to say, 'I don't doubt you love me and I love you. Love can cope with imperfections and failings. However right now everything is swirling around me and I need a rock to cling to, I need to know I can trust you, everything you say. No lies or deceit,' she took a final breath before plunging into the deep, 'and the trouble is I have at times doubted you. I've seen you shift and change as if hiding things from me.'

Their eyes were locked, Matthew transfixed and cold from the truth of her words, she hot from the intensity of her need, both silent. Then Lizzy burst in, demanding that her parents come and see the puppets they'd made and the show they'd prepared about two princesses and a lonely dragon – Aunt Wanda being cast as the dragon.

# Chapter Twenty-One

Michaela Naidoo was waiting for Matthew at Wapping police station when he arrived. She filled the small public waiting area: with a bag on one chair, her coat on another and her ample frame on a third. She had waited patiently, watching with perceptive interest the comings and goings of the front desk, her mind wondering about the small dramas being recounted before her.

'This will have to be quick,' Matthew told her, taking her to an empty interview room, 'I'm on my way to a briefing.'

'I'll get to the point then,' Michaela put her things down on the table but didn't take a seat, leaving Matthew to stand as well. 'We have a deal over your giving me an exclusive into Towers's murder in return for my providing you with any useful information I come across.' It was a statement rather than a question, though she obviously wanted Matthew to confirm how things stood between them.

'I'm sure we can develop a relationship that is mutually beneficial,' Matthew said, guessing that her current police contact had summarily cut their connection with her, so leaving her high and dry. Although his puzzled frown showed her that he wondered why she needed to have spoken to him now to confirm this.

'Good, as I have something for you,' she pulled a plastic folder, a half dozen pages thick, from her bag and handed it to him. 'Mrs Wellend on a plate for you.'

'That's good of you,' he responded, his puzzled expression deepening, 'but her complaint against me has been resolved.'

'I did wonder if you'd heard about the further developments yet,' Michaela shook her head, much as a teacher would when confronted with a student who'd failed to do their homework. 'She isn't giving up, but intends to take out a civil suit.'

'Shit,' Matthew said under his breath, getting a sympathetic look from Michaela.

'Hmm, it would be deep shit,' Michaela agreed. 'I spoke to her yesterday and she's obviously hoping for as much press coverage as she can get. Of course, it's not supposed to influence her son's trial but you know how these things work. However, I decided to give you the benefit of the doubt as I think that sexist-cop routine you pull at times is just an act.'

'Thanks,' Matthew wasn't exactly listening as he glanced through the file, but what he read was showing him he owed her his thanks.

'It's not the first time she has done this,' Michaela told him, her face breaking into a grin, more than satisfied that he now owed her a debt of gratitude. 'She made a similar complaint about a social worker and a deputy head teacher, both supported by the same local councillor, it stopped her son being taken into care on one occasion and being permanently excluded on another.'

'Great, I'd offer to buy you breakfast but I really must go,' on top of everything else he didn't want any more distractions at the moment and the file she had handed him would stop a major one in its tracks.

'Ohh, one other thing,' Michaela said, over her shoulder as she went out of the door he held open for her, 'I heard you are looking for Todd Barrett to help with your inquiries.'

'Yes, he's linked with Ricky Towers in some way,' Matthew explained, his mind still on the contents of the folder she'd given him.

'Well he's gone north to try out a new drag act,' she said, heading for the front of the station, 'I don't know where but Victor Thorsson should be able to tell you.'

'What?' Matthew asked, only just realising what she was telling him as he opened the security door to let her out into the public area.

'Thorsson, runs the Blue Bird Agency, he handles Tina's act,' she stated, giving him a backward wave. The door closed on her and she didn't see Matthew bang his head two or three times on the inside of the door, wondering how he could have missed the obvious. *He really did need to get with it*, he thought, with a final bang of his head.

'Make certain you hang around after the briefing,' Swift told Julie as he caught up with her in the corridor on the way to the meeting, 'The chief wants a quick word with you, she caught me when she first came in.'

'Do you know what about?' Julie puzzled, noticing Matthew rapidly approaching from the other direction, looking very much like a bloodhound that had caught a scent as he strode purposefully towards them.

'She said it was to do with your acting role,' Swift said, pushing the briefing room door open as Matthew caught them up, 'probably wants to discuss options and offer some advice.'

Any further comments were cut off as they entered the room and took their places. Chief Superintendent Green was sat at the head of the table, having called the meeting partly to keep a grip on what was being done – as she didn't entirely trust Chief Superintendent Harvey of the NCA – but also so she could demonstrate to her boss the proactive stance she was taking in overseeing the parallel investigations. Harvey and Patel sat to her left, with their back to the window which overlooked the choppy, blue grey Thames and, in the distance, Old Stairs; the latter was rapidly disappearing under the incoming tide. While Swift and Julie sat to her right leaving Matthew, who was the last to enter the room, to take the seat directly opposite Green. Which he did, with a nod and a smile towards Green in the belief that it never hurt to make your boss feel like a human being.

'I was just saying that, despite appearances, we seem to be making headway,' Green began with a summary of how things stood. 'The key seems to be how these different attacks and murders are linked. They all involve the use of a motorbike, a Honda X-ADV, using falsified number plates in each case. We do not have a great deal of physical evidence but Julie believes DNA found on a rope links Micheal Stennard, despite his having an alibi, to the killing of Mr Gerald Driver. Stennard also fits the general description of one of the men involved in the acid attacks, for which he has a potential motive. Another suspect, Todd Barrett, not only provides Stennard, and thereby himself, with an alibi but it has also been discovered that he met regularly and secretly with Ricky Towers. As such Julie is looking to further question Barrett, unfortunately he has disappeared.'

'Yes, ma'am,' Swift agreed, wanting to ensure Julie got the credit she deserved. 'She and her team have checked with all his known associates and work colleagues but no one seems to know exactly where he has gone off to. He'd resigned and worked his notice so his leaving might not be that suspicious.'

'The best lead we have is that he has taken a job with a cruise line,' Julie informed them, picking up the thread at Swift's nod. 'However, none of the main cruise lines that dock in UK ports have him on record, so we are trying all the other European cruise lines. Although we can't find any record of him having left the country either, so our line of inquiry is rapidly closing down.'

'This chasing down the small fry is excellent and may prove of use at some stage, to fill in the gaps,' Harvey acknowledged, his sarcasm more biting than he'd intended but he was convinced that the officers in front of him did not grasp that it was the fact of Towers's murder that was significant and not the identity of the person hired to do the deed. 'However, this is increasingly looking as if Towers's death was orchestrated from within the family.'

'On what basis do you make that judgement?' Green asked, happy for her colleague to put his views forward but expecting he could back them up with some facts, especially as she couldn't escape the feeling that he often kept things back.

'Though it is still early days there has been no sign of any outsider interventions,' Harvey tapped the table to emphasise his point. 'Whoever is ultimately responsible for removing Ricky Towers would need to quickly start to take over, while the family are still in shock. The only evidence we have of such a move taking place has been Bobby Towers moving into Ricky's Wapping offices and apartment, apparently taking it over late last night. The existing security staff, Gary Towers's men, have been replaced with Bobby's, most of whom seem to be recruited from the white supremacist gang that Bobby's involved with.

'This morning we,' by which Harvey meant Nisa Patel and her surveillance team, 'have been seeing some of the more prominent people in the Towers organisation turning up at the offices. These actions, although they don't constitute proof, certainly suggest that Bobby Towers is behind everything and he's moving to secure his place as head of the Towers family empire.' Harvey paused, only briefly, for the impact of his words to hit home, before continuing so as not to lose the initiative he thought he'd gained. 'Inspector Merry, were you able to discover anything when you visited the family yesterday?'

'I didn't attend in person,' Matthew noted Harvey's look of exaggerated surprise although, as an NCA team were watching the family home and the comings and goings of those attending it, the reality was Harvey already knew the answer to his own question. 'However, my informant was there and reported back that the family seemed as confused about who was responsible as we are. In fact, everything Bobby said or did seems to confirm he doesn't know what is going on.'

'I am sorry,' Harvey seemed perplexed, 'but weren't you instructed to go and observe the family?'

'There seems to be some misunderstanding as to my relationship with the family,' Matthew jumped in, hoping to save Swift the embarrassment of having to fudge an answer. 'My presence would have been no more welcome than that of any other officer. While my contact was able to pass unremarked.'

'So,' Harvey's exasperation was clear, 'we only have this third hand information to set against the actions we have directly witnessed Bobby take.'

'My contact has known the family for most of his life and knows Bobby and Gary of old,' Matthew stated, watching Harvey whose body language showed he put no faith in what he was hearing. 'He doesn't think Bobby had motive or the balls to go up against Ricky and, despite all appearances, my contact believes Gary and Ricky remained very close, so Gary is an unlikely suspect.' If Matthew had any doubts that Harvey was Michaela Naidoo's police contact an almost imperceptible nod of agreement showed that Harvey was well aware of how things stood within the Towers family, confirming he had insider knowledge.

The realisation allowed the pieces to fall into place. Ricky and Gary were pretending to have fallen out but were keeping in touch via Todd. And, through Michaela, they were supplying Harvey with information about Bobby. Ricky and Gary both wanted an end to the criminal side of their organisation or at least to be able to walk free of it. Lucrative it might be but it was simply too dangerous for the brothers who only wanted to enjoy the lifestyle they had achieved. This meant Bobby had to go – sent down by Harvey for whom such an arrest would be a considerable feather in his cap – before he dragged the family into even deeper waters. The question was could Bobby have found out and acted first by killing Ricky? It was possible Mike Stennard had learned something from Todd Barrett, about Ricky and Gary's duplicity, and passed it on via his old gang to Bobby. Matthew realised this is exactly what Harvey thought and, with Ricky dead, the chief superintendent no longer needed Naidoo to act as go-between and had cut her off.

'Who is your contact?' Patel asked, interrupting Matthew's reverie.

'Donald Key, he doesn't have any direct links with the Towers family but …'

'I'm aware of who he is,' Patel stated, 'one of Ricky's old gang, when Ricky used to lead from the front.'

Both Patel and Harvey knew that Donald Key was close to the family, a sort of surrogate cousin, but Harvey knew of no reason why the man should give an honest appraisal of the Towers family to any police officer. 'He's hardly a sufficiently trustworthy source to base our assessment of what the various family members know or don't know about Ricky's death,' Harvey concluded testily. 'The evidence shows that our focus should be on Bobby.'

'Actually, sir, I think you are right,' Matthew conceded, ignoring the surprised stares of the others in the room, 'Bobby is just delusional and fanatical enough to do something like this but his role would have been to pull the strings rather than the trigger. Therefore, unless I'm misunderstanding the situation, looking into the Towers organisation and the ramifications of Ricky's killing really falls within the NCA remit, while finding the actual killer or killers sits with us.'

It was Amanda Green who was quick enough to retake the initiative, she might not fully understand what was behind Matthew's thinking but it offered clarity on a way forward that would stop Harvey trying to continually to take control of both operations. 'I believe that's a good place to wrap this liaison meeting up,' she said, with a smile that allowed for no disagreement with her, 'I need to speak with Julie but her focus should be on finding Todd Barrett, anything we get that shows a link with Bobby Towers, or anyone else, Malcolm will pass on to you.' She nodded to Harvey, who seemed surprised if pleased at having so easily achieved what he'd wanted all along – sole recognition for the eventual arrest of Bobby Towers – the MIT East officers could have the small fry. 'I take it that the NCA team will be interviewing all those who meet with Bobby and, in due course, with Bobby Towers himself.'

'Yes,' Harvey readily agreed, with a gracious if self-satisfied tinged smile, even as Swift and Matthew were rising to go and Green was turning to speak with Julie.

'It's very good of you to say so, Amanda,' Julie didn't think that Green looked like an Amanda, she looked very much like Chief Superintendent Green or even Ma'am but not an Amanda, still she'd been told to use first names for their informal chat, so Amanda it was.

'You seem to have learned a great deal from both Malcolm and Matthew during your time in MIT East,' Amanda said, 'they have both given you excellent reviews.'

'I believe we all work well as a team,' Julie settled for a response that she thought truthful as well as diplomatic.

Green almost asked what Julie thought of Matthew Merry but decided it was an unfair question and would potentially distract the conversation. 'Without further beating around the bush the reason I wanted to speak with you is partly to offer some personal advice, one ambitious female officer to another, and also to alert you to a possible opportunity.'

'I'm always grateful for any advice,' again Julie spoke truthfully, though in practice the only thing she believed she had in common with the chief was her gender, beyond that they were as different as a pea from a bean.

'Despite things having moved forward a great deal over recent years, there is still a tendency to see female officers operating in certain roles,' Amanda confided, 'and, though the walls are coming down, the more we push at them the better.' Green paused to take a file out of her briefcase, 'The Counter Terrorism Command is, as I'm sure you are aware, expanding and they are looking for another inspector to join their ranks and set up a specialist team.'

'CTC?' Julie's surprise came more from her never having given serious thought of working in this branch, despite Swift's advice, rather than any doubts about her ability to do so.

'Details of the post are in the folder,' Green explained, not detecting any hesitancy in Julie's surprise, 'it is being advertised as we speak and the interviews will be competitive so make no assumptions. That is, of course, if you decide to apply. It is your decision to make but I wanted to tell you that I think you will make a strong applicant and should give it some thought.'

Matthew had tried to be succinct in summing up what his thoughts were on the case and the rather slender evidence he had to back them. Malcolm Swift, who was hearing them in the order Matthew related for the first time, asked only a couple of questions for clarification and had otherwise quickly grasped the nettle.

'So, Todd Barrett and Tina Barron are the same person. And Barrett may be in league with Stennard, as Julie suspects. Plus Stennard could have passed on information to Bobby Towers causing him to act, as that dick-head Harvey believes,' as unprofessional as his words were Swift felt his description apt for the chief superintendent who'd given him so much grief over the last couple of days. 'Either way finding out exactly what Barrett knows, what he has been up to with Stennard on the one hand and with Ricky and Gary Towers on the other, seems key to the whole thing.'

Matthew shrugged, 'It's the best lead we have at the moment,' although he was still unclear about the degree of Barrett's involvement. 'He's escaped our notice so far by his using his mother's maiden name of Barron and, at times, by passing himself off as a woman. Although whether this and his involvement has been innocent coincidence, intentional deception or a mixture of both I can't say.'

A call to the Blue Bird Agency quickly revealed that they had not arranged any gigs for Todd Barrett, whom they knew as

Chris Barron – stage name Titillating Tina – since his disastrous appearance at the Lea Way pub. When Matthew asked to be put through to Victor Thorsson the receptionist, whom Matthew assumed was the same effete youth he'd previously met, told him that Thorsson hadn't come in that day or yesterday nor had they been able to contact him.

'Is that normal?' Matthew asked.

'No, not at all, he usually tells us if he won't be in and how he can be reached,' the young man calmly stated, without any curiosity or concern about his boss's whereabouts. 'But as he is the boss, he can do what he wants.' The receptionist passed on Thorsson's home address without any thought and, as Julie was still in with Green, Swift delegated Matthew to go speak with the agent. While he galvanised the remainder of the team to chase down every other possible lead on Barrett's whereabouts.

'Come on, Harry!' Matthew called out, as he and Swift breezed into the incident room, disturbing the work-like hush, 'get your coat, we are off out. The game's afoot!' The constable knew not to hesitate or stop to question, smiling at the joke made at his expense, he grabbed his coat and the inspector's, which he half threw and half passed to him, and headed out.

'As soon as Julie is finished speaking with the chief,' Swift called out to Matthew's retreating back, 'I'll go with her to question Gary Towers, I'm beginning to think he may know more about where Tina is than he let on to your contact.' Matthew waved in acknowledgement as he went through the door, realising Swift's thinking was probably spot on. Although, if nothing else, it would allow Swift to legitimately step on Harvey's toes, a fact his governor seemed to be relishing.

# Chapter Twenty-Two

Kathy Merry was sat in front of her laptop, staring at the empty, white filled screen. It wasn't as if she *wasn't* resolved on what she wanted to do. However, if her decision was as much based on reason as on emotion, she thought, then her reviewing her direction of travel was sensible and not a hesitation. She had considered the consequences to her daughters and then to Matthew, now she reviewed them as they would impact on her. In each case the negatives revolved around loss of earnings, which seemed a relatively minor thing compared with what she expected to achieve. She was, she thought, in the process of shedding the skin of a passive victim and taking on the mantle of a fighter for justice.

'You can't just sit back and expect everyone else to fight for you,' the female barrister had told her some days, seemingly a lifetime, ago. The barrister was someone Matthew knew, Malcolm Swift's ex-partner, someone who had grown a reputation for defending the undefendable: paedophiles, rapists and sex-offenders. 'You must take up the fray yourself, be clear that you are not in any way to blame for what your attacker did, be straight forward in stating that your version of events is more truthful than his. You must not hesitate nor give even a scintilla of credence to any counter claim he makes. Your truth is the only truth.'

These were stirring words, she had thought, but was only now beginning to understand how to put those words into action. Even her dreams had been betraying her. Their common theme was of her running naked through the school chasing the man who had taken her clothes. Every so often she caught up with the thief, his face unseen, and had sex with him in return for her clothes; which he would run off with once again and so the chase would go on. However, in real life she knew she had not been a willing participant nor had it been a game. Her memories were still jumbled but she had no doubts that her assailant was Lance Fulbright and, at times, she could even feel him on her, his thrusting, even the very smell of him.

Angry with herself, at any doubts she'd had or concern as to her own responsibility for being attacked, she had been bad tempered with everyone else that morning. Both Lizzy and Becky had gone off to school with their aunt, their eyes red with tears. Matthew said little and had gone early, clueless how to deal with her. There was no doubt that Matthew thought she needed *dealing with*, he could not conceive of simply standing at her side, just being a mute rock inscribed 'I'm here when you need me'.

Then there was the phone call, her deputy and long term friend, Jeremy, who hesitantly explained what had occurred the day before. 'The chair of governors asked me to convene a special staff meeting at the end of the day,' Jeremy's tone was embarrassed but determined, concerned that he was doing the right thing and not making matters worse. 'He told everyone that you will be off indefinitely, that you have had a serious breakdown. He's asked me to be acting head, supported by Lance Fulbright, as you were.' There was a pause as Jeremy waited for her to comment. Then in the face of her silence he went on in an even more hesitant tone, 'There was no one from HR there, which I thought odd, plus his being explicit about your reasons for being off. It just didn't seem right. So, this morning I phoned HR and they seemed confused about your being absent. They are going to phone you but I thought you should hear this from me first.'

Again a pause, again another silence, in the end causing him to add, 'Whatever you need Kathy, myself and the rest of the staff are behind you, just let us know.'

She thanked him and asked him to pass on her thanks to the staff, she would wait to hear from HR before commenting but she wasn't off due to a breakdown, she simply needed time for herself. It was as she said 'herself' that she realised what she needed to do, for once her needs were paramount.

The person from HR, when they called, got the first clarion call. They began with the usual rote phrases: 'we are here to support', 'we are on your side but need to clarify the situation' and, most importantly, 'this is the agreed policy and how it will apply to your situation'. However, the representative from HR quickly found herself floundering and unable to respond to Kathy's clear, precise catalogue of the wrongs done to her, the lack of support she'd received and what the police investigation was looking into.

'I've been sexually assaulted, raped, by a colleague. My attacker was appointed by the chair of governors, who has now informed the staff that I've had a breakdown and may not be returning while my attacker continues in post. Although I explained this to Paul Stoppard and that he should contact you for advice he obviously hasn't done so. There has been no misunderstanding, as you suggest, nor any lack of clarity in what I have told the chair of governors. Given the misinformation he has given to the staff I now feel forced to resign,' Kathy's machine gun litany left no room for any interruptions or comments, the brief silence of confusion which followed her words was enough for her to end the call with a curt 'thank you'.

As she typed her letter of resignation, with copies to her professional association, the chair of the staffing committee and HR, she realised this was just an excuse. She'd known for some days that she didn't want to return to work, she needed a different purpose in going forward. Her first goal was to obtain justice but beyond that she needed something else, she needed to be heard.

Thorsson lived on a newish housing estate, of three and four bedroom semi and detached houses designed for the upwardly mobile professional person, not far from Debden tube station. Had it not been for the office block looking college building standing at the rear of his house he would have had nice views of the slopes down the Rodding Valley along which lay, ruler like, the M11. Thorsson's house was one of the detached ones, with a garage on the left of the property and a side gate, on the right, leading to the rear. Matthew was trying the bell for the third time, followed by a number of loud knocks, he'd also tried shouting and looking through the letter box. Harry had peered in through the front window and, having grown more impatient than his boss, decided to climb over the side gate.

The gate, set into arched brickwork, was a small obstacle for the athletic Harry, who simply hopped up onto the low adjoining wall between the properties and from there, using the neighbouring garage wall for support, clambered over and dropped into the narrow side passage. His way forward was blocked by a covered up motorcycle, which he quickly revealed to be a battered Honda X-ADV. Before he had time to call out to Matthew, Harry heard a noise from the rear of the house and stepped forward to further investigate. It wasn't so much how odd Todd looked, as he turned around the corner of the house, as the fact that he was holding a shotgun that startled Harry. While Todd, in his turn, halted in surprise at being confronted with the young constable that had recently questioned him.

Todd's lifting the sawn-off shotgun, he'd picked up at the first ring of the front doorbell, and pulling the trigger was a reflex action and for Harry his dive for cover behind the motorbike was equally instinctive. Matthew, who was standing just the other side of the gate, didn't give much thought to what he did either but jumped up on the joining wall to peer over the gate. Matthew hardly had time to take in the shocked looking Todd, and the prone but screaming Harry, before Todd hurled the empty shotgun at him and dashed back into the house.

Matthew ignored the shotgun, which had bounced harmlessly off the gate, and calmly got down to help the injured constable.

Both of Harry's legs were bloody but, after briefly probing, Matthew decided the worst of the blood was coming from the left one and used his tie as a tourniquet. Matthew barely recognised himself as his training kicked in, telling Harry to hold the improvised tourniquet in place and to stop squawking. Then he phoned 999, giving his details and location, for an ambulance, armed response unit and at least eight mobile units to close off the surrounding area. Finally telling the operator to ensure the senior officer at Debden nick and his own superintendent and chief superintendent were informed. He then handed Harry his phone and told him to keep the dispatch operator informed of events.

Having ensured Harry was not that badly injured he left him speaking to dispatch, as much to distract him as to impart any useful information, and Matthew went round to the rear of the house. He threw a small rock at the locked French doors without any noticeable effect. After a moment's thought, he picked up a large patio container and, using both hands, swung it at the glass door, again to no effect. Thinking himself an actor in some farce he pondered his predicament, lifting his cap to wipe the sweat from his forehead. Then paused again, this time to tell a neighbour peering over the fence to return indoors and stay out of harm's way. Finally he hefted a large, solid concrete statute as a battering ram to smash his way in. Much to his chagrin he cut his arm, a shard of glass slicing through jacket, shirt and flesh, as he reached in to open the door. It wasn't a life threatening injury but searingly painful all the same.

Once inside the house he could hear shouting and what sounded like an affray coming from upstairs. Halfway up the stairs Matthew could see Barrett, wearing Tina's blond wig askew, trying with limited progress to hack his way through the front bedroom door with a large kitchen knife. Thorsson, who must have locked or barricaded the door, was screaming for help from inside the bedroom.

'What the fuck are you up to, Tina?' Matthew shouted, Todd was in trainers, jeans and a shirt and didn't look as if he'd shaved that morning but his wearing the blond wig had given Matthew the idea to call him by his female name.

'No closer, don't come any closer!' Todd, startled, jumped round to face Matthew, his back to the door and the knife he held in both hands in front of him pointing forward.

'Don't worry about that,' Matthew said, hoping his voice sounded calm, though aware his heart was racing, 'I'm staying right where I am.'

For a moment or two the pair looked at each other, wondering what their next move should be, but it was Matthew who spoke first. 'You know I think I prefer you dressed as Tina and not Todd,' Matthew stated, easing himself into a sitting position, holding his cap to staunch the blood dripping from his injured arm, knowing if Todd went for him he could easily retreat down the stairs.

'Ohh,' Todd breathed more easily now, lowering his knife, 'I did notice you stared at my legs.'

'Not the actions of a gentleman, I'm sorry to say,' the inspector admitted, noticing Thorsson had fallen silent, no doubt wondering behind the door what was going on. 'You do realise that in the next minute and a half this place will be overrun with coppers, most of them armed, don't you.' As if to emphasise his words a distant wail of a siren could be heard, 'Better you put the knife down.' Todd looked uncertain, looking at the knife, then down at Matthew and then lifting his head to better hear the approaching sirens. 'Fuck, Tina, just put it down,' Matthew sounded peeved, much as he might sound as if scolding one of his daughters. 'Then sit down and just do as they say, it'll be over before you realise, without any more fuss.'

Todd complied, sliding down the door to sit on the floor, carefully laying the knife in front of him and clasping his arms around his knees.

'Well done, son, well done,' Matthew quietly commented, as the front door burst in and four uniformed, armed men charged in shouting warnings. Two, piling up the stairs, dragged Matthew out the way and secured Todd before releasing Thorsson from the bedroom.

Julie arrived at the hospital slightly ahead of Kathy, both finding Matthew, his arm now stitched and bandaged and doing his best to look the modest, injured hero, sat in the A&E waiting area.

'Harry is OK,' Matthew explained to Julie. 'They took him straight to surgery and removed all the pellets, his legs are a bit of a mess but nothing vital was hit so they are expecting a full recovery. He's in a side ward, still asleep from the anaesthetic and they'll let us know when he comes round.'

With Kathy he found it harder to maintain his bonhomie. He could hardly compare his own relatively minor physical injury with what she had been going through and, despite all, he felt guilty at having dragged her all the way over to the hospital. 'It was good of you to come,' he told her with a strained smile, sounding as if he were speaking to a thoughtful colleague, rather than his wife.

'Don't be stupid,' she said, giving him a cautious hug, taking care not to knock his bandaged arm. She felt on surer ground now she'd sent her letter off, her way forward more clearly marked and, for better or worse, she felt she could devote some time and sympathy to Matthew.

'The governor will be along later,' Julie informed the pair, surprised at the hesitancy they showed towards each other. 'He's with Barrett, who's been charged with assaulting Thorsson and wounding Harry, plus firearms charges, for now. We expect to start questioning him tomorrow. In the meantime I've sent Hayden to pick up Stennard, an ARU has been dispatched to assist, if called on, as the chief doesn't want any more *dramatics*.'

'How is Thorsson?' Matthew asked, settling his good arm round Kathy, who seemed content to rest against him, her presence giving him as much physical and emotional support as he needed.

'Shaken,' Julie explained, still watching the pair. 'He'd been left, tied to a chair in the front bedroom and when he heard the shot from the back he managed to throw himself over so he blocked the door from opening. Saved his life it seems.' She was taken by Matthew's and Kathy's unthinking, born from habit, physical intimacy which seemed at odds with their seeming inability to speak with each other. It was so different from how she felt about her own partner, from whom she would have wanted to hear every detail about how Yvette felt as well as wanting to hug and comfort her. Was it possible to reach a stage where words were no longer needed in a relationship, that a simple touch or look was enough to tell all? Or had things dwindled to a point of not really caring and simply sitting next to each other was all the enthusiasm they could summon to support the other?

'I should go,' Matthew told Julie, looking at Kathy to confirm she agreed. 'Either everything is catching up with me or whatever they gave me for the pain is making me drowsy but I feel I should lie down. You'll let me know what happens?'

'Of course,' Julie responded with a smile, nodding a goodbye to Kathy. She watched them leave, Matthew a little unsteady on his feet but, at least, he had his arm around his wife's waist and she had hers around him, each supporting the other.

Matthew had taken the day following the incident at Thorsson's house off sick but later in the day had been contacted by Swift.

'He says he will only speak with you,' Swift told Matthew, sounding unconcerned at the request which indicated to Matthew that his governor was confident a confession wasn't far off. 'His solicitor, whom we think is being paid for by Gary Towers – which might change once the truth comes out – has asked about a deal over prison. They've tried to establish that Todd should be treated as a female but CPS have said *he* doesn't meet the criteria so the most we are offering is that he'll be treated as a vulnerable prisoner under Rule 43. As a result he has signed a statement confessing to the charges made so far, but won't discuss anything else except with you.' Swift paused before adding, 'He says he can trust you, that you understand how he thinks. I don't know what that means exactly but I always had you pegged as a warped degenerate, so it must be that you have in common.'

At least Swift appreciated his own joke while Matthew wasn't feeling overly happy. His concern was that Kathy appeared to be waiting for him to say or do something for her, something she expected him to understand but yet he was failing to see.

# Chapter Twenty-Three

Todd, dressed in a coverall as his clothes – even those found in a suitcase at Thorsson's – had all been taken by forensics to be examined for evidence, looked much more chipper than Matthew had expected. Todd's solicitor looked like a million others of his kind, he had a gravitas born from a lack of any emotional attachment with the proceedings other than ensuring his client's legal rights were not infringed. Swift had gone through all the usual formalities on starting the tape running and, then moving the folder of evidence in front of him to one side – as he did not expect to refer to it that much – being confident that Barrett was ready to tell all, he now turned to Matthew to begin the questioning.

'How are you, Todd?' It wasn't the opening Matthew had agreed with Swift, but seeing the young man sitting confidently before him had changed his mind, he'd expected him more confused and uncertain of himself.

'Fine, I slept well, I didn't think I'd get off but was out like a light. You?' Todd asked with a smile, he almost winked but knew that Matthew understood that, despite all outward appearances of being dressed as Todd, in reality it was Tina talking.

'Tossed and turned,' Matthew shrugged, 'my arm's still very sore,' knowing that all Todd/Tina really wanted was a friend, a sympathetic ear to listen. 'So, let's start with the attacks on Lionel Wong and Perry Cheung, it was you who drove the bike wasn't it?'

'Yes, I drove it although it was Mike's bike,' Todd confirmed, 'a replacement for one he brought to the lock-up one day, when I was thirteen.'

'That is Micheal Stennard, who resides at Shearsmith House, Whitechapel?'

'Yes, I've known him since secondary school.'

'He's a bit older than you though, isn't he?' Matthew asked, thinking it worth confirming the pair's exact relationship as it might help explain their joint participation in some of the crimes.

'When I started at secondary things were difficult for me,' Todd explained, thinking back without emotion, 'I didn't fit in. I was a loner and didn't have any real mates. Mike took me under his wing, stopped the others from bullying me.'

'Why did he do that?' Matthew wanted to know, remembering his own years as a bookish, introverted twelve year old.

'He just liked me,' Todd shrugged. 'He left school the year after but he'd hang around and make sure I was alright. By then he was well in with a gang and it was a reason for him to show the school kids he wasn't to be crossed.'

'What about the bike?' Matthew brought things back on track.

'We used to hang out at my mum's old lock-up,' Todd smiled at the memory. 'She had it for the stall she used to run, until she got ill, but as the payments were still being kept up I hung onto the keys. It became our Bat Cave, that's what Mike called it, he was Batman and I was Robin.'

'Sounds fun,' Matthew said, thinking that Mike Stennard had been something of a late developer, 'and that's where you kept the bike?'

'He'd got it from a mate and it needed doing up, over the years it was rebuilt a couple of times, mainly from parts we'd nicked,' Todd explained. 'He used it to do things for the gang he was in. You know, run drugs round the streets, act as look out, that sort of thing. Being on a bike made it harder for anyone to chase him. As

I got older I started to help out and would even drive it for him, with him on the back.'

'Never bothered to get a driving licence, I take it,' Matthew stated, sharing a sly conspiratorial smile with Todd over the misdemeanour.

'What about the shotgun?' Swift injected the question. Slightly startling Todd who was focused on Matthew, searching the inspector's face for understanding and acceptance as he told his story.

'That came later, it was meant as back-up if we ever got cornered.'

'Did you ever use it?'

'We tried it out over Rainham Marshes,' Todd grinned, he'd found the noise and power of the gun, as it shredded bushes or tore a hole in an embankment, reassuring. 'He had a dozen shells, we used six. Then tried it again on the bike, it sent us flying so we knew to take care about how we used it.'

'So that left you four shells,' Swift, who had undergone weapons training, understood the sense of power such a weapon could bestow but was equally horrified by the damage they could do.

'One got bust, damp had gotten into the box, then two more got used on Towers and the other on your man,' Todd paused at the thought, he had not the slightest qualm about killing Towers but had regretted his rash action in wasting his last shot on the young police officer. 'I hope he's alright, I fired without thinking. He took me by surprise.'

'His legs are badly torn up,' Matthew had no intention of understating the injuries, 'but he is awake and comfortable. They expect him to make a full recovery but he's going to be off for a couple of months.'

Todd nodded thoughtfully before stating, 'My legs are my best feature, you know, everyone says so, even Mike.'

'Have you always liked to dress in female clothing?' Swift and Todd's solicitor wondered at the relevance of Matthew's question but neither objected to it.

'Mum always liked to dress me up. I don't remember much about my dad but after he left I would put on little shows for her. She was always telling me what a great voice I had and I was a lovely dancer, so graceful,' for a moment Todd was back in those more innocent times, moving his hand slightly to the beat of a song that only he could hear. Then pulling himself back to the present, he went on, 'Mike thought so too. But I couldn't perform in front of others, not even in school plays, but for Mum or Mike it was different. I used to dress up for him in the cave and dance with him, he said I was more like his girlfriend than his mate. I was so happy then.'

'So, you were more than friends?' Matthew concluded, his mind going back to his friendship with Ricky. They had become increasingly physical, touching and acting lewdly with each other, boyish things perhaps but had they not fought Matthew wondered just how far things might have gone.

'We used to play around, he'd bring some dirty mags to the lock-up and we'd look at them. It was fun, blow jobs and screwing, we didn't think anything of it just the pleasure it brought. Though I knew he didn't like to be called gay, he'd beaten a boy up who'd called him that. He never told his mates in the gang about me and he'd go out with girls. Tarts, he'd call them, said they weren't half the fun I was.'

'Was this from when you first met him?' Swift asked, realising they might now consider additionally charging Stennard with having sex with a minor.

'Pretty much, I still remember the first time …'

'So you were both close from the start,' Matthew interrupted, again pulling them back to the matter in hand, 'helped him with the crimes he committed?'

'At first he always drove the bike on his own, doing stuff with the gang he'd gotten involved with, but when I was about fourteen, when he was out on his own, he used to let me drive and he'd go pillion, so he could get on and off quicker,' Todd explained. 'He'd gotten hold of some plate making stuff and we used to change the number all the time. If we thought things were getting hot we'd nick another bike.'

'The last one being the Honda?' Matthew assumed.

'That was me, after he got out of the nick,' Todd told them, looking less happy, 'but he weren't interested. He said he was never going back inside and that a mate of his was getting him hooked up with a job. He even said he was going to marry some girl he knew.'

'Was the mate Bobby Towers?' Swift asked, it would help with Harvey's investigation if Bobby could be linked to these cases, any leverage they could find would help their case.

'Not that I know,' Todd was clearly surprised at the question. 'It was one of the guys he used to hang around with, someone from his old gang, a real hard case or so Mike said.'

'Is that how you got your job at the Blue Snake?'

'No, Mike wasn't working there when I first started,' Todd told them. 'I got the job after college, I'd done a media course. College was so much better than school, I could be myself more, but it wasn't until I started at the Blue Snake that I began to think I could live and work as Tina. Barron is my mum's maiden name, it was the name she had the stall in, and when I dressed up for our little shows she'd often call me Tina, it was the name she'd picked for the daughter she never had.'

The interrogation was halted at this point, Swift formally stopping the tape and stepping out of the room to take an urgent message, leaving Matthew to ask Todd and his solicitor if they wanted tea or water, both of which were declined.

'I have just been informed,' Swift stated, having restarted the tape, 'that Mr Maximilian Dwight has died of his injuries. As we discuss your part in his attack we will now be considering murder charges.'

Todd just shrugged at the news, saying, 'I never wanted to kill him but I did want to see him suffer. Mike said I'd gone too far.'

'Are you admitting to being responsible for Mr Dwight's death?' Matthew asked, it was no surprise to him or Swift, but they wanted to capture it for the tape.

'Yes, that was me, Mike knocked him down but I had the bottle,' Todd matter-of-factly explained, 'I barely knew what we'd done to Lionel and Perry and I wanted to see Max's face when I emptied the bottle over him, wanted to see him suffer.' There was no anger in Todd's voice, he showed virtually no emotion at all and he spoke to Matthew and Swift as he might to friends over a pint as they discussed the weather or the latest episode of a TV soap.

'Just for clarity,' Matthew continued, 'it was you who drove the bike in both attacks and Mike rode pillion?'

'Yes.'

'And he threw the acid in the first attack.'

'That's right, it was Perry he was after,' Todd smiled at the irony of the situation, 'he was really pissed with him over a fight they'd had. I'd suggested I could help get his own back, but he came up with the idea. He'd overheard about a club they regularly went to and thought the faggot needed a lesson. We should have practiced, I suppose, basically the stuff went everywhere except where he wanted. It suited me though, Lionel getting it instead.'

'Why is that?' Matthew wanted to know, feeling another puzzle piece fall into place.

'When I started at the club, it was literally like a new world opening up for me, especially Geraldine.'

'You met Gerry Driver at the club?'

'I met *Geraldine* and was bowled over, she was so nice. I was in awe of her and could hardly speak to her. I was always the one picked to help her with her props and dresses. I couldn't believe she was a bloke, I didn't just fancy her, I wanted to be her,' Todd's voice rose as he relived his passion for the female impersonator. 'I idolised everything about her,' then his voice fell again, becoming flat and tinged with anger, 'but she didn't *see* me, not the real me, you understand. I was always "darling Todd" to her, but everyone was her "darling". I was nothing special, just another nobody fawning on her. Not like Ricky Towers when he came round.'

'You're jumping ahead, somewhat,' Matthew wasn't certain he was doing the right thing but he wanted to keep a degree of order to the questioning that they were fast losing. 'What about Lionel and Perry?'

'I met Perry shortly after seeing Geraldine,' Todd explained. 'He had me pegged straight off, knew I was gay, that I loved to dress up, even my infatuation with Geraldine: "Who doesn't love her?" he said. "Who doesn't want to be her? Who doesn't envy every ounce of her?" He laughed all the time, talked about everything and showed me everything: how to dress, put on make-up, how to walk and sit. He even bought me my blond wig and he gave me the confidence to try it out. We'd go to pubs with Lionel and life was great.' Todd sighed, pausing at the memory, then screwed his face up in disapproval, 'Then Lionel got jealous. It was stupid really, Perry worshipped the ground Lionel walked on, with me it was just a bit of fun. Perry had done so much for me I only wanted to give something back, it was just a BJ not proper sex.' Again Todd shrugged, but this time there was a decidedly feminine air to the gesture, a dismissal of Lionel's insecurity of Perry's love for him.

'So you were more than happy to help Stennard, despite him being after Perry and not Lionel?' Matthew tried to make sense of what Todd was telling them, thinking he should have pushed Perry harder about his marital infidelities.

'Perry was quick to turn on me, said I was just a cheap bit of skirt, a talentless wannabe, I hated him for those words,' Todd's voice dropped, his tone low and intense, 'just like Geraldine later on.'

'What about Dwight?' Again Matthew pulled Todd back on track.

'Before our falling out Perry had introduced me to Thorsson. He said he'd take me on if I did a trial gig for him and I got good reviews.'

'Only things didn't go well,' Matthew knew the story already.

'No, I'd practiced and practiced, in front of Mum and at the lock-up. But I was so nervous,' Todd scowled, managing to look both angry and bewildered at the memory of his dreams crashing and burning, 'I thought I might just be pulling it off when I realised they weren't shouting "get 'em off" but "get *him* off". Dwight said nothing to me except that some people weren't cut out as performers but I heard what he said to the agency, shouting down the phone. Nearly all the staff and half the customers heard him as well. I couldn't stop crying. Then when Mike was talking about other people he had a grudge against and Dwight's name came up, I just thought it's your turn to cry.' Todd stopped, asking for water, and Swift decided to pause for a break.

'So, you've explained about the acid attacks,' Swift began the interview again, after he restarted the tape as previously. 'What led you to killing Driver?'

'I followed Geraldine around, whenever I could, dressed as Tina so he wouldn't recognise me. I found out where she lived, heard how everyone thought Gerry wasn't gay and how his dressing up as a woman was just for the act.' Todd began confidently, retelling events from the clarity of his own perspective. 'I ended up going to one of the clubs where he was performing and saw him with Ricky Towers and knew, at a glance, it was all a lie. I met Gary the same night, and his infatuation with me enabled me to get close to Geraldine. Gary and Ricky were keeping their distance, pretending they had fallen out and I ended up as their go-between. I didn't mind, passing information back and forth between them as well as passing on what they wanted the police to know about Bobby Towers. Ricky wouldn't say so, but he was in love and wanted out, he wanted a settled life with Geraldine. While Geraldine basked in Ricky's admiration, lapping up all the opportunities Ricky could lay before her.'

'Opportunities denied to you,' Matthew believed he now understood Todd's motivations.

'Yes, Gary was really nice and leaned on Thorsson to give me another chance. He also asked Geraldine if she could give me some pointers. When he heard, Ricky said he'd work something out for me if Geraldine thought I had any likelihood of success, even in a small way.' Todd's face had gone blank and hard, his voice again angry, 'Geraldine was very polite, said I had a raw talent that needed time to be nurtured and moulded.'

'That isn't what she really thought was it?' Matthew pushed as Todd fell silent.

'No, I overheard them talking, Geraldine saying I was a talentless, tone deaf, clod-hopper and no amount of training could make any difference,' it wasn't clear if Todd was angry at their duplicity or whether he felt their words to be an unfair appraisal, perhaps his anger arose from the humiliation of knowing that what was said about him was true.

'So, you decided on your revenge?' Matthew concluded.

'At first I thought to simply drop him in the Thames, I knew he was terrified of water and I wanted him shit scared and humiliated. Then when I was getting the stuff for his act out of his car I came across a little bag with his toys in and the stuff he wore with Ricky and, well, the rest you know.'

They went through Driver's killing step by step getting Todd's confirmation for the tape, even how he'd disposed of the bag and lingerie he'd found, though leaving the sex toys for all to see, and the nylon orange rope he'd used having come from the lock-up.

'What made you kill Ricky Towers?' Matthew finally asked.

'When I met with Ricky afterwards I expected him to be devastated,' Todd explained, now starting to sound tired, 'but it was like he'd simply lost his pet dog. He didn't seem even slightly put out.' Matthew knew the years of beatings Ricky had taken from his old man for showing even the slightest sign of weakness and if anyone could completely hide his emotions, even the deepest grief, it was Ricky.

'I decided there and then to put the shotgun to use,' Todd continued, 'it'd been wrapped in a backpack under some junk in the lock-up but now it had a purpose again. I didn't really have a plan, I just thought to trail around after him, once he'd been to the barbers, until an opportunity arose. It all happened like it was meant to: a knock on his car door, my visor up and then, the second he wound the window down, blam! Then I was away.'

'What about Victor Thorsson?' Matthew asked, seeing Todd looking pleased at the thought of his murderous handiwork.

'It had all been arranged,' Todd stated with a small laugh to himself at the irony of events, 'I'd handed in my notice weeks before, on the basis that Thorsson, as a favour to Gary, was finding me work, something on a cruise ship or a couple of gigs up north, to get me started. I'd packed and left mum some money in the pot, not that I think she understood. Then he phoned me to say he hadn't been able to get anything, he couldn't risk upsetting the few contacts he still had but if I could wait he'd keep trying. He agreed to put me up for a couple of nights until I could sort things out, he obviously thought Gary would come to my rescue. But Gary had been good to me and I didn't want to ask him for anything more.'

'So why did you delay and not kill Thorsson as soon as you got to his place?'

'I was going to, what I intended was to sit down with him over a cup of tea and then give it him straight in his bullshitting gob. Thing was, he kept on and on about how terrible it was that Geraldine was dead, that it was such a loss. It was hilarious listening to him, going on about this wonderful, talented person, such a lovely man, not at all gay and yet could be so feminine. I just had to listen, knowing that the incredible Geraldine was just another gold-digging queer out for what she could get and happy to use her arse to get it.' Todd shook his head, laughing at the hypocrisy, the betrayal of his ideal, as he saw it. 'Anyway, it was all he talked about and I was just getting bored with it when you turned up.'

# Chapter Twenty-Four

Julie Lukula had not felt so nervous about attending a briefing since she had first left Hendon and been a probationer. Although at least two people, at the full mid-morning briefing at the Wapping incident room, already knew her news she still thought the others would be very surprised to hear it. She had timed things so as to arrive just at the scheduled start, thereby ensuring she could give her news at the end, only to be told they were running late as Matthew was returning from the scene of another suspicious death.

'There was a fire last night, in Newham,' Swift was explaining to Green, as Julie approached them, 'the fire service have now said it was arson and the Gangs Unit have pointed out the address was known to them as being the residence of a known drug dealer and gang leader.'

'He's in hospital with third degree burns, I believe,' Green checked her facts of the case, 'it was his baby daughter and his girlfriend who died?'

'Yes, he'd been asleep downstairs and got out the rear, he claims the stairs and hall were an inferno when he awoke. I sent Matthew over there on his way in but I will need to discuss with you how we will allocate a team to him as I'm very short staffed currently.'

'Having Harry Bainbridge off and now Inspector Lukula deserting the ship can't help,' Green smiled indulgently at Julie.

'Yes ma'am,' Julie responded with a wan smile, 'that's exactly how I feel.'

'You'll be sorely missed,' Swift told her, 'but we will manage, no one is indispensable.'

'I take it you want to announce your news at the end of the briefing,' Green stated, once again exhibiting a degree of emotional intelligence. Julie barely had time to nod when Matthew entered the room with a bustle, though his attempt at trying to show he'd rushed was rather undermined by his holding a to go cup of coffee which he'd obviously stopped off to buy.

'Good morning all,' Swift started crisply, the remnants of his lilting Welsh accent gave anything he said an additional resonance that was oddly calming, 'I'm glad to inform you all that the considerable effort you have made, both individually as well as a team, has resulted in some very positive outcomes on this case.' Swift paused, while Green led a brief applause at the statement, nodding and mouthing her own 'well done' at the team.

'Before we recap, can I remind everyone that any outstanding paperwork needs to be completed today,' Swift's tone became business like, 'Ray will be tying up the loose ends and winding up the incident room, however, if he needs to chase anyone it will be in my name,' Swift glanced at Matthew, knowing his new case would be taking the inspector away and he didn't want him getting delayed by helping Ray, but Matthew was busy reading a text to confirm a meeting with an inspector in the Gangs Unit.

'Hayden, perhaps you could start by bringing everyone up to date with Mike Stennard's involvement in all this,' Swift asked, smiling. His was the only really black face in the room, Julie's light skin and that of an Asian officer were pale in comparison, he wasn't always comfortable in such situations, especially when with other senior officers, but here he felt at home. This was *his* team and he shared their successes and took the brunt of their failures.

'By the time Stennard's lawyer arrived and we started the interview,' Hayden began, her voice gravelly from her years of smoking, her notebook open though she barely glanced at it as she spoke, 'we already had news that Todd Barrett had copped for the acid attacks and had implicated Stennard. After a brief chat with his lawyer he readily confessed to being guilty of the charges of Murder, ABH and GBH,' muted applause and muttered approval greeted this. 'In his version of events Barrett was the instigator but in most other respects the confessions match. He says he had no idea about Barrett being responsible for killing either Driver or Towers and, on balance, I tend to believe him, he seemed stunned at the idea. He claims the acid attacks were motivated by his loathing of homosexuals. He also denies any sexual relationship with Barrett, either now or before his previous jail time. I suspect, from the number of times it was brought up, his lawyer will be looking for mitigation based on his client's well documented difficult childhood and his being groomed to join the neo-Nazi biker gang. However, from Stennard's point of view, having decided to confess his guilt, he seems focused on being portrayed as a *hard man* so as to increase his kudos when inside.'

'Are we looking to charge Stennard with the sexual assault of a minor?' Green asked, more of Swift than Hayden.

'I've had a brief conversation with CPS on that and they want something more concrete from Barrett, more clarity on the timeline,' Swift explained, ensuring everyone heard his reply. 'I will be interviewing him again, to confirm details, but I suspect from his attitude in the interview Matthew and I conducted that he isn't going to want to drop his mate in it. He remembers those years with affection, despite what Stennard has since become.' Matthew, from his seat at the rear, nodded in agreement, Swift's words echoing his own feelings for Ricky Towers.

'CPS won't want to muddy things, given the confessions you have otherwise secured,' Green commented, concurring with the CPS viewpoint, 'after all it is hardly likely to increase Stennard's sentence.'

'It might have an influence on Stennard's quality of life inside though,' Ray muttered to Hayden.

'As for Todd Barrett,' Swift continued his summing up, 'he has been charged with and has confessed to three murders, two cases of ABH and one of GBH. He had already confessed to various firearms charges and GBH for wounding Harry. Whom, by the way, expects to be released as an outpatient tomorrow.' Cheers and applause drowned out Swift as he added, 'Though it'll be sometime before he is out of a wheelchair and can return to work.'

'He'll have time to study for his sergeants exam,' Hayden pointed out, causing a swell of laughter; as well as smiles from Green and Swift. The latter indicating that Harry's actions, which had landed him in hospital, were not being considered rash or likely to be the subject of any disciplinary action.

'As for Barrett's motivations,' Swift pushed on, knowing both he and the chief had busy schedules for the day, 'on the whole his actions seem to stem from his need for acceptance and affection. He seems to have had those in spades from his mother and, at first, from Stennard, although after he was released from nick Stennard doesn't seem to have initially renewed their friendship. While those from whom he might have expected the most support he only received ridicule or contempt. Lionel Wong, Perry Cheung, Maximilian Dwight and Victor Thorsson all ended up branding him as worthless. He must have felt it as a deep betrayal.

'In practice Driver did the same and, worse still as Barrett saw it, did so hypocritically by denying being either gay or a transvestite. Despite this I think Todd still revered Driver, Geraldine was his feminine ideal and the person he wanted so much to be. So, when Towers showed no emotion over Geraldine's death it was too much for Barrett, yet another betrayal he could not stomach. Does that sum things up as you see them Matthew?'

Matthew paused for a moment, considering the options, then answered, 'I think you are spot on, sir, that forensic psychology conference you went on has obviously paid off.' Even Green laughed at the joke, one that perhaps only Matthew could get away with, and Swift also laughed, not above being the butt of a joke.

'Thank you for that, Matthew,' Swift brought the dying laughter to an end. 'Which reminds me, we need to talk about resourcing your new investigation.' Then addressing everyone, 'So, as I've already said, we need everything tied up now as quickly as possible.'

Julie caught Swift's eye, who was expecting her to make her announcement, instead she asked, 'What is happening with the NCA's case against Bobby Towers, now we know he wasn't involved in killing Ricky?'

'Well,' Swift glanced at Green whose slight nod approved his divulging what had occurred. 'Given Barrett's confession, though he clearly excluded his boyfriend from any involvement, I interviewed Gary Towers to confirm this. Despite everything, Gary claims he will stand by Tina, that is Todd, and he holds himself responsible for bringing Todd into Ricky and Geraldine's lives. He also claims that since leaving the army to help his brother he has worked to get Ricky to give up his criminal ways.' Swift paused, when Gary had told him this in his slightly clipped, military fashion he'd thought him naive but the more Gary spoke of his brother the more Swift had seen the man's aim to be a realistic one.

'Gary,' Swift continued, 'hated his father as much as his brother did. However, all the beatings they received pushed them in opposite directions, Gary determined never to be like his father while Ricky ended up emulating him. However, Gary was convinced that Ricky loathed himself for being his father's creation and he'd been making slow headway with him to change. Then Geraldine came on the scene and Ricky's outlook completely altered. As Gary saw it, Ricky started to believe he could be the man he wanted to be and not what everyone else expected him to be. All the while Gary kept himself clear of the family's criminal exploits but kept records of all they were up to. And some of this he and Ricky had started to pass to the police, via various intermediaries, including Tina/Todd.'

The murmuring at this revelation caused Swift to pause then, signalling for quiet, continued, 'To cut to the chase, Gary has agreed to hand over various documents to Chief Superintendent

Harvey about the Towers's money laundering and other criminal operations. It is very early days as yet but Harvey believes this is the final nail he needs to put Bobby, his brother and father away for a long time. If he's right they will be facing lengthy jail time and seizure of their considerable criminal assets.' Again there were muted cheers and applause, the team were in no doubt they'd been instrumental in achieving a significant outcome, a real dent in criminal activity, from what had started as a suspicious drowning.

'Right, on that note of celebration,' Swift pushed on, knowing he and Green needed to be leaving, 'I pass you over to Inspector Lukula.'

Julie knew she couldn't put the moment off any longer and stood to squarely face her colleagues, 'I just wanted the opportunity to invite you all to my leaving do, next Friday.' There was a surprised and expectant hush. 'This morning I received confirmation of my appointment as an inspector in the CTC, to head up a specialist investigation team. I'd like to particularly thank the Chief Superintendent and Superintendent Swift for their support. I do feel torn at leaving the team, then I thought of Matthew,' Julie turned to look directly at Matthew, 'and I knew I'd disappoint him if I didn't take the job.'

Matthew made no response as Julie was swept up in the others' congratulations, her announcement only adding to the growing celebratory mood. He'd never really seen himself as Julie's mentor, and they'd have time to talk before she went to pastures new, but at that moment the tinge of pride he felt at her words only added to his resolve to do the right thing by his wife.

Matthew had found it hard to concentrate for the remainder of his working day, his mind kept coming back to what he had to say and how this might play out with his wife. He rehearsed what he would say, not just the words he'd use but the gestures and even the tone needed to reinforce his meaning. His aim was to ensure that Kathy knew he could be trusted and that he was prepared to stick by her through thick and thin. He'd even, against the norms of professional conduct, phoned Sergeant Gillian Raynaud to ask for an update – officer to officer.

'I won't hold you to anything but I want my wife to have the right level of expectations,' Matthew explained, knowing Raynaud wouldn't be happy at being put on the spot, especially off the record, like this. 'If it isn't likely to go to court then I'd prefer not to build her up more than I should.'

'OK,' Raynaud took a breath knowing she should only give him what she'd already told his wife, but having worked with Matthew a couple of times she took the chance of trusting him. 'Officially it is too early to say, our suspect has been interviewed and he has given alternative answers to all the evidence we have in your wife's case. As such, things are in balance as to whether or not it will go to court, although I'll be pushing for that outcome as I believe your wife's testimony more strongly supports the evidence, than the suspect's account.'

'I see,' Matthew was downhearted but held out for the straw of a 'but' that he saw coming, 'and unofficially?'

'We've been through his computer and found some porn but, frankly, nothing of any concern, nothing that is going to shock a judge or jury,' Raynaud explained. 'However, one of our techs noticed something about the photos he'd taken of places where he'd worked as a consultant. He'd taken the photos to use on his blog, as a testimonial to the work he'd done and those were fine, but he also had a large file on six schools, including Kathy's, out of the dozen or so he has worked at. The technician noticed something about the photos in these files, that one particular female in each school occurred in every picture he'd kept. Your wife, for example, was in each photo he'd taken and kept of her school, she might be at the forefront or in the background, but she was in each one.'

'So, it was a record of all the women he'd been attracted to?' Matthew jumped to the conclusion Raynaud had already reached.

'Exactly, and it didn't take much effort to track down the women in the other five sets,' Raynaud stated, 'even though three of them had subsequently moved. Of the five, three have denied any involvement with Lance Fulbright, they wouldn't even entertain the idea. However, the other two have now made accusations, in both cases they had originally doubted what they recalled and couldn't believe it had really happened. I'm still in the process of interviewing them, confirming details and trying to collect any evidence, which is minimal if non-existent.' Raynaud paused, letting what she had said sink in.

'Even so, you feel you have something?' Matthew asked, picking up on Raynaud's muted yet positive vibe.

'There is a pattern emerging,' Raynaud explained. 'The women work at all levels, two were new to teaching, two are heads of department, one a deputy. –' *The bastard's working his way up the hierarchy*, Matthew thought to himself; his anger flaring as he struggled to control himself and listen quietly, professionally, to what he was being told. – 'However, the two women who have come forward both describe a late night meeting, Fulbright hanging back to speak with them, then a blank until the following day, followed by many months of flash backs, self-denial and uncertainty. I'm expecting to be in a position, in the very near future, to put these accusations to Fulbright. I expect him to deny the charges and perhaps even offer similar explanations as he has used about your wife, even so my expectation is that I will be charging him.'

'It's basically the weight of the three accusations against his denial that you have?' Matthew was no fool, he knew that this was far from conclusive; especially given the delay in the victims coming forward, it never played well with a jury despite it being a consequence of the drug used by the perpetrator on his victims.

'I intend to reinterview the other three women, I'm hopeful that at least one more will come forward once they know how things stand,' Raynaud explained, she knew a good defence lawyer could still get Fulbright acquitted but she was doing all she could to stack the odds in favour of the victims.

'Thank you,' Matthew's words were heartfelt, his tone was reward enough for Raynaud having put her trust in telling him, 'I won't give Kathy any details but at least I know I don't have to play things down more than I need to. It's a help to know.'

Wanda had returned to work and her own home the day before last, leaving the family to regain a more normal level of domesticity which, unfortunately, eluded them. Kathy was oddly distant, not uncommunicative nor unwilling to hug her daughters at any moment they seemed to need it but there was nothing spontaneous or natural in what she said or did. It was as if she had to momentarily think through every word or action, to check that her instinctive reaction was the right one or needed to be modified in some way, to be tempered so as to avoid too emotional a response. The girls also struggled for normality, their inability to understand the veiled emotional maelstrom in which they now lived causing unexpected outbursts of anger, tears or both. Matthew, through it all, remained passive, like a clam trying to stay shut inside himself while clinging to the rock of his family.

However, finally, Matthew went as far as insisting that Kathy join him on the sofa, once the girls were in bed and asleep, rather than retiring early on her own as had become her habit.

'It's a positive move forward,' Matthew finished, having told her that there was a growing expectation that Raynaud had discovered a pattern to Fulbright's action, one that might lead to other victims coming forward. 'If they can also link him to purchasing the drug he used it would be conclusive but he seems to have covered his tracks too well. Even without that, he'll find it hard to maintain his innocence against three accusers.'

'She'd told me that things were progressing, I remain hopeful,' Kath said, sounding to Matthew like someone who was hopeful it would snow at Christmas, there was no indication of any emotional attachment in Kathy's words. 'We will have to wait and see.'

There was a brief pause as Matthew threw all his resolve and rehearsed words out the window and took an entirely different course of action. 'We need to sort out some counselling, some type of support.'

'I don't need that, not just yet,' Kathy stated emphatically, making a cutting motion with her hand to suggest the topic was not up for discussion.

'I don't mean just for you, I mean for us, together,' Matthew's tone, which had been hesitant, was suddenly insistent. His wife's emphatic denial was the final straw in breaking the back of his belief that somehow things would simply come right. 'I can't go on like this, even if you can, nor can the girls. We need help in sorting this out between ourselves, then we need to include the girls, help them through it.'

Kathy said nothing, she didn't need to as her expression told him everything: *this isn't your problem, it is mine to deal with. If you don't like me as I am then go.* Though unspoken it could not have been plainer.

'So do we have sex?' It wasn't what he'd intended to say but it got to the heart of the problem and came from his heart. 'Every night I want to sleep with you, because I love you, want to be that close to you again. But I don't know if that is what you want and, even if you do, is it too soon?'

'Is that all you care about?' Kathy felt her anger rising, a scream forming inside her – *go, leave now and never come back!* – barely contained, cutting off her breath and stopping the unformed words.

'No, it's all the basic stuff, even down to eating together, using the bathroom at the same time, even just being in the same room,' Matthew was on a roll, a train speeding down the tracks out of control but now started he was going to finish. 'One minute you're hugging the girls, the next you are ignoring them. I don't know what to do, what to say or even if I should say anything. I need help, the girls need help even if you don't. And, yes – I want to make love to you. There was a time when we used to enjoy each other, it was a source of wonder between us but that ended months, even years, ago long before what has happened recently.'

The scream inside her had dissipated as Matthew spoke, it was still there but no longer in a form that was ready to be spoken. 'OK, I agree, if you can find someone and make the arrangements, I promise I will go with you.'

'I'll do that, but we will take things at your pace,' Matthew reassured her, wanting to take her hand in his but was terrified she might pull away. 'I just don't want us slipping further away from each other, we always used to do things together, it was always *we* not me and you. You want that back don't you?'

'Yes I do,' she admitted, a small smile forming on her lips. Deep down his words, and the small tears forming if not falling from his eyes, had pleased her. Though she kept her hands firmly in her lap, she could not as yet abide the thought of his touch. 'But it might take time, getting back to being one half of *we* isn't going to be easy for me.'

It was by tacit agreement that Matthew would continue to sleep on the couch although neither, as yet, had given up on the idea that it was only a temporary solution.

As Matthew drifted into sleep, his thoughts of his wife lying naked in bed turned to a dream of her flesh melding into one with his. Until, finally, he was on his own, a fleshy little limpet contained and protected within its hard, closed shell, buffeted by the black, cold, stormy sea swell. Even so he was content, his shell stuck fast to the rock that was his family. However, even as he dreamed this, the rock was changing becoming pliable and taking on the form of pink, sweaty flesh that began to engulf him as Kathy's naked body wound around him and intruded itself into his sleeping dream.

# Thoughts

'Never be bullied into silence. Never allow yourself to be made a victim. Accept no one's definition of your life, but define yourself.' – Harvey Fierstein

'Your gender identity is who you are. Sexual identity is who you bounce that off of.' – Andrew Solomon

'Cross-dressing is more of a set of actions or behaviours and not synonymous with gender identity (straight, gay, bisexual, transgender, among others).' – Steven Petrow

*

Finally:

If you have enjoyed this book then please leave a review, your thoughts are much appreciated.

# End Notes

The author is a member of the London Crime family
www.londoncrime.co.uk – @LondonCrime1

The author can be found on Twitter at: @JohnMeadAuthor

Further information and support on issues connected with the plot line:

**TRUE VISION** – support and advice on Hate Crime
http://report-it.org.uk/what_is_hate_crime

**THE BEAUMONT SOCIETY** –
http://www.northernconcord.org.uk/other.htm

'The Society was founded in 1966 as a self help and social organisation for transvestites and transsexuals.

The Society is run for, and by, people who are transgender, covering the spectrum from occasional cross dressers to post operative transsexuals. We are a national organisation run on a regional basis. There are members throughout the UK, with local groups in many areas, there are also members overseas.'

**CROSS TALK – THE MAGAZINE** –
http://www.northernconcord.org.uk/cross.htm

**FREEDOM HOUSE –**
https://freedomhouse.org/issues/lgbti-rights

'Freedom House is an independent watchdog organisation dedicated to the expansion of freedom and democracy around the world.

Lesbian, gay, bisexual, transgender and intersex (LGBTI) people around the world face discrimination, persecution and violence simply for expressing who they are and choose to love. Consensual same-sex conduct is criminalised in more than 70 countries, with punishment including fines, flogging, and imprisonment and in seven countries, the death penalty.'

**THE CONSORTIUM –**
http://www.lgbtconsortium.org.uk/

'Little specialist infrastructure exists to support LGBT groups and organisations, and existing voluntary sector infrastructure organisations have often failed to acknowledge or provide support for lesbian, gay, bisexual and transgender projects.

The Consortium was set up in 1998 to address these gaps; and to nurture the development of an LGB sector. In 2003, the desire for greater diversity from members saw the Consortium expand its brief to include transgender voluntary and community organisations.'

**RAPE – ADVICE AND SUPPORT**
https://rapecrisis.org.uk/
https://www.met.police.uk/advice/advice-and-information/rsa/rape-and-sexual-assault/what-happens-after-you-report-rape-or-sexual-assault/